THE CRIME

ALL IN SERIES - BOOK THREE

MAGGIÉ COLE

PULSE PRESS

This book is fiction. Any reference to historical events, real people, or real places are used fictitiously. All names, characters, plots, and events are products of the author's imagination. Any resemblances to actual events or places or persons, living or dead, is entirely coincidental.

FREE GIFT FOR YOU

PSST - I have a short story that you're going to love and I want to give it to you for free! It's The Rule 1.5!

This short story sequel is a follow up to Tom and Liv's story, so don't read it until you have finished reading Book One of the All In Series, The Rule!

Grab it now so you have it!

www.authormaggiecole.com/therulesequel

From time to time, I'll email you juicy new freebie stories and let you know about my new books. But don't worry, I'll keep your email safe and won't share it with anyone or abuse it.

Promise!

Don't forget to check out The Lie, Book Four of the All In Series. The blurb, prologue and part of chapter one are included at the end of this book for a sneak peek!

Also, I have a huge favor to ask you! If you enjoyed reading this book, please leave me a nice rating and review on the platform you bought this novel.

Thanks so much for all your support!

Maggie Cole

For D.M.

Thanks for always being honest!

And knowing your S's!

XOXO

PROLOGUE

Covered in sweat, filled with terror, I woke up as the visions of what I had seen were still fresh in my mind.

Women and children wept; tears streamed out of their fear-filled eyes. My ears rang with the echo of their cries and the sinister laughs that mocked them.

Nausea overcame me, and I ran to the bathroom and violently threw up. As I hugged the toilet, a cold sweat rushed through my body. I closed my eyes as the tears flowed out, and I began to sob.

I had wanted to help them, I really did, but the gun pointed at them suggested that if I tried, I would have been shot. So I chose the coward's way out.

After telling the men in charge, that it wasn't my scene, I left as fast as I could.

Those sick assholes are my business partners. The thought sent my stomach pitching again.

I must have been in shock because my mind was a black hole. Somehow, I had arrived back at the hotel even though I didn't remember the drive. When the valet opened my car door, it had snapped me back into reality.

I had felt like a zombie as I walked to the elevator and pushed the button to my penthouse suite. I'm not sure how long I sat on the chair and stared out into the black night. My body shook (probably from shock), as their faces played on repeat in my mind.

At some point, I must have dozed off. When I woke up from the nightmare, the sun peeked out over the bay. The water sparkled and glistened with different-colored blues as if everything was right in the world.

Would anything ever be right again?

In the morning light, it became clear what I needed to do. It didn't matter if they were connected to me. If I was held responsible for their crime then so be it, but they needed to be stopped.

I picked up my phone and googled the number.

The phone rang a few times. "FBI," a woman's voice answered.

"I need to report a crime..."

1

Maddie

"One key or two?" The front desk clerk didn't even look up.

The hotel lobby was buzzing and packed with guests checking in. Several big conferences were in town and hundreds of people wore lanyards with nameplates.

My immediate response was to say two, when I remembered that I no longer, as of this past weekend, was a package deal. "Just one," I told her, as I felt the independence of the words roll off my tongue.

Mike and I were together for six years, and it was strange to suddenly be alone. I left him only a few days earlier, but if I was honest, I should have left him years before. Surprise hit me, as, once again, relief washed over me that we were done.

Why couldn't I have been strong enough to break up with him years ago?

It would be a long time before I even dated again, I told myself. I needed to be by myself for a bit.

The front desk woman quickly wrote my room number on

the back of the card envelope. There were two wings to the hotel: east and west. My room was in the east wing.

"If you want to eat in any of our restaurants, I suggest you get a reservation now, as we are full this week. Otherwise, Coastal has some appetizers and drinks if you don't require anything extensive." She pointed to the bar area.

I thanked her, quickly grabbed my room key, and headed toward the elevators.

It didn't take long for me to reach my room. I entered the room, surprised by my view of Tampa Bay. The water glistened with multi-colored blues and sparkled from the bright sun.

I happily flipped off my shoes and climbed into bed. The cheap ticket I booked required several layovers, and my day had begun pretty early. It was nearly 4:00 p.m., and a nap sounded pretty good.

I quickly fell asleep, and woke up when it was dark. The skyline was mostly black with stars, and I could no longer see the bay. The clock on the nightstand read 7:23 p.m. I debated whether or not to stay in my room, but my stomach rumbled, and I decided to head to Coastal.

After I looked in the mirror, I decided to jump in the shower. I freshened up my long black hair with some dry shampoo and put on some makeup.

A new pink sundress sat inside the top of my suitcase. I grabbed it, threw it on and slid my feet into a pair of flip-flops. My laptop bag was next to my purse, and I slung it over my shoulder, thinking that I could get some work done while I waited for my food.

I double-checked that I had my room key and made my way through the hotel. It didn't take me long to get to Coastal, and I was escorted to a quiet table for two at the back of the dark bar. A piano player strummed keys to a slow melody. Candles were lit on each table, and gave off a romantic glow.

I grunted to myself at the thought of 'romance'. *Had I ever had any romance with Mike?* I tried to throw that thought out of my head and reminded myself that I needed to stop beating myself up for staying—it wouldn't change the situation.

It wasn't super busy yet, but I assumed it would be as the night progressed. I opened my laptop, ordered a glass of Chardonnay, and looked at the menu. I tossed the menu aside, no longer really hungry and not sure if I even wanted to order any food.

A glass in, I needed to use the restroom. The people at the table next to me agreed to watch my laptop, and I took the chance that they weren't thieves.

The waiter pointed me in the direction of the bathroom. No one else was there. I washed my hands, freshened up my lipstick and headed out.

As I stepped out, I bumped right into a man's chest, and nearly fell backward, but he put his arm around my back and embraced me tightly, so I wouldn't slip.

My nostrils filled with his scent, and my heart started to thump in my chest. I could feel his tight biceps around me and his hand around my waist. I slowly gazed up, and discovered his dark hair and piercing dark brown eyes.

His rugged good looks screamed he was high-powered, and I could tell his suit was expensive. *Is he a GQ cover model?* I felt the outline of his chest muscles through his suit, and I immediately wondered what it would be like to feel his bare skin against mine.

"Are you all right?" His deep, sexy, and commanding voice asked, and as his smile grew, a set of dimples appeared on his cheeks.

God gave him dimples too?

I tried to find words. My eyes locked into his, as currents of hot electricity pumped through my body. I managed to mumble a yes.

Someone needed us to move so they could get through. He

stepped aside but still held onto me. My heart wasn't the only one that raced—I could feel his beating through his suit.

I licked my lips. He intently stared at me and his smile grew bigger. I couldn't help it and grinned back at him.

I'm not sure how long we gazed at each other, but several people tried to get past us. He reluctantly released me. Disappointment at the lack of his touch coursed through my body.

"Thanks for keeping me from falling; I'll let you pass now," I somehow squeaked out.

"My pleasure." He winked at me and walked into the men's room.

Jack

I walked into the men's room as my mind reeled. My senses registered high alert—she was the most stunning girl I had ever laid eyes on. When she stared at me with her big blue eyes, and her jet black hair brushed softly against my hands, I had held myself back from leaning into her and kissing her.

I studied my reflection in the mirror. I wondered if she would still be in the bar.

Was she here by herself or with someone?

Please, let her be by herself.

I only went to the bar to use the restroom. There was a long line of people in the lobby, who waited for the elevators. The plan was to use the bathroom and go up to my room. Over a year ago, I stopped using women for my pleasure, and the bar no longer served me.

A shock had pulsed through my system when I held her. She felt perfect in my arms. I wanted to pull her closer. The only reason I let her go was because people needed to get past us.

I wondered where she was from and what her name was. Was she here on business or pleasure?

God, the things I want to do to pleasure her.

Stop it! I told my reflection in the mirror. She could have any guy in the place, and I was sure they were better guys than me. I didn't deserve a girl like that.

She wasn't only the most beautiful girl I had ever seen, but she seemed sweet and innocent. Every fiber of my body wanted to find out more about her.

I tried to talk myself out of it. It wasn't a good idea. If she knew what I had been a part of, she would definitely run.

If only I could have met her after my dealings with the FBI were over. Maybe then we could have had a chance. Surely, it wasn't right to get involved with her while I was still dealing with this crap.

Jack, walk straight out of the bar and up to your room.

It was decided. I would *not* pursue her.

I walked out of the restroom. My brain told me not to look for her and to go straight to my room. But my dick won. I glanced around to see if she was still in the bar. I spotted her, in the back, by herself with her laptop open. She had her perfect legs crossed and a glass of wine in her hand.

She was eloquent, classy, and drop-dead gorgeous. When I gazed at her, I couldn't walk away.

Before I knew it, I was at the bar, ordering from the bartender. This was not in the plan, but I had to get to know more about her.

Maddie

I DEBATED WAITING IN THE HALL FOR HIM TO COME OUT, BUT MY

common sense returned. I scurried back to my table. My mind raced, as I stared at my blank computer screen, not sure how a stranger could make me feel so excited.

I had booked the trip to Tampa to spend a week by myself. I wanted to detox men from my life, and here I was, with jelly insides at the first gorgeous guy I saw. "Damn it, Maddie," I cursed myself. "You aren't here for men."

I took some deep breaths and tried to regulate my heartbeat. I had never felt a jolt like that—with any man. I tried to convince myself it must have been because things were so bad with Mike for so many years.

Why did you stay so long? Once again, the question I couldn't answer flew through my mind. I sighed. I was a doormat for so many years. I had tried to do whatever I could to make him love me when he never would and put his happiness over mine.

But why did I stay?

The waiter came over and put a bucket with ice next to the table, which snapped me out of my thoughts. I shot him a confused glance.

He proceeded to open a bottle of Cristal Champagne. He filled a glass then handed it to me.

"I didn't order this."

"Madam, Jack Stevens ordered this for you and would like to know if he could join you?"

"Jack Stevens?"

The waiter nodded toward the bar. The jolt once again shot through me as our eyes met. My heart rate skyrocketed up again as I tried to comprehend the situation.

Jack lifted his eyebrows at me, as if in question about whether he should come over. My brain reminded me that I had sworn off men and that I needed to be by myself and figure out who I was first...but my body betrayed me.

I managed to point to the chair opposite mine.

Crap. What am I doing? My insides started quivering. *Where could this possibly lead? I'm several states from home and in a resort hotel bar.*

The waiter smiled and filled another champagne glass before he set it down across from me and left. I had little time to compose myself before Jack arrived.

"Jack Stevens." He held out his hand.

"Maddie Burns." I grabbed his hand and shook it.

"I hoped you weren't here with anyone." He sat across from me, dimples popping out as he grinned, and his eyes shined from the flicker of the candles.

I blushed, not sure what to say, and finally grabbed my glass and held it up. "Cheers then, I guess."

He clinked my glass and took a sip. "Maddie," He enunciated my name into a sentence, and let it hang in the air. "Are you here for business or pleasure?"

"Pleasure," I replied, a little too quickly, then blushed again at the thought of pleasure with him.

His smile deepened. "Pleasure is good."

My flush swept across my cheeks and heated up so much I wanted to go hide.

This was so out of character for me. I didn't go to bars alone. I didn't get picked up by men who could be cover models and oozed power and confidence. I wasn't sure how to play this cool.

The thought of pleasure with him made my insides pulse.

I continued to sip my champagne. Somehow I managed to get out, "And what are you here for, Jack Stevens?"

He laughed a bit. "Business...and maybe some pleasure."

My face was officially in flames as images of our naked bodies filled my mind. I tried to concentrate on breathing calmly. As I sipped my champagne, I realized that I was halfway through my glass.

Setting my glass on the table, I asked, "What do you do…for business."

"I guess you could call me an entrepreneur. I'm in town

assessing a few businesses to buy. What about you, Maddie? Where are you from?"

I sized him up, wanting to know everything about him. He felt mysterious, and I was drawn to him, almost like a magnetic pull I couldn't control. My eyes wouldn't leave his. "From California, but I live in New York City now."

I didn't think his smile could get any bigger, but it did. "Well I guess we both have that in common. What part of the city?"

My stomach did a happy flip. *He lives in New York City, too?*

"Right now I'm in the Meatpacking District. I'll be moving...just not sure where yet." I regretted the words that came out of my mouth the minute they left.

"Oh?" His brows lifted in question.

The last thing I wanted to do was talk about my breakup. I quickly decided on a different route: "Roommate issues."

"Boyfriend or friend?" He drilled me. "And I'm hoping if it's a boyfriend that it's an ex...no offense."

"Ex and no offense taken."

He sat back in his chair, cool and in control, and watched me with the same intensity and huge grin.

"What?" I shifted in my chair.

"Dumb guy to let you go," he stated matter-of-factly.

I rolled my eyes.

"Don't roll your eyes at me," he flirtatiously teased. Then, he leaned in, with a serious expression, and lowered his voice. "*Really* dumb guy."

Heat flew into my face. I wasn't sure how to respond, but I didn't really have time. There was a massive commotion from the front of the bar and it made us both turn.

The entrance of the bar started to flood with people. They sounded hostile and I looked back at Jack in question.

His eyebrows drawn together, he jumped up. "Stay here. I'll be right back."

He swiftly walked to the bar and talked to the bartender. The noise grew louder and the people's voices were angrier. Within two minutes, Jack was back at the table.

"Maddie, what wing is your room in?"

"East, why?" A bad feeling flowed through me.

"They put the East wing on lock down. The smoke and carbon monoxide alarms have malfunctioned and everyone is being evacuated from the entire wing. The hotel is sold out. They have nowhere to go. Grab your stuff." He pointed to my laptop and bag.

I didn't move and tried to process what was happening.

"Maddie, we don't have a lot of time. Come on. That crowd is pissed off, more people are coming in. This isn't going to be a safe place to hang out. Let's go," he instructed.

"But where..." My head snapped as I realized the crowd had gotten larger and angrier. They pushed past the hostess and the bar became standing room only. Glass shattered and people started to push and shout.

Jack grabbed my laptop and shoved it in my bag. He pulled me up. "Come on, Maddie."

Swiftly, he drew me into him, planted his arm firmly around my waist, and escorted me through the bar, as we stayed close against the wall. We moved through the lobby, which was louder than the bar. People were yelling at the staff, and security were trying to calm them down. Jack pulled me closer and into a crowded elevator for the west wing. He pushed his card in and hit the penthouse button.

It dawned on me that he was taking me to his suite. I nervously glanced up at him. He brought his lips to my ear and whispered, "Don't worry. It's okay."

I wasn't sure what to do. The logical part of my brain told me to get out of the elevator, but I wasn't sure where I would go. The emotional part of me wanted to sink further into Jack's muscular, warm body.

People in the elevator discussed the chaos in the lobby. I stood quietly, and wracked my mind about what to do. Jack kept his arm tight around my waist, even in the safety of the elevator.

I sank into his chest and inhaled his sexy scent, completely paralyzed except for my racing heart.

People left, one by one. There slowly became room to spread out, but neither Jack nor I moved. Finally, there were only the two of us in the elevator, and we waited for the final stop.

I fixated on my fidgeting hands. "Jack, I..." What the heck was I trying to say?

His thumb stroked my waist. "Don't worry, Maddie. It's only a safe place to go. You don't have to do anything you don't want to, I promise."

I inhaled slowly and was pretty sure I knew what the deeper connotations of that meant. But, I felt completely safe and secure with Jack. I only just met him, but I didn't want to be anywhere but with him.

Lewd thoughts raced through my mind, along with how I didn't know this guy, and that I was taking time off from guys right now. I tried to push the thoughts away, but my mind started spinning.

The elevator stopped and opened into the penthouse hallway. We slowly stepped out of the elevator. Jack held the door open for me.

I walked in and did a double take. The penthouse was huge. The skyline twinkled and there had been turn-down service already. Slow, sexy music played, and the lights were soft and dim.

Jack turned toward me, then held my face in his hands; his thumbs caressed my cheeks. "Make yourself at home. You can stay as long as needed. There are several bedrooms. Don't stress. I promise I'll be a gentleman." His eyes were worried, and I realized that he understood my thoughts. Well, not all of my thoughts...

But what if I don't want you to be a gentleman?

I bit my lip. "Thank you."

He winked at me and gave me a dimpled grin. "No thanks needed. I get to spend more time with you now."

Jack

I wanted her to know that she didn't have to worry. I wouldn't try anything. She was safe here.

I walked into the kitchen and opened the fridge. "You hungry?"

She gave me her million-dollar smile. "I'm starving actually."

"I would order room service but I have a feeling the hotel is going to be a little understaffed tonight." I pulled out some chocolate-covered strawberries, nuts, cheese, and crackers.

"Yum. That works!"

"What can I get you to drink?"

She thought for a brief minute. "Can I have a water?"

I pulled out two waters. *Probably better if we don't drink,* I thought.

I opened one up and handed it to her, set the other bottle on the counter, and removed my suit jacket and tie. *I really need to get out of these clothes. They're suffocating me.*

When I unlatched my top three buttons, her eyes drifted over my body. I don't think she realized it, she was that innocent, but she checked me out and slightly licked her lips, which sent my dick into overdrive.

You promised her you would be a gentleman.

The last thing I wanted to do was scare her. I saw her eyes in the elevator, and there was no way I wanted her to run out of here.

As I watched her ogle me, I wondered what she would think if

I sat around all night with an ice pack on my dick. *I am definitely going to have blue balls.*

"I'm going to go get out of this suit. I've been in it since 5 a.m.. Help yourself to anything you want...but don't disappear while I'm changing." I wagged my finger at her.

She threw her head back, laughing, and her beautiful black hair bounced all over her back. "Where would I go?"

"I don't know. I'm just saying." I shrugged my shoulders. Then I turned and walked into my bedroom.

I shut the door and leaned against it as I took deep breaths. I would not try anything. I would not put her in any uncomfortable position. *I only want to get to know her better.*

I wasn't sure how long she was in town for, but maybe I could take her out while she was here? Maybe when I was back in New York she would consider going out with me?

I shut my eyes, and reminded myself that I wasn't supposed to have pursued her. But now that I had, there was no way I couldn't see where this could go.

I'm not going to sleep with her tonight, I told myself, again. *I'll just get to know her more.* I wondered if she was really over her ex.

Please be over him.

Don't fuck this up, Jack.

2

Maddie

THE CHOCOLATE-COVERED STRAWBERRIES LOOKED GOOD, SO I grabbed one, along with my water. I walked over to the skyline and realized there was a balcony, I opened the door and stepped out into the sharp, February, night air. The balcony was huge, with a hot tub off to the side.

The water glowed pink from the light, and I put my hand in it to feel its warmth. I don't know if it was all the champagne I drank, or my newfound independence, but without even thinking, I untied my dress. It fell to the floor, and I stepped out of my sandals.

I heard a soft whistle and turned to see Jack in a pair of shorts and a t-shirt. His eyes surveyed my body, as I stood in my neon pink bra and thong, which matched the water in the hot tub.

Frozen, Jack continued to stare at me, as if wrestling with his mind, before he walked toward me. His eyes continued to scan my almost naked body, and I exhaled slowly as my insides pulsed with desire.

Jack gulped, hard. "You're making it a little difficult for me to stick to my promise to be a gentleman."

I don't know where the courage came from, but I gazed in his eyes, "Maybe I don't want you to be a gentleman."

Way to send him mixed messages. So much for my elevator worries.

I'm not sure how long we stood there, eyes locked. Jack struggled with whatever was going through his mind. Finally, he stepped forward, put his arms around me, and bent down to slowly kiss me. As if savoring me, his tongue rolled into mine, slowly at first, then faster, with urgency and heat.

My entire body lit up in flames as I melted against him.

Jack pulled back first, and disappointment surged through me, as I breathlessly tried to regain my composure.

I must look like a panting dog.

Jack Stevens was one hell of a kisser.

With a small step back, he removed his shirt and shorts, so he only wore his boxers. I gazed at his chest and ab muscles, dying to touch them. My eyes trailed to his crotch, and caught a quick view of his semi, before I realized he knew I was gawking. He softly laughed, before he stepped into the hot tub.

"You coming in? I mean, I have no problem staring at you all night if you prefer..." he teased and sat back with his arms stretched across the back of the tub.

"Ha ha." I twisted my long black hair, tied it up in a knot, and joined him in the hot tub. Without hesitation, I plopped down next to him. He casually put his arm around my shoulders and pulled me a bit closer.

It was strange. I only met Jack about an hour earlier, but I was so comfortable with him. In fact, I was more comfortable with him, than Mike.

How can that be?

On one hand, nervous butterflies swarmed in my stomach. On the other hand was a calm sensation. Strange and surprising all at once.

"Why are you here in Tampa?"

I sat and thought for a moment, and wondered if I should make something up or tell him the truth? I must have paused too long, because Jack answered for me, "Ahh. The breakup. It's super fresh, isn't it?"

Crap. I didn't really want to get into this, or think about anyone but Jack. And definitely, *not* Mike.

"Last weekend. But it's been over for a long time."

I think he sensed I didn't really want to talk about it. "So...why Tampa?"

I shrugged my shoulders. "Some deal popped up on my Instagram feed and I thought, why not."

Jack laughed. "So people actually do that?"

"Do what?"

"Go at the spur of the moment to random places?"

I jerked my head back, "You've never done that?"

He shook his head.

"Why not?"

Jack thought for a minute, "My businesses keep me pretty busy. Life can be...what should I say without sounding so boring you'll get up and take your chances in the lobby…?"

I raised my brow at him.

Jack continued, "... scheduled."

"Well, that *is* boring!" I attempted to get up.

"Oh no you don't!" He pulled me back and sat me on his lap.

I giggled and gazed at his face. I could see little wrinkles in the corner of his eye, but something told me it wasn't from age, but maybe the stress of a demanding career. "How old are you, Jack?"

"Thirty-six. You?"

"Thirty-two."

"You ever been married? Have kids?"

"No, but if I had been, or had kids, what would you say?"

"Dumb guy, lucky kids."

I rolled my eyes, smiling. "What about you?"

"Almost married once, no kids." Did I detect some sort of sadness in his eyes? Maybe it was the memory of his ex-fiance?

He changed the subject, "Tell me, Maddie, what were you working on when I interrupted you in the bar?"

"Honestly, nothing. My mind wasn't really working after I ran into you." I surprised myself at how openly my words flowed out of my mouth.

Jeez, why don't you tell him you want to jump his bones?

He gave me a cocky smile and licked his lips. "If you hadn't almost knocked me over, what would you have been doing?"

"Ha ha!" I playfully punched his shoulder. "Writing ad copy. I work for a PR firm. My friend, Liv, convinced me to join her. I moved from California about six months ago."

"Liv Marko?"

"Yes. You know her?" I straightened up a bit.

Jack nodded. "New York is known as a big city, but in reality, it can be small. Her husband Tom, and I; we have a few companies together. Liv does the majority of my company's marketing and PR."

I slid off Jack's lap.

"What's wrong? Did I say something to offend you?"

"No, nothing offensive. But if you're a client of the firm, I don't think this is a good idea." I tugged at my hair.

Jack grabbed me and slid me back on his lap. He put his arms around my waist. "Maddie, I've known Tom for a long time. I know Liv really well, too. As long as we disclose this...whatever this is…" he took one hand and moved it back and forth between him and me, "...then it will be fine."

I sat in his lap and bit my lip, not sure what to do. My heart raced. My head told me this wasn't a good idea, but my body screamed out to be part of his.

His forehead pressed against mine, and our eyes locked. "Maddie, trust me, okay?"

I bit my lower lip harder. I don't know why, but this man,

who I had only known a little over an hour, I trusted. "Okay," I whispered. I leaned in and found his lips, then parted them with my tongue and explored every inch of his mouth.

Jack moved his hands to my head and pulled the knot out, so my hair cascaded around my back. His fingers laced through it, and he gently pulled at my hair with one hand and pushed my head closer with the other, which caused me to slightly moan.

I hadn't been touched in forever.

My womanhood pulsed. My knees parted and spread across both sides of his hips as I sat on his manhood and felt it bulge at my presence. His lips fluttered across my chin, then my neck, before he pulled my head back and lightly sucked on my collarbone.

A louder moan escaped me. He bulged further at the sound.

I ground my body on his and squeezed my arms around him. I tried to bring him closer to me and nibbled at his ear lobe. I felt his heartbeat thumping like mine. My hands moved over his chiseled chest and outlined his muscles while fondling his nipples between my fingers. I kissed his Adam's apple as it throbbed at my touch.

"Maddie, I want you in my bed," he whispered in my ear. He gently bit it and caressed my back with his warm hands.

"Then take me to your bed," I whispered back, not knowing where my courage came from.

He groaned. "I promised you I'd be a gentleman."

"That isn't what I want or *need*." It flew out of my mouth, while I kissed around his earlobe.

Jesus, Maddie, when did you learn to be so forward?

I couldn't help it. I wanted nothing more. I'd never had a one night stand, but I wasn't going to be a prude about this. I felt more alive with Jack than I had in the six years I was with Mike, or anyone else for that matter.

Jack stopped, put his forehead against mine, and locked his eyes with me. "What do you need, Maddie?"

My blood pumped through my veins, and my chest heaved with every breath. *What do I need?*

I closed my eyes, and opened them to see Jack's eyes scanning mine. "Tell me what you need, Maddie."

"Whatever you're willing to give me."

How desperate do I sound?

Jack didn't make me feel bad or hesitate. In a swoop, he picked me up and set me on the ground, before he stepped out of the hot tub himself. He led me over to the outdoor shower and positioned me under the warm water. He slowly removed my thong and bra, then shimmied out of his boxers.

He turned my back to his chest and massaged the soap into me. Jack kneaded my shoulders, then down my spine, and cupped my ass with his hands. He kissed the side of my neck before he turned me around and took a step back.

"You're stunning, Maddie."

I glanced back at him in the moonlight. Water dripped off his chiseled body, and his chest and ab muscles rose with each breath.

I was naked, wet, and didn't feel an ounce of self-consciousness. Something about Jack made me feel sexy, confident, and fully wanted. Mike denied me so many times, and rejected me like trash. Jack's eyes, on the other hand, seared through me with lust and desire.

I wanted this man to make me orgasm, but the way his eyes fixated on me, made me want to please him, too. I wondered if I was capable.

What am I doing? I don't have the experience to be with this guy.

It's a little too late for backing out now.

Past sexual encounters filled my brain, and I pushed the thoughts of all the disappointments out of my head. I stepped closer to him as I caressed soap onto his body, then rubbed my own against his, as my tits grew harder in the process. Fire blazed through every vein in my body as I gazed up at him and stood on my tiptoes to claim his mouth as my own.

"You're delicious," he murmured to me, which sent volts through my nerves.

"Just tell me what to do to please you," I mumbled into his neck before I knew what I was saying.

What is wrong with my mouth tonight?

Jack's head pulled back a bit. I bit my lip; heat rose to my face. I tried to focus on his nipples and felt him stare at me.

He pulled my chin up to his face. "You're perfect, Maddie. Just relax and tell me if you don't like anything, or want me to stop at any time."

Don't like anything? Want him to stop? Like that would be possible with this guy!

I realized he wanted me to answer him. "Don't stop," I begged him as I stared into his eyes.

Jack nodded, and put his lips once more on mine. His hard-on pressed against my stomach, and my vagina throbbed at the thought of him in me. He turned the water off, grabbed towels, and wrapped me up before himself.

He guided me inside a door I hadn't noticed, and into a room with a huge bed. He quickly threw his towel and mine to the floor. His mouth and tongue claimed mine, and my hand stroked his gigantic dick. A low groan cascaded out of him.

His mouth found my chest. One hand gently squeezed my left breast. His mouth encompassed my right breast, and his tongue rolled my nipple, which created a ripple of pleasure through my nerves.

How can a stranger make me feel so good?

I pulled at his hair, and he groaned again. My body vibrated with anticipation, as my lower region dripped with my juices, waiting for his arrival.

His lips were on my belly and fluttered across it. My hands made their way to his shoulders, and dug into them. In one move, he put both hands between my legs and cupped my butt cheeks. Then, he picked me up and sat me on the bed before he slung my legs over his muscular shoulders.

I gasped as he opened me up with his long fingers. One at first, then two, then three as his thumb circled my clit. "That's it, baby," he crooned. He bore into my eyes before he dipped his head and kissed my inner thighs.

"Oh, God," I gasped, as he continued to expertly insert and remove his fingers while circling my clit.

Maddie, don't cum on his hand.

A small grin played on his lips. He kept his fingers on me and came up to my ear once more. "I can't wait to taste you."

My clit pulsed against his fingers, and I started to let out a moan, but caught myself and tried to stop it.

"Don't stay quiet. You're sounds make me so hard." He moved his hips so I could feel his dick on my thigh.

Does he somehow know I only had quiet sex in the past?

Jack's lips frolicked all over my skin, as he worshiped my body and woke up every nerve I had.

My sexual encounters were limited in excitement. But this man I barely knew, expertly knew *exactly* what I needed.

His tongue started gliding over me and stole my breath before his lips enclosed on my womanhood. I whimpered, my breath shook, and my mouth hung wide open.

"You're lovely, Maddie," Jack mumbled against my skin, then swirled his tongue all over me.

My sex started pulsing. Each throb took me a notch higher, as Jack's fingers continued to slide in and out of me.

I dug my heels and calves into his back, and propelled my body further into him. "That's it, baby." His tongue flicked faster against me, and his fingers went deeper. My head got a tad dizzy. My vision started to blur.

Is this what this is supposed to be like?

Oral sex with Mike was horrible. My boyfriends before...well, it was okay. Nothing compared to Jack Stevens. I actually enjoyed it. In fact, I had only dreamed of moments like this, and I started to lose all control of my words.

"Jack...oh my God... Jack...oh God...Jack..." I got louder and louder as he played my body with his expertise. He glanced up at me, fondled my nipple in his free hand, and made every inch of my body scream for him.

I couldn't control my emotions. I heard myself begging him to not stop. Loud. Uninhibited. Desperate to fly.

And I didn't care. My normal, self-conscious, quiet-in-the-bedroom self, did *not* care.

I hadn't lied to him. I didn't only want it, I *needed* it.

Dextrous fingers curled within me, rubbing, swirling, pushing against my sweet spot, while my walls gripped him desperately. And as his mouth sucked on my nub, the fire scorched within me, screaming out to explode and soar into ecstasy.

"Jack!" My body convulsed, and my eyes rolled into the back of my head, as adrenaline rushed through my veins. I shattered against him and grabbed his hair, then pushed him further into me, as I tried to make it last forever.

When I thought I couldn't take any more, I tried to pull back on him, but he grabbed my ass and pulled me back into him, ferociously eating me out and sending me soaring back up.

In the aftermath, I continued to tremble...exhausted from my high...exalted from this man. A perfect stranger who gave me something no other man ever had.

I should have felt awkward. I always did in the past and I didn't know him. This was an intimate act. But all I felt with Jack was cherished.

He slowly made his way up, his mouth doted on my stomach, breasts, and neck before claiming my mouth, kissing me with a new heat—like I was his everything, and he couldn't get his fill.

My heart was still racing from my climaxes, but I desperately sought out his tongue, tasting my orgasms on him as my nerves continued to hum. I reached around his shoulders and lightly ran my nails across his muscular back.

"You're so delicious," he repeated, and sent my ego to the sky.

Underneath him, I felt his cock against me, and I never wanted anything more than at that moment. I was wet, ready, and a new desperation raced through my veins.

He was my candyman and I wanted another hit.

Jack must have grabbed a condom from somewhere. He put it on while still on top of me, but briefly stopped. "You all right with this, Maddie?" He looked me straight in the eyes.

"Please...," I managed to somehow get out, my voice a tad hoarse, which made him smile. He rolled me over, so I was on top, and slowly slid me down on him. I closed my eyes and whimpered, as I allowed my body to wrap around him.

Aside from the fact, I hadn't had sex in a long time, Jack was bigger than anyone I had ever been with. I sat on him for a minute, recalibrated, and felt his girth against me.

"You okay, baby?" Jack's eyes scanned mine as I continued to whimper.

"Mm-hmm," I nodded with labored breath. Then, cautiously, I started to move my hips. My body quickly found a rhythm with his, and we melted into a perfect concoction of pleasure.

Jack moaned a sweet sound as my walls gripped his manhood. "Oh, your sweet." He leaned up and sucked my breast.

I arched my back and grinded into him deeper and deeper, then circled my hips on his dick.

He moaned...loudly. Then started to mutter words like, "Beautiful," and "Fucking sexy," and "God, keep doing that," and "Please, Maddie, don't stop."

I felt like a caged bird freed. I soared, my insides a sea of fire, and felt pleasures I hadn't experienced in all thirty-two years of my life. The normal clumsiness I felt during other sexual encounters was nowhere to be seen—just Jack, me, and our heated bodies that pounded each other with gratification.

"I want to feel you shatter beneath me." Jack sat up, grabbed me, and threw me on my back. He pushed my heels up to my buttocks and rammed into me while his tongue wrestled with mine.

I didn't think his dick could go any further into my body than it was when I was on top of him, but I was wrong. He urgently thrusted, and hit my G-spot which I hadn't know existed prior to him, over and over again.

"You're so good," left my mouth and "oh...oh...oh..."

My vagina was a volcano ready to explode. Jack's body continued to slide into mine, as he teased and taunted my nerves. His lips fluttered against my neck, then his eyes locked into mine.

One more thrust and I tumbled. I fell over the hill and spilled all the way. I shook and cried out his name, as he released into me, and sent me further into my spiral. I clawed his butt cheeks and left marks, as I dug my desire into him.

When our bodies stopped spasming, he put his arms under my back and flipped me on top of him, still inside me. He pulled me close to him and hungrily kissed me like he hadn't just rocked both our worlds.

"Maddie, you're amazing," he breathed between kisses.

I couldn't get any words out and held him tighter. My chest heaved from it all, and my breath started to slow. My pride beamed from his praise.

Jack finally pulled out of me, removed the condom, tied it in a knot, and threw it in the trash can next to the bed.

We laid worn out in each others arms. Jack told me again that I was delicious and caressed my back as I drifted off to sleep.

Jack

. . .

I TOLD MYSELF I WOULDN'T TOUCH HER. WHEN I SAW HER BY THE hot tub, her body glistened in the moonlight, I couldn't help it. I felt like I was being pulled to her and I had to taste her.

I pulled out of the kiss, sat in the hot tub, and reminded myself I would only get to know her. But she was too tempting. Her body was on mine, and I didn't mean to tell her I wanted her in my bed, but it rolled out of my mouth. When she told me she needed whatever I would give her, I wasn't going to deny her.

What a dickhead her ex was. Any real man wouldn't let this woman be in need of anything.

She was sweeter than I thought she would be. A heavenly piece of pleasure. Of all my one night stands and sexual encounters, I had never experienced anyone like her.

And she was worried about pleasing me? Yep, her ex must be a total douchebag.

Mesmerized, I watched her fall asleep in my arms, knowing that there was no way she could only be casual. Although I had sworn off casual a year ago, I couldn't go back to my old ways...not with her.

Perfection was defined when she was created, I thought, as I stroked her back and looked at her sensual curves, amazed that she didn't even know it. I wondered what kind of a man would not tell her how special, perfect, or amazing she was and let her go—obviously, a total moron.

I didn't know how long she was in Tampa, but I wanted to see more of her and wracked my brain to figure out what I could do that was nice for her. Picking up the phone, I called the front desk.

"Mr. Stevens, this is Susie, how can I help you?" The front desk clerk sounded cheerful, even though it was around midnight.

I twisted the old-fashioned phone cord in my hand. "Hi Susie. Is the east wing still closed?"

"Yes it is, sir."

"Please, bring Ms. Maddie Burns's luggage to my room."

The receptionist became uncomfortable. "Sir, I'm so sorry but we can't do that without Ms. Burns's permission."

"She's sleeping. I don't want to wake her up," I replied, rather annoyed.

"Yes, but...but it's our policy, sir," she stuttered.

I rolled my eyes. "Please let me talk to Greg." Greg was the manager, and I had dealt with him quite a bit, as I was in Tampa a lot these days.

"One moment, sir."

I waited and looked down at Maddie, who slept peacefully.

"Mr. Stevens," Greg boasted.

I turned on the heat. "Hey, Greg, I have a situation. I need it taken care of. I'm assuming, as much as I book out your penthouse that you could understand the position I'm in and help me out, especially since your hotel is the cause of this issue?" I didn't mean to be that type of dick, but it wasn't totally false. The only reason Maddie was in my room was because of their east wing issue...although I felt like I should have been thanking him for that.

Greg was silent for a moment. "What can I do for you, Mr. Stevens? You know we appreciate all your patronage. We absolutely want to continue serving you as our guest."

"Thank you, Greg. I need Ms. Maddie Burns's suitcase...and any contents she may have taken out of it, packed back in it and brought to my suite, please."

Greg was silent again. I could hear his brain turning. "Right away, Mr. Stevens," he finally agreed.

"Thank you, Greg. I appreciate your help."

I snuggled into Maddie and reminded myself not to screw this one up.

3

Maddie

AT 3 A.M., I WOKE UP AND SAW MY LUGGAGE. I LOOKED OVER AT Jack, who slept with his body half in the sheets, half out, glistening in the dark.

His body could make the Greek Gods jealous, no doubt.

I sat on the edge of the bed with a silly grin on my face. As I admired his body, I held myself back from touching him and wondered how this man could not be taken.

Maybe he felt me ogling him, because he slowly opened his eyes.

"Maddie? Something wrong?" His sleepy face filled with concern.

I crawled up next to him. "I'm fine. My luggage is here?"

"Yes," he stated, like it wasn't a big deal.

"How did that happen?"

"We are both naked and you want to know about your luggage?" He raised his brow at me in a mischievous way.

My grin grew bigger. "Yep."

"I called the front desk and arranged for it when you fell asleep. I thought you would want some fresh clothes this morning. Not that I have any problem if you want to stay naked in my room for the week," he teased and rubbed his hands on my naked back.

Hmmm...a naked week with Jack Stevens...now that is something to think about. But surely he's joking?

Jack leaned over, and his tongue found mine with a new passion. My body responded, and I wondered, once more, how this total stranger could feel like a natural piece of heaven?

Probably because you're on vacation. Is this what they mean by a vacation fling?

Well, at least a one-night fling, I reminded myself. While I was inexperienced in one-night stands, my gut told me that Jack was a pro. Not that I was judging.

I felt him stir to life, as his body pressed against mine, hard and warm.

I wanted to taste him. No, I *had* to taste him. His dick was smooth and throbbed against my hand. I could feel a vein as I played with his shaft. I shimmied down his body, took in his amazing pecs and abs, and listened to his breath increase with each new kiss I placed on him.

I approached his manhood, and instead of licking his shaft, I started to suck his balls. Pride gushed through me when he grunted in delight.

I didn't have tons of experience in the blow-job department, but I desperately wanted to give Jack as good of head as he gave me.

Dear blow-job gods, please send me top skills right now.

An unfamiliar need rushed through me...to feel him in my mouth...to taste the salt of his cum...to make him beg as much as I had begged him. So I moved my tongue to his shaft, licked slowly from the base to the top, sucked on his tip, and took my time fully engaged in the process. I listened intently to his moans and words of encouragement, and let them lead me through the journey.

Jack put his hands through my hair and pushed me on his tip, "Please, Maddie," he begged, which gave me an adrenaline rush. I fully embraced him. Inch by inch, I sucked, licked, and twisted. Where the skills came from, I didn't know, but somehow, my body knew what he needed.

He panted and mumbled incoherent words as his hips moved with the rhythm of my mouth. His hands caressed my head, then gently pulled my hair, then pushed me, then pulled me again.

And I loved it. For the first time in my life, I loved giving head. I moaned in appreciation of this man and his beautiful, hard, smooth, ready-to-burst dick. The taste of his pre-cum made me want more. In that moment, I left the old Maddie that hated to give head and became a woman who felt the power of what I could do to this sex god of a man.

My moans turned Jack on more. I could feel him swell and he was close to rupturing. He tried to pull me off him, and warned me that he was about to cum. Normally, I would have removed my mouth, but not this time. I wanted all of him…every drop of his orgasm…a prize for the pleasure I was able to reciprocate back to him.

"Maddie...oh God, I'm gonna cum, baby," he cried out. His voice warned me, and his hands attempted to push my mouth off him.

I was high from how much he needed me in that moment to finish what I started. Determination overcame me, and I pushed his hands away and sucked him off harder. I listened to him moan as he started to shake and then violently explode in my mouth.

I devoured him. I swallowed and drank like a hungry girl. I never let up, as I brought him to ecstasy and listened to him call out my name and curse with pleasure.

His body finally stopped ricochetting. I removed him from

my mouth, and slowly looked up. Jack grinned at me, dimples on both cheeks, as his chest heaved, and a drop of sweat dripped down the side of his face.

"That was incredible," he boasted. "I give you permission to do that anytime you want."

Joy jolted through me that I could make him feel so good.

I slid back up to him and squatted over his waist. My bare breasts laid on his chest, my lips were inches from his as I grinned at him. "Thanks for getting my luggage."

Jack let out a roaring laugh and rubbed my bare ass. "If that's all I have to do to get that kind of blow job, please give me a list of anything you want me to do for you."

"I'll start my list tomorrow then," I teased.

He took my face in his hands. "Seriously, that was amazing."

My ego once again shot up.

He kissed me and my body started to heat up again. "Thank you, it's my turn now."

A surge of adrenaline ran through my body.

He flipped me on my back. Jack's talented hands started playing with my breasts, as his lips moved between my neck and mouth.

"So fucking beautiful," he muttered.

"You're not so bad yourself," I whispered and grabbed the back of his neck and pushed him further into my mouth.

Jack stopped for a minute and stared me in the eyes. "You're fucking delicious, Maddie. I mean it."

My cheeks heated. I had full carnal knowledge of Jack, and he literally made me blush, as I laid naked in his arms. I tried to pull him to me again but he stopped me.

"I want to watch you cum, Maddie. I want to see your eyes roll, and know you're reacting to my touch. I want you to lose control and call out my name and not even know you're saying it." He gazed into my eyes, searching for my reaction.

My cheeks grew redder. In fact, they burned as my vagina

twitched in anticipation, and my heart raced. I knew that was exactly what he would do to me.

No man ever talked to me this way before. Not in the bedroom or out of it. The way Jack talked before, during, and after sex, was a major turn on. I found it sexy and freeing.

Jack saw me blush, kissed both my cheeks, and pulled back to look into my eyes, "Do you want me to do that to you, Maddie?"

I bit my lip and nodded. If anyone else on earth stated they wanted to do that to me, I wouldn't have the nerve to admit I wanted them too. But I couldn't hold back with Jack.

"Tell me then." He continued to drill his eyes into mine.

"Make me cum, Jack. Please," I whispered.

His mouth hit my neck. He sucked and gently bit and sent ripples throughout my spine. His hands found their way to my lower region. "Do you want one or two?" He bent one finger in me, then pulled it out and slowly twisted in two, before repeating it over again.

"Shit, Jack," I cursed at him. I closed my eyes and tried to steady my breath, as I knew he was only getting started with me.

"Or, maybe you want three, baby?" Those intense, sexy eyes never left mine, as he inserted three fingers at once, then rubbed, glided, and twisted against my insides.

I whimpered against him.

He continued to finger-fuck me with his one, two, three sequence. He didn't miss a beat, and intensely gauged my reaction.

The side of my leg felt his erection spark to life again. Apparently, it turned him on to watch me. I grabbed his dick and tried to stroke him.

He sat up, pulled his fingers out of me, grabbed my hand, and moved it to my other hand. Then, he took my wrists and held them over my head.

"I want full control of your body. Can I have it?"

Did he seriously say that? My entire body fluttered. I let out a shaky breath, bit my lip again, and nodded. Anything to get his fingers back in my body.

"Do you want that, Maddie?" His lips were inches from my mouth, and his eyes drove into mine.

I nodded again.

"Tell me," he demanded.

"Please, Jack." I would beg if that is what he wanted, desperate for his touch once more.

He secured his hold on my wrists above my head, then started his finger rotation once again. Over and over, he teased my G-spot then pulled back, as I moaned and closed my eyes.

"Open your eyes, Maddie. I want to see you."

I opened my eyes.

"Good girl. Now you get more." He put his thumb on my clit and rubbed me slowly, effortlessly, with enough speed to take me up, but not enough to push me over. He released his thumb whenever his finger would swipe my G-spot.

I was in heaven. I was in hell. I was up, but not enough, and on the cusp of exploding. Yet, he continued to hold me back.

"Oh God...please...don't stop...oh, please...Jack," I cried out. Not able to think anymore, as my eyes tried to stay open, but I had to blink repeatedly. My body became his to control.

"You want it, Maddie?" he questioned and pushed my wrists higher up so my body was stretched further. Thumb on, thumb off. Fingers in, fingers out.

I nodded, not able to talk, groaned loudly, and tried to breathe. I begged him with my wild and crazy eyes. The lower region of my body swayed back and forth, and moved into him further.

Jack had a full-blown hard-on now. I could feel it pulsing against my leg. I glanced at it and Jack saw me.

"What do you want, Maddie? Do you want my fingers or my dick?" Jack shifted his head so his lips were right up against mine.

"Fingers. Dick," I cried out not able to decide or comprehend.

My brain was a foggy mess. I wanted to cum, but Lord, his dick was hard.

"Why don't I give it all to you? Would you like that?" His eyes beat into mine.

Like a dog salivating, I was eager for it all.

"Tell me you want it all," Jack calmly instructed me, his lips so close to mine, but he held back, as I tried to grab them with my own lips.

"Want...all," I managed to get out, breathless and crazed for him to give me whatever he saw fit.

Jack smiled, then quickly put his thumb on my clit and his finger on my G-spot at the same time. I spilled my sex all over the place. I was a bomb that erupted everywhere. My eyes rolled, and my body violently convulsed, as Jack watched my face the entire time.

I didn't get a rest. The minute my orgasm slowed, he slid in me and the climb up the mountain started again. This time, I was still quaking and my eyes hadn't regained focus.

"Jack…you're so…good."

"Ah… you're heaven, Maddie."

"Oh…fuck," I screamed out, as his girth shimmied against my walls.

Jack released my wrists and I wrapped my arms around him. I dug my claws into his back, while still trembling as he entered and exited me. Tightly, I wrapped my legs around his rock-solid body and started to orgasm again.

"You're...fuck...Maddie." He found my lips and claimed my tongue.

I think he knew I couldn't go much longer. He pumped hard in me, called out my name, and God knows what else.

I was delirious. I don't know how long we laid there, but the sun started to rise. We were in a pool of sweat and body fluids, exhausted from our efforts.

Jack's phone alarm rang. My head jerked. He laughed. "Time for my workout."

"You have to be kidding me."

We probably just burned a thousand calories apiece.

An amused Jack shook his head, "Nope." He leaned over, kissed me on the lips, and whispered, "*You,* Maddie Burns, are fucking amazing." Naked, he jumped out of bed and walked out to the balcony.

4

Jack

SHE WAS SWEET AND INNOCENT BUT WILD AND UNINHIBITED, TO MY surprise. I couldn't get enough of her, and I wanted to keep pleasing her.

Once outside, I jumped in the water, and my body took delight in the cool temperature. I swam laps, back and forth, my mind in more motion than my body.

I have to see her again.

My mind raced about how I needed to make sure she wouldn't go back to her side of the hotel, and that would be it. I wondered if she, like me, wanted to see where this could go.

She was fresh out of a breakup, but she sounded adamant that it had been over for a while. I prayed she wouldn't make that a reason she couldn't continue to see me.

I hadn't put my heart out there...not since Kelly. There wasn't anyone I would have even considered seriously dating. But Maddie was like no other woman I knew, and if she slipped through my fingers, I would officially be the biggest idiot on earth. I hardly knew her, but I knew that in my gut.

I don't deserve her, but I have to have her.

I swam to the wall and dove under, turned, and kicked my feet off of it. My body skimmed through the water, and I rose to the surface to catch a glimpse of her. She sat in the chaise with a robe on and watched me.

Well, she hasn't left, so that's a good start.

What is she thinking? I wondered. *Will she want to see where this can go or will she only want this to be a one-nighter?* She didn't seem like a one-night-stand type of girl, but who knew. Not that I was judging if she was. Lord knows, I was no saint.

My past. I was such a dick. It would serve me right if she did tell me it was only for one night.

The more I swam, the more I started spinning out, my demons starting to catch up to me with no amount of exercise to burn them out of my mind. I really didn't deserve her, but I would fight for her if needed.

Maddie

It took me a minute to register that he was naked on the balcony. I stood up and walked over to the sliding glass door. There was a pool I hadn't seen the night prior, and Jack swam laps in the nude.

I threw a robe on and planted myself on a lounge chair. Jack's body effortlessly cut through the water, back and forth, over and over again. I watched him like a guilty pleasure.

Damn, he's so hot.

An hour later, he jumped out of the pool, wrapped a towel around himself and sat in the chair next to me. "Enjoy the show?"

"Why yes, I did." I smirked at him.

Jack licked his lips, lightly laughing. "So what are your plans today?"

"Zero, zilch, nada."

"Ah, the life," he teased.

"Don't you ever take time off? It is, after all, Saturday."

Jack sat further back in the lounge chair. He turned his head toward me, and gave me a slight smile with a hint of sadness in it. I could see his mind churning, as he chose his words carefully.

"It's not that easy for me, Maddie."

I didn't understand. "What do you mean?"

"My work is who I am. It's part of me. I'm nothing without it."

Squinting my eyes at him in question, I tried to understand what he meant. "That's a pretty bold statement to make. What's really behind that?"

Jack stood up and leaned over to kiss me. "Nothing. I need to get ready for my meeting." He turned and walked away.

Obviously, I had struck a nerve and wondered what the heck it could be. The realization that I had only known Jack for less than twelve hours—and while last night was the most amazing sex ever, I didn't know anything about him—hit me. Well, except for the fact that he had accounts at my employer's firm.

Crap. I had forgotten about that. That meant, at some point, I might run into him during work. And, he made a pretty large statement that work was everything to him, so there was no way he would jeopardize anything professional.

After spending six years with a workaholic and being in second place, I wasn't about to do it again. Jack was nothing like Mike in the bedroom, but he sounded exactly like him in his career. I wasn't about to journey through that disappointment again.

No, Jack was a god in bed, but no way he would want more. *You just got out of a relationship. This is called a one-night stand, Maddie. Be grateful for what it is and move on.*

Suddenly, I felt like I shouldn't be there. I grabbed my wet bra and underwear that were still outside from the previous night, and threw on my dress that laid on the concrete floor next to the hot tub. Flashbacks of our night riveted through my head.

But I quickly pulled myself back to reality and slid into my sandals, walked into the penthouse, and found a pen and paper pad in the kitchen.

JACK,

Thanks for a great night. Have a great rest of your trip!

Maddie

FROM THERE, I WALKED INTO THE BEDROOM, GRABBED MY suitcase, and started wheeling it away. I reached the door but didn't make it out.

"You're leaving?" Jack sounded hurt.

Paralyzed, I stood still and didn't turn around. Suddenly, I wasn't sure what the hell I was doing by leaving like this.

"Maddie?"

I turned to see Jack in a towel, and he looked at me like a wounded bird.

"I left you a note," I managed to get out and pointed to the kitchen.

Jack walked over and read the note. "Seriously?" He glared at me.

Speechless, I gaped at him, and the longer I stood there, the sillier I felt. The feeling I screwed something up surged through me. But what did I know? *What exactly is one-night-stand proper etiquette?*

"I thought I would see if my room was fixed now and get out of your hair," I attempted to fib. I was always a crappy liar.

"Bullshit, Maddie." Jack called me out. "What's so bad that you have to sneak out of here while I'm in the shower, with your bra and panties in your hand and nipples all fucking erect under that dress?"

My eyes drifted to my body. Yep, my nipples were erect under my dress, my hands full of my undergarments, and my suitcase in my hand.

Oh jeez, I was an idiot.

"I think my nipples are my business, thank you," was all I could muster.

"That's funny, I remember them being *my* business less than a few hours ago," Jack fired at me.

I couldn't argue that one. I was out of words. Jack walked toward me, and I froze. Unable to move, I wasn't sure how to get myself out of this one.

His eyes pierced though mine as he reached above my head and shut the door. I didn't even realize it was still open. His eyes and voice went soft, "If I gave you any impression that I wanted you to leave, then I apologize."

"You didn't," I quickly told him, then regretted it the instant it came out of my mouth.

He took his fingers and stroked my cheek. "Then what has you running out of here, like this?"

"I don't know." Again, another lie.

Jack grabbed my suitcase out of my hands and moved it to the corner and came back to the door where I still stood. He grabbed my hand and led me over to the couch. "Sit."

"Now I feel like a naughty schoolgirl or something."

Jack grinned. "Don't get me started on fantasies right now."

I laughed and felt my body start to relax a bit.

"Maddie, let's get something straight, shall we?" His eyes penetrated mine.

I stared at him, not sure what he would say.

"Please, don't ever leave me a note like that or try to sneak out on me again." Jack grabbed my face and scanned my eyes.

Again?

"There's something here—between us. I know it."

I stared at him, unsure how to respond. If I was being honest with myself, I was up for a replay with Jack, no doubt. He gave me the best night ever. But, as I silently tried to comprehend his words and the meaning behind them, I couldn't deny those weren't words of a one night stand. They were words of something more. *But I just got out of a relationship.*

"Can we agree on both those things?"

I almost agreed but stopped myself.

"What?" He sensed there was something I wasn't saying.

"Jack, what do you want from me? Last night was great...this morning was great...but honestly, I don't expect anything from you. It's okay," I reassured him, giving him an out.

He didn't answer the question but flipped it back to me. "Does this have to do with your ex?"

"What? No!" I denied, but inside, I knew that was definitely part of it. He looked at me like he didn't believe me.

It wasn't that I wasn't over him; I was. I had been for months…actually, the truth was Mike and I had been over for years.

But if Jack was asking me to get into a relationship with him, was I ready to get back into one? How could it be possible for me to meet someone I could be in a relationship with this soon? And what about his work addiction?

"Why don't you answer my question? What do you want from me?" I repeated.

Jack shook his head and inhaled deeply. "Honestly, Maddie, let's start with your phone number. You not sneaking out of my room. Maybe a dinner date tonight, and tomorrow, and I don't know what else, but maybe see where this goes?"

The truth was out. He wanted more, and it was now up to me to say yes or no.

Visions of me as I waited in restaurants by myself flashed into my mind. "I can't Jack. I've done the 'date the workaholic' before." I decided honesty was the best policy here.

"Ah. I see. So this does have something to do with your ex."

I couldn't deny it, I guess it did, as much as I didn't want it to. I fidgeted with my fingers and focused on that.

"What was the worst thing about dating a workaholic?"

"I always came second. I won't do that again."

"And you shouldn't. Maddie, do you feel you came second last night?"

I thought about it. There was no way I could say that I felt anything but Jack's priority last night. "No, of course not. But it's not the same thing."

"Really? Did your ex make you feel like I did last night?"

I blushed. "No."

"Did you think I was attentive to you in the bar or only in my bed?"

I couldn't deny that I was the only thing he seemed to care about last night. "All night. You put me first all night."

"Then don't you think I deserve a chance to show you that I won't put you second, and I'll put you first if we try to see where this goes?" Jack's long fingers stroked my leg, as his eyes begged me to give him a chance.

I thought about it for a few minutes. Fear and excitement boiled up in me. I didn't say anything at first.

"Please, Maddie. Give me a chance. I'm not your ex."

One thing was right, Jack was nothing like my ex when it came to the bedroom or even how he made me feel last night before we had sex.

As much as I thought I should swear off guys for a bit, and needed to figure out who I was, I couldn't deny I wanted more of Jack.

"Okay. But don't disappoint me, because I don't want to feel like a stupid girl anymore."

He smiled, relieved, happy and content with my answer. "He's the dumb guy. You're not the stupid girl. And I won't, I promise. But for God's sake, cover your nipples up because I need to go to work, and I'll miss my meeting if you keep them out like that."

I smacked him in the arm, not able to hold back my laughter.

"Seriously. Stay here as long as you want. Here's the extra key for you." He grabbed the extra key off the table, then vulnerably admitted, "I like having you here."

I grinned like a schoolgirl. "I like being here with you, too."

"It's settled then. Give me your phone number and I'll see you tonight for dinner?" He reached over to the table and grabbed his phone.

I agreed and put my number in his phone.

He kissed me, dressed, and left.

5

Jack

THE WHEELS OF HER SUITCASE ROLLED ACROSS THE WOOD FLOOR just as I stepped out of the shower. Panic ran through me. Sure enough, I caught her as she tried to leave.

She agreed to give me a chance. I know I didn't deserve it, but I wanted to keep pursuing her.

Whatever guy she had been with was a serious douchebag. He put her second? What kind of man would ever put her second?

A complete douchebag.

Maddie made her requirements clear, and I would do everything I could to make her feel like the precious darling she was.

My new partner was late. I wracked my brain about where I should take her for dinner. I opened my laptop and searched for places we could go.

Everything seemed so boring. I needed to find somewhere special. Somewhere to show her that I was committed to making her number one. That she deserved more than whatever her ex did for her, and that I would be the guy to give it to her.

I sorted through all the places I visited during my trips to Tampa. Nothing stood out. I thought about how Maddie scrolled on Instagram and booked her trip. The thought made me smile.

She was adventurous and my schedule sounded like a bore to her. Well, if I was honest, it was...

I sighed. *How to show an adventurous girl she's my priority,* I thought and tapped my fingers on the table.

Then it hit me. I knew what I would do.

My new partner walked in.

I looked over at him. “Can you give me a recommendation?”

Maddie

Apparently, the east wing was open again, so the resort was full of happy people. The madness of the night before was nowhere to be seen. So I spent the day doing random things. I walked the resort, then hung by the pool and talked to a few strangers who were on vacation.

Reluctantly, I wheeled my suitcase back to my side of the hotel. My gut told me Jack wanted me to stay, but I needed to think about some things.

Giving Jack a chance was one thing, but was I really contemplating a new relationship?

My brain told me that I was getting myself into a similar situation as I had been in with Mike...and I didn't want that. Factually, I should have told Jack no and left it at that, but I couldn't deny how his actions felt so different from the way Mike ever made me feel.

The sex was unreal...surely it was a one-off thing, and I would be disappointed the next time? Was it possible to have mind-blowing sex with the same person, for more than one passion-filled night?

The reality was, I didn't really know Jack and I felt like the sex was blurring the lines. Almost as if, I couldn't really see anything but good because I was under his sex spell or something.

Men like Jack Stevens don't really exist, do they?

He will surely get bored with me after tonight.

I was lost in thought when my phone rang. It was a blocked number, so I let it go to voicemail. A few seconds later, I received a text.

"Tried calling you, but it went to voicemail. Can you call me back?"

"Who is this and what is your number?"

"Jack. Forgot my number is blocked—555-6289."

The phone rang once. Jack picked up. "Why is your number blocked?"

"Business purposes. Put my number in and it won't pop up blocked anymore."

"Okay. So what's up?"

"What are you doing tomorrow?"

My heart sank. Once again, I was going to come second, probably to his work. He was going to blow off our dinner.

Well, at least he's calling, and you're not sitting in a restaurant waiting.

"Canceling our date already, huh?" I tried not to sound disappointed, but I also couldn't deny I was a bit pissed off.

Jack roared with laughter.

"I don't think it's funny." I started to get more upset.

"No. As a matter of fact, I am *not* cancelling our date. I am extending it." I could sense the smug look on his face through the phone.

"Good. In that case, nothing. Remember, I don't have any plans. I'm not scheduled like you." I teased, as relief shot through me.

He exhaled, "Good. Can you pack an overnight bag and meet me in the lobby around five o'clock? Will you throw my stuff in there, too? There is an overnight bag in the closet."

"Ummm...sure...can you tell me where we are going?" I didn't tell him I was back in my room.

"Nope. I'll text you a list of what to pack. See you at five."

I glanced at the time—two hours till then—I better pack and go back to his place.

Sure enough, Jack sent over a list of items:

Bathing suits

Sunscreen

Casual outfit for tomorrow—shorts and t-shirt for me

My sandals, your sandals

Wear something dressy casual for tonight

My toiletries bag

Whatever toiletries you need

I texted him back. "You forgot the condoms."

"Shit! How could I forget that? In my suitcase, inside pocket."

"I was kidding."

"No you weren't," he responded, along with winking and fist-bump emojis.

I sent him an eye-roll emoji back. *Yep, he's right, I most definitely wasn't kidding.*

I decided it would be easier to roll my suitcase back to Jack's. So once again, I wheeled my way through the hotel. The desk clerk gave me a smirk. I ignored her.

Back at Jack's, I put my bag together and rifled through his closet and drawers. I felt strange going through his stuff.

I texted him. "I feel like a snoop going through your stuff."

"I asked you to, remember?"

"Still feel like a snoop."

"Do you want me to punish you for it later tonight?"

I'll get in line for that punishment. "Ha, ha!"

"Can you grab a pair of underwear for me too, please."

"What if I want you panty free?"

"I can free ball it, if that turns you on."

I sent him a GIF of a guy bowling and knocking down all the pins.

"OUCH!"

I packed everything—including a pair of his underwear, quickly showered, and started getting ready. I put on my other new sundress, heels, and jewelry. When I had finished my hair and started applying my makeup, my phone rang.

"Hello?" I answered without looking.

"Maddie, I'm running a bit behind. I'll be there in five minutes."

"Shoot. Jack, sorry, I lost track of time. Don't rush, I'm about ten minutes behind."

He chuckled. "And here I was, thinking you were going to tell me I was putting you second."

"I'm not *that* unrealistic." At least he took my demand seriously.

"I'll see you in ten then."

I finished getting ready and headed out. I grabbed our bag. Hmmm...that was strange...*our* bag. Less than twenty-four hours after meeting this guy, and I'm packing our bag to go to some random place...

I pushed the thought out of my head. *Isn't this what vacation is supposed to be all about?*

6

Maddie

JACK WAITED FOR ME IN THE LOBBY. A SCHOOLBOY GRIN GREW ON his face when he saw me. He wore a white button-down shirt with his sleeves rolled up and khaki shorts. Not sure how it happened, but he seemed to have gotten hotter since this morning. He greeted me with a long, lingering kiss.

After snatching the bag from me, he put his hand on my back and led me out to the car. He opened my door and I got in. After he pulled into traffic, I turned to him and smiled. "Where are you taking me?"

"You ever been to St. Pete?" He glanced over at me.

"Nope."

"Good. Me neither."

"Rather crazy for your scheduled self, isn't it?"

He gave me a full dimpled smile and shrugged his shoulders.

"So what are we going to do there?"

"We're going to have a nice dinner, then I'm going to feast on your body all night, and we're going to spend the day at the beach tomorrow."

My face flushed at the thought of him feasting on my body. "You aren't going to work tomorrow?"

He raised his brow at me. "Do you want me to work tomorrow?"

"Nope."

"Then I'm not working tomorrow."

"Really?" I didn't fully believe him. "Not even some laptop or phone time?"

"I didn't bring my laptop and I'll turn my phone off. I think I've earned a day off, and I can't think of anyone else I would want to take a day off for..."

I gave him a giddy grin. "So when did you concoct this plan?"

"When I was sitting in a meeting, thinking about your blow-job skills instead of listening to important details of my newest merger."

I slapped his arm. "Hey there! Don't blame the blow job for your lack of professionalism."

"Maybe it was when I was thinking about how I made your eyes roll to the back of your head..."

I slapped him again and giggled as a new shade of maroon crept up my face.

"So what did you do today?"

"Not much. Lounged by the pool. Talked to some random strangers. Walked around the resort. Nothing special."

"Sounds relaxing."

"It was. So what kind of company are you merging with?"

"You really want to talk about work?"

"Yes. I want to know what you do."

Jack peered at me to see if I was serious. "Okay, but I didn't bring it up."

"Fair enough. Promise I won't hold it over your head."

"Can I trust you to keep this between us?" He shifted in his seat, tapped the steering wheel, and nervously glanced at me.

What was the big secret? My curiosity was now officially killing me. "Yes, I won't tell anyone, I promise."

"It's a sex club."

"You're lying."

"No, I'm not."

I burst into laughter. "How on earth does that even happen? Do you own other sex clubs?"

"Yes, but not a lot of people know about those. Liv and Tom—they don't know—so please don't bring it up."

"I won't say anything, but why keep it a secret? I mean, if you're going to do it, what's the shame in it?"

"It's not shame, I just don't want to be seen as *that* guy."

"What do you mean by 'that guy'?"

Jack tapped the steering wheel, "You know. The perverted guy who is in the sex industry."

"So you aren't the perverted guy? I mean, you did some pretty perverted things with me last night."

"That wasn't perverted, but I can show you perverted tonight if you want," Jack promised.

I wasn't sure what that meant. *But you can show me perverted all night long if you want.*

"So you aren't the perverted guy but you are? I'm getting confused,"

"Look, I own a portfolio of companies. A few years ago, I was introduced to a guy who needed help with his club over in Miami. I turned it around and it's making a fortune. So every now and then, I find another gem that I'm able to turn around and make a lot of money on. But I don't want to be known for that."

"What *do* you want to be known for?"

"The guy who takes over companies and turns them around. The one who saves jobs and creates better lives for others." His eyes were focused on the road, but I knew without seeing them that this was something important to him.

Wow. He cares about more than only making money.

"That's noble." I put my hand on his thigh.

We didn't talk for a bit. Finally, I asked, "So how often do you go to these sex clubs?"

"Maddie," he replied sternly, like it was a topic I shouldn't breach.

"What? I want to know! Is that where you'll be late at night?"

"Funny," he mumbled, but he didn't seem amused. "I don't go when they're open."

"What! You don't go?"

"No. My partners run them. I deal with the backend stuff and only go in during closed hours."

"Well, Jack Stevens, I never would have thought it, but you're a prude, aren't you?"

Jack checked me out, licking his lips. "I definitely wouldn't consider myself a prude."

"But you won't go to a sex club, even though you own them?"

He glanced over at me. "Would you?"

I shrugged my shoulders. "With you? Sure, why not?"

Jack laughed. "You're serious?"

"Yeah, why not? Could be fun! I mean, I've never been to one but it could be interesting. Think of it as taking me to work."

Jack glanced at me in disbelief. "I can't even believe we are talking about this right now."

"Why? Because you're a prude?"

"No, because you are serious about me taking you to a sex club."

"I think it could be kinda hot."

"You're serious?"

"Yep."

He shook his head as we pulled into the hotel. The valet came to take our keys, and Jack snatched the overnight bag from the backseat, walked around the car, grabbed my waist, and led me inside. He quickly checked us in.

When we arrived at the room, Jack dropped the bag. He pulled me out onto the balcony that overlooked the beach, "Wow. That's a beautiful beach. Thanks for planning this."

Jack pulled me to him, kissed me, and grabbed my ass with both palms. He wadded my dress up, and took a finger and moved my underwear aside, then slid it into my pussy. It caught me off guard and I inhaled sharply.

"You're so wet. All that talk about the sex club has you worked up?" He raised his eyebrows at me.

I tried to catch my breath as his finger moved against my walls, and caused me to stand on my tip toes before I sank back on his hand.

"We have reservations, so this is going to be quick, but I'm going to make you cum, and then I'm going to lick my fingers, so I taste you all night long. Is this a good start for perv?"

Apparently, he was on a mission to show me he *was* a perv. I stared at him, and I tried not to smile but didn't accomplish that goal very well.

Jack didn't wait for me to answer and began to work me into a high. He went right to my G-spot, and my lip started shaking. I lost the ability to stand. He grabbed me, turned me around, and held me tight around the waist, before he pushed me up against the balcony so I faced everyone on the beach below.

We were on the twentieth floor, so no one could probably see my face contort or hear my muffled cries, but the fact that someone might watch and hear stirred something in me.

As if he could read my mind... "Do you like the thought of someone seeing you? Hearing you?" Jack whispered into my ear, while he tapped my G-spot and made me inhale sharply.

He tapped, tapped, tapped, and I thought I would explode. Totally different than the night before or this morning. How this man knew how to do all these different things to my body was a mystery to me.

"Oh, God," I breathed out.

His teeth pulled my sundress string, and my dress fell. The arm that was around my waist inched up but stayed secure, while his hand reached up and slid under my bra, then rubbed my nipples. Jack's tongue flickered on my neck.

Whimpering against him, I was putty in his hands, as I melted into his every touch.

"Do you stay this quiet, or let everyone know you're being pleasured?" he whispered, tapped me hard, and sent the first set of small tremors throughout my body.

My voice became a reflex, and I cried out his name as I lost any remaining ability to stand. A ragdoll, held only by his arm, and the wall as the heat from his body coursed through my backside, and his cock pulsed against my ass.

I had little room to move, but I pushed my backside as hard as I could against his cock and ground into his hand. Dizzy from the heat in the air and Jack's warm body next to mine, I closed my eyes, heard the waves crashing below me, and seagulls calling out.

Jack's lips murmured in my ear, "So many things I want to do with you."

"Jack…I..." I latched my arms behind Jack's neck as my body repeatedly clenched his fingers, unable to stop. My lungs vibrated, and my head leaned back, further into Jack's neck, while my eyes flickered, and my breath puffed out of my mouth.

It's so hot. Please make me fly.

"I'm going to make you cum now, and then I'm going to taste and smell your deliciousness all night." Jack tapped me some more and swiped my clit with his thumb.

I peaked almost instantly, cried out his name, and didn't care who heard me or saw me. My body burst in his arms, and I shuddered savagely against Jack and the wall. Over and over, my high rippled through me.

When I was done, he turned me around so I could watch him suck on his fingers, before he pushed them into my mouth.

"You *are* a perv," I whispered to him, a massive grin on my face.

Jack gave me a cocky eyebrow and tied up my sundress. "Let's go."

7

Maddie

THE ELEVATOR DOORS OPENED TO A ROOFTOP BAR. LIVE MUSIC pulsed through the air, and a view of the sunset drew a crowd with standing room only. Jack had reserved us a VIP area and we were led to a cabana room with a table and couch. We sat on the couch, Jack's arm around me, as I leaned into his chest.

The waitress came over and we ordered drinks.

"How did you know where to go if you haven't been here before?"

"I asked Roy."

"The sex club owner?"

"Yes."

"So I really do think we should go check this out one night while we are here," I told Jack. I had never thought about going to a sex club before, but to my surprise, I was curious, and I figured it would be fun with him.

"Maddie, I'm not taking you to a sleazy sex club. If any other dude tried to touch you, I'd beat his ass."

I laughed. “Easy there, killer.”

“I’m not laughing, Maddie.”

"What if a girl wanted to touch me?”

Jack’s eyes widened. “Are you into that?”

Ignoring the question, I asked, “Would you beat her ass?”

“Very funny.”

“I don’t see the difference.”

Jack shifted in his seat. “You know, you’re right. There isn’t a difference in some ways. I wouldn’t want to share you with anyone.”

“You’re not telling me, if I wanted to have a threesome with another girl, you would say no?”

“I would one-hundred percent tell you no,” Jack firmly declared.

“You must be the only guy on the planet who would say that.”

“Have you had a threesome before or been with a girl?”

“No. But you’re really surprising me here. I really didn’t expect your prudish ways,” I teased him.

Jack’s face was serious. “I will never share you with anyone.”

I wasn’t done teasing him. “Prudish and possessive then?”

Jack rolled his eyes, a faint smile on his face. “I’ll agree with the possessive, and I’ll show you again how you’re wrong about the prudish.

I laughed. He could keep trying to show me how he wasn’t a prude... I rather enjoyed it.

“So don’t you think in order to make improvements you should go experience it first? How do you know what it really needs if you don’t really know what it is? And why do you think it’s sleazy? It’s not like it’s a whore house. It’s people who want to have sex. How is it any different from you and me?”

“Look, I’m not judging the customers. I’m just not into hooking up with a bunch of random people. Been there and done that.”

"You're being a hypocrite. That is exactly what you and I did last night." I pointed out.

"That's different."

"How?"

"I didn't want to hook up with you. I wanted to get to know you."

I gaped at him in disbelief. "Are you saying you don't pick up women in bars and have one-night stands?"

Jack shifted uncomfortably then sighed deeply. "Listen, I'm not saying I'm an angel. But I never had the intention of hooking up with you. Is that what you wanted from me? Just a one-night stand?"

"I've never had a one-night stand before. And I was in a relationship for six years, so not really sure what I expected, but you pursued me, remember?"

"Fair enough. But you've really never had a one-night stand before?"

I blushed a bit. "Nope."

"I was the first guy to ever pick you up in a bar?" Jack's cocky grin filled his face.

I backhanded him on the shoulder. "Don't get cocky now."

Jack leaned in closer. "So you've never had a one-night stand, but you want me to take you to a sex club?"

I shrugged my shoulders. "I don't know. I never really thought about it before, but why not?"

Jack laughed. "You, Maddie Burns, are full of surprises." He leaned in, his lips met mine, and his tongue slowly and expertly explored my mouth.

There was something so arousing about Jack's kisses. Whether he went slow or fast, it made my skin stand on edge and millions of butterflies release in my stomach.

The faint smell of my balcony orgasm was on his fingers, and I tasted it on his tongue as the beer he drank didn't fully cover it up. I don't know what it was about this man, but I couldn't get enough. Was it because I was with Mike for so long and this was exciting? Or was it that he was different? But it couldn't be this easy, could it?

Jack pulled me onto his lap, and I pushed my thoughts out of my head. He ran his hands through my hair and slightly pulled it, as his mouth fluttered on my neck. The bulk of his erection pushed against me, and I stopped myself from straddling him because of where we were.

We were getting hot and heavy when someone cleared her throat. We pulled out of the kisses to see that the waitress was standing over us, smiling.

I blushed and probably looked like I was caught with my hand in the cookie jar. Jack, ever so confident, had a happy grin on his face—not one bit embarrassed—as though it was perfectly natural to be passionately kissing your date in the bar.

The waitress wanted to know if we were ready to order.

"Maddie, you like oysters?"

"Love them."

"Dozen oysters please."

The waitress left and I turned to Jack. "So what part of New York do you live in? I didn't get to ask last night."

"Over in Chelsea."

"Do you like it there? I still don't know the different parts of New York very well."

"Yes. It has a good vibe to it. So..."

"So...what?"

He spoke slowly, as if he wasn't sure he should be asking, but it obviously was on his mind. "What is the situation with you and your ex?"

"What do you mean?"

"You still live together, but you're moving out, right?" His possessive side showed up.

"Yes."

"And it's definitely over?" Jack's voice had a bit of vulnerability in it. I found it rather sexy and sweet.

I smiled and leaned closer to Jack. "Totally over. We never should have moved to New York together."

Jack gave me a relieved smile. "I don't want to be nosy, but can I ask you, besides feeling like you came second, what else didn't work?"

I thought for a minute. "That is an interesting way to pose that question. What didn't work...jeez...where do I start?"

"That bad?"

I shrugged my shoulders. "It wasn't bad at the beginning and I did stay six years..."

"But?" Jack cocked his head to the side and waited for me to give him more intel on my failed relationship.

"It was fun at first. I was only twenty-six when we started dating. We grew apart. Mike became a workaholic, and slowly, we drifted. I felt alone the last few years, if I'm being honest. When Mike decided to move to New York for work, I thought maybe a new change in scenery would bring us back to a good spot.

"Liv, for years, kept offering me a job, so I took her up on her offer. But all New York did was drive a wedge between us further. Mike became even more obsessed with work. I never saw him. Whenever we had plans, he would show up hours late, cancel at the last minute, or not even tell me, and I'd be sitting in a restaurant or somewhere else, waiting, feeling like a loser.

"Last weekend, as I sat in a restaurant and after being stood up again, I decided I needed to move on. It would be better to be by myself, and figure out who I was without him, than stay and continue this charade."

Jack processed my admission. I wasn't sure what was going through his mind.

He probably thinks I'm a pathetic loser.

He finally spoke. "That's shitty, Maddie. I'm sorry you experienced that. I think I now understand why you freaked out this morning."

"I'm sorry about that. It was horrible that I did that to you... that note." I rolled my eyes.

Jack laughed. "Yeah, it was definitely a Dear John letter..."

"Sorry." I gave him my best 'I'm sorry' face.

Jack leaned in and gave me a kiss. "All's forgiven."

"Thank you." I kissed him back.

"Maddie, do you really not know who you are?"

I shrugged my shoulders. "I don't know. Most of my adult life has been Mike and Maddie...even when Mike wasn't there. So much of my life, I put Mike first...his career...his family. Where he wanted to live. Everything was always about him and I let it be that way."

Jack rubbed my back. "So why do you need to move out? Why not make him?"

"Honestly, I hate our place. He didn't even ask me what I wanted. He signed the lease and told me to pack up. I thought we would have picked a place together, but nope. Typical Mike. The lease is in his name, so it's a bonus that I can leave and move on. I need to figure out where. But, I don't really know my options."

Jack paused a minute. "When we get back to New York, why don't I show you around some neighborhoods? You can get a good feel for where you want to live?"

"Really? Are you going to have time to do that? I know you're super busy."

Jack laughed. "I think you have me pegged a little wrong, Maddie."

I pinched my brows together. "I'm sorry. Please, tell me what I have wrong."

Jack didn't say anything for a minute. He took a sip of his beer, stroked my back with his other hand, and stared at me with a small but content grin on his face.

"What?" I couldn't understand what was behind that grin.

"I'm super busy, Maddie. You have that right. But what you don't understand is that I decide what I do and don't do, and I will make time for you...because I want to. And if showing you around New York helps you find somewhere to live that makes you feel good, then I want to help you find it. Plus, I'm not going to lie, but the thought of you going back to New York and spending even one night under the same roof as your ex has me going crazy right now," Jack told me calmly.

It was so sweet, but I laughed. "So you're jealous, huh?"

"Damn right."

"Trust me on this, nothing is going on with Mike and me. We are over."

"And what does he want?" Jack raised his eyebrows as if he already knew the answer.

I didn't say anything. Jack answered for me. "He wants you to stay with him, doesn't he?"

I rolled my eyes. I couldn't deny it. "Not going to happen."

I could tell by Jack's face that he didn't fully believe me.

"Anyway, can we change the subject? What about your ex...or exes, I'm assuming." I rolled my eyes.

"Nothing to talk about. Other than my ex-fiance, I usually do more casual dating."

I felt a stab to the heart. Here I was, telling him I wanted to be on my own to find myself, and he was telling me that he only does casual, which should have been perfect.

I would have been able to handle the one-night stand, but I can't do casual dating...not with him.

I think my face gave away my disappointment. He grabbed my face and pulled my forehead to his, so we were eye to eye. "Hey, I'm not saying I want casual with you, I want to see where this goes, but I'm being honest about my past."

"Okay." Relief washed over me and I gave him a kiss. That was fair. "So why didn't you get married?"

Jack's fingers tapped his beer bottle. His face hardened a bit. "I was twenty-eight. Kelly was pregnant...we were already engaged when she became pregnant, but we lost the baby and...it tore us apart."

There was a sadness in Jack's eyes. It was the brief glimpse of sadness I saw the other night when he first mentioned his ex-fiance and the fact he didn't have kids.

I caressed his cheek. "I'm so sorry. That had to be difficult."

He shrugged his shoulders but I could see his pain. "It is what it is. I kind of jumped into my work and didn't get too attached after that."

I didn't know what to say, so I leaned in and kissed him. Once again, the waitress came in to catch us lip to lip. She gave us the oysters, refilled our drinks, and left.

The sun set and it was dark. The night sky was full of stars. The music was blaring in the air, and the rooftop bar was filled up. But Jack and I remained in our own world, inside our private little cabana.

We ate our oysters mostly in silence.

"What would you be doing tomorrow if you weren't here with me?"

Jack laughed. "Probably being a pathetic loser, sitting on my balcony, and working on my laptop all day."

I decided to tease him. "Yep, you're right. Totally pathetic."

"You, meanwhile, would be at the pool with all the guests. Running around, driving all the men mad in your bikini."

"Ha ha!"

"Jack, is that you?" A man's voice flew into the cabana.

Jack's face hardened. "Jim. What are you doing here?"

Jim walked fully into the cabana and sat next to me. Jack instinctively reached around my waist and pulled me closer to him.

"Well aren't you a pretty one?" Jim sized me up as if I was a piece of candy he could eat.

"Easy there, Jim," Jack warned.

Jim waved off Jack's warning, "Relax, Jack. Such a stick in the mud, isn't he?" He leaned in and I could smell some sort of hard alcohol...whiskey maybe? I didn't say anything.

"Jim, what are you doing here?" Jack repeated, not very friendly.

Jim looked up, as if he heard Jack for the first time. "Business...a little fun..." He took his finger and traced it on my thigh. I jumped and instantly felt dirty.

Jack stood up, face beat red. "What the fuck, Jim?"

"Easy there, killer. I'm only having some fun. You remember what fun we used to have, right, Jack?" I wasn't sure what he was referring to, but I didn't have a good feeling about it.

"Those days are over, Jim. Time for you to move on." Jack moved closer to him and pointed for him to leave.

Jim threw his head back and laughed hysterically, "Have it your way, Jack. I'll see you on the next trip." He walked out.

Jack was red with anger, his fists still clenched. I stood up and grabbed his fists, and tried to calm him. "I'm sorry about that asshole." Jack's face was enraged.

"It's okay."

"No, it's *not* okay. If he ever touches you again he will leave here in a body bag."

"Who is he and what did you mean by those days are over?"

Jack sat with his finger tapping on his leg. "Look, Maddie, I told you I was no angel and I meant it. I've done a lot of traveling with business men over the years and there's been a lot of late nights and partying. I really don't want to get into it. That guy is a complete asshole and I hoped I would never have to see him again."

I wanted to know more, but I decided it was best to drop it. What was in the past was in the past. It wasn't my business. "Okay," I moved onto him and straddled him, no longer caring that we were in a public place.

I put my hand on his face. "Let's forget about him and go back to you and me."

Jack smiled at me and I could see him relax. "Perfect. Thank you." He pulled my head toward his and our lips connected in a hot fire of lust. My knees dug into the couch. I pulled my body forward into his, and wanted to be as close to him as possible. I wasn't sure where this notion of *us* was going, but I decided to be in the moment and fully enjoy him.

The hip-hop music blasted out, and outside our cabana, people were everywhere, but Jack and I sat in our corner, oblivious to our surroundings...except the rhythm of the music and each other. The music was raunchy, and dirty, and my body wanted to grind into Jack's, so I did something totally out of my character. "Do you have a condom?" I whispered.

Jack's face was first one of surprised confusion, then a slow grin formed. "Right here?"

"You don't want to?"

"No, that's not it. You sure?" He was already pulling a condom out of his wallet.

I grabbed his free hand and pulled it under my dress. "I want you right now, Jack."

He pulled his hand out, and stuck his fingers in my mouth. With his other hand, he tore the condom wrapper with his teeth. He unzipped his pants, slid the condom on, and then moved my panties to the side. He adjusted my dress so it floated over our bodies.

And while earlier on the balcony, I had been excited at the thought of being caught, it no longer plagued in my mind. I just had to have Jack. It didn't matter where we were, or the fact that anyone could walk into our little private cabana at any time. I needed to have him and I couldn't wait.

I glided onto Jack in the hot night air. There was a bit of a breeze and the music encouraged my every movement. I watched his face change from amusement to pleasure to ecstasy.

His girth and depth filled me up, and the couch let me sink into him, as he held my back close to him. Our lips locked, and our tongues darted in and around each other. We were in a moment of pure lust, as our need and desire took us to a place that only we knew.

The music changed and I slowed my grind as Jack moaned and cried out, "Just like that, Maddie...you fit so perfect...holy shit that feels amazing." His words filled my pot of courage, and I forgot that anyone or anything besides him existed.

Our eyes were intensely locked between kisses; our breath quickly turned into pants; Jack moved his hands on my hips and controlled our speed. We both began to sweat as our faces flushed. He moved to nibble my neck and I arched my back to get into him further.

With every beat of the music, I felt Jack's hardness as I clutched and released and basked in the sensations he gifted upon me. "So good," I heard myself say, not sure how loud it was, or if Jack could even hear over the music.

My thighs squeezed around Jack's legs, my knees tried to go deeper with every push he gave me, as his manhood pounded my sweet spot over and over, in perfect unison with the music.

I sucked on Jack's neck so hard I was pretty sure he would have a bruise.

His lips grazed my chest. He took one hand, unbuttoned the top of my dress, and pulled out one of my breasts. He sucked on it tenderly at first, then harder, and sent surges through my already electrified body.

"Jack," I blurted out, "Oh God," and, "I'm gonna cum."

In my ear, "Wait just a bit longer, baby, I want to cum with you..."

"Oh God, Jack, I..."

"Just another minute, baby."

My labored breath increased, my nerves stood on the top of the mountain, and waited to jump off.

"Good girl, I want to savor you...you feel so good," he praised me, eye to eye, forehead to forehead.

And that's when I broke. A tremor started to ripple through me, slowly at first. Jack thrusted quicker, and my adrenaline gushed through every cell of my body. I felt Jack pump hard inside me, as his body shattered into mine with fury. Our arms held tight to each other, as we were two souls in the night that danced among the heated flames.

We rose together and we fell together. It was beautiful. And we clung to each other at the bottom, we whispered words like, "thank you" and "incredible" and "so delicious" and "I can't get enough of you." Who said what, I don't know. I was still incoherent from my high.

I slowly came out of my fog and realized Jack was still inside me. I lifted myself off of him and resettled on his lap. Jack grabbed the condom, wrapped it up in a napkin, shoved it in his pocket, and zipped up his pants. He moved my underwear back to the center and gave me a sweet lingering kiss.

"Where have you been all my life, Maddie Burns?" He sweetly brushed my hair off my cheek.

I smiled, and wondered where *he* had been, and could this really be? I gave him another kiss before I removed myself from his lap and sank into his chest. I felt Jack's and my heart beats slowly return to normal.

"Well, you've fulfilled all my fantasies of rooftop bar sex," Jack joked.

"Is that right? Been dreaming a long time about that one?"

"Something like that." He kissed the top of my head and gave me his dimpled grin.

Jack

. . .

How dare he touch her. My stomach flipped when I saw him and my anger started to bubble when he sat next to Maddie. Then he touched her.

I wanted to kill him, but I knew I couldn't make things worse for the investigation. The last thing I needed to do was make anything harder or last longer. We were a year into it and I needed it to be over.

It took all my strength not to kill him when he touched her.

I lied to her. The truth was too gruesome and shameful. Maddie could not ever find out. She would surely realize I was not worthy of her and that would be it.

My blood boiled, but Maddie wouldn't let Jim's out-of-line actions ruin our night. She surprised me once again, when she wanted to have sex on the rooftop bar. I seriously didn't know where this girl came from, but I was officially the luckiest guy in the world.

Maddie shocked me with her openness to the sex club and threesomes conversation. I assumed she would have judged me, but she didn't. Instead, she teased me about being a prude, and that made me think of more things I would do to show her I wasn't. And while she was innocent, she was adventurous, inside and outside the bedroom, and that turned me on more.

It wasn't only the mind-blowing sex. Maddie was so much more than someone to fool around with. After we ate a little bit more food, we walked the beach. It was dark and the beach was empty. The moonlight was over the ocean, and lit our path, as the waves crashed at our feet.

We walked on the wet sand, strolled hand in hand, and talked about all sorts of things. Maddie's childhood in California, mine in New York, her career, my career, and what she loved so far about New York.

"You are going to stay in New York, right?" It dawned on me, now that she broke up with her ex, maybe she would want to move back.

"Yes. I really like my job and New York is exciting."

A wave of relief hit me. Most of my travels kept me on the East Coast, so if she moved back, that would make it more difficult to see her.

"What do you find exciting?"

She shrugged her shoulders and laughed, "I think it's the energy!" She twirled around so fast the skirt on her dress swirled up, and she eventually fell into my arms.

She was carefree, the opposite of me, and I felt calm around her. I leaned into her, and devoured her mouth. My arms were around her, one hand cupped her butt, and the other hand pulled her head into me.

"I want to see you when I get back to New York," I told her when I pulled out of the kiss.

"I thought you were going to show me around neighborhoods?"

"I will. I mean take you out."

"You better. I did after all, fulfill your rooftop sex fantasy." She took off running, as I chased after her.

8

Maddie

I WOKE UP TO THE SOUND OF THE WAVES CRASHING, OPENED MY eyes, and saw Jack standing naked on our balcony. I walked over to him, and put my arms around his waist. “Penny for your thoughts?”

Jack stretched his arms behind me and cupped my butt cheeks before he turned around and kissed me. “Morning, Gorgeous. Did you sleep well?”

I laughed. “Pretty much think you thoroughly exhausted me last night.”

“Sorry, but not sorry.” Jack winked.

“Not complaining! What were you lost in thought about out here?”

“Nothing,” but I wasn’t convinced.

“Do you feel guilty about not working?”

“Maddie, I have a girl I’m crazy about naked in my arms, and a perfect day of sun, sea, and sand in front of me. I absolutely don’t give a fuck about work today.”

"So you're crazy about me, huh?"

Jack's face was serious. "One-hundred-percent full-blown crazy."

I gazed into his serious eyes and wondered again if he was real or only a vacation fantasy playing out? Would Jack Stevens actually exist outside of this trip?

He leaned in and kissed me. A passionate kiss that made me believe that he wanted more than a vacation fling.

"You're so freaking hot." I didn't realize I said it out loud.

Jack laughed and my face burned red. "Let's shower, get our suits on, then go grab some breakfast and hit the beach."

I gave Jack a sly smile. "I do deserve to be scrubbed down after last night's activities."

A naughty grin consumed Jacks face. "Well, let's not miss an inch then."

An hour and a half later, we finally left our room after some pretty intense shower games. We found the beachside cafe and ordered coffee and breakfast.

"This place is beautiful." I glanced around and took it all in. The waves crashed gently against the shore and the sand was pure white.

"Crazy, all the times I've been in Tampa and I've not been here before." Jack looked around absentmindedly.

"So Tampa isn't a one-off thing? You're here a lot?"

"Enough." Jack shrugged his shoulders like it wasn't a big deal.

"Do you travel all the time?"

Jack thought a minute and put his hand over mine, his fingers trailed over my hand. "Yes. But I don't have to be gone as much as I am."

I didn't say anything for a minute. The gravity of his words hit me. He was telling me that he would change his schedule to be with me more. "That won't hurt your business?"

"No. I can rearrange my schedule to be tighter when I travel."

Something occurred to me. "Do you intentionally stay away from New York?"

Jack shrugged his shoulders.

"Why do you stay away?" I wanted to know.

But Jack wouldn't tell me. He shrugged again.

"Jack—"

"Maddie, I'm telling you that I can be in New York more, to be with you, because I want to. Can you give me some credit and leave it at that?"

I backed off, not sure why Jack wouldn't tell me why he stayed away, but I wasn't going to push any further. Hopefully, one day, he would tell me.

"Okay."

Jack put his hand back on mine. "Hey, I'm sorry if that came out mean."

I put a smile on my face. I didn't want to spoil our day. "It wasn't. All's good."

Jack picked up my hand and kissed it. "Okay, delicious girl. Let's get on the beach, shall we?"

We were soon in lounge chairs, under an umbrella. Jack eagerly rubbed sunscreen all over my body.

"I see your perv self is back."

He raised his eyebrows at me though his sunglasses. "You thought it left?"

I giggled.

The rest of the day we spent doing fun beach activities. We rode on jet skis, swam and made out in the ocean, snorkeled, and took advantage of the hotel's Hobie cat sailboat.

When we set off to go back to Tampa, the sun was setting. Jack opened the car door for me, but instead of getting in, I turned around and wrapped my arms around him. "This was the best date ever. Thank you." I gave him a long kiss.

His dimples popped out as he grinned. "You can thank me later tonight when we get back."

I licked my lips. "What do you want?"

He winked at me. "Whatever you want to give me."

"Aren't you easy?"

"Yep." He kissed me again.

We drove back mostly in silence, tired from our sunny day, happy, and content. The time we spent together was fun and easy. I thought of all my wasted years with Mike, when I worried about where he was, if he would show up, and who he was with.

Jack was refreshing. While he kept telling me that he wanted to see me back in New York, I decided right then and there that if this was only meant to be a vacation fling, then I would still savor it as a gift. Jack Stevens brought me back to life, and for that, I would always be grateful.

He caught me with a silly smile on my face. "What's the big smile about? You look so happy right now."

"I am. You put this smile on my face."

Jack grinned like a schoolboy. "Good. Is it better than getting your luggage in the middle of the night? Because I liked that reward..."

I swatted him playfully.

We sat the rest of the car ride in a happy and content silence. It was pitch black when we pulled up to the hotel.

"Mr. Stevens. Ms. Burns. Welcome back." The valet greeted us when we pulled up.

Quickly, we got to the penthouse and when we entered the room, I washed my face and brushed my teeth. I grabbed one of Jack's t-shirts, threw it on, and crawled into bed. I was exhausted and must have fallen asleep, when Jack was in the bathroom.

In the middle of the night, I woke up when I heard the phone ring. It took me a minute to realize the buzz was my phone.

I jumped out of bed and found it on the charger in the kitchen. Without looking at the screen, I answered it.

"Hello?" My voice cracked, and I tried to stay quiet so that Jack wouldn't wake up.

"Maddie, where have you been?" Mike accused me.

Irritated, I replied, "Seriously, Mike. It's the middle of the night. Why are you calling me?"

"Maddie, where the fuck are you?"

"None of your business. My life is no longer your concern."

"This game of yours is over, Madelin. Get your ass back home now."

"I'm not playing a game. We're done." I forgot about Jack in the other bedroom, as my voice rose with anger, and my face heated up in flames.

Mike hissed. "What about all your stuff? It seems we aren't quite done yet, Maddie."

Panic filled my chest. "Mike, leave my shit alone. As soon as I find a place, I'll remove it. I gave you six years, you can give me a few weeks."

Mike laughed.

"I'm hanging up now. Don't call me again." I hung up, threw my phone on the counter, and brought my shaking hands to my face.

Suddenly, I felt Jack's arms around me. "Hey, what's going on?"

I leaned back into him and sighed. "I think Mike might destroy all my stuff before I get back. He's pissed I broke up with him."

"What a dickhead."

"Yup."

Jack turned me around. "Listen, I own a moving company and a storage facility. Why don't we send them over the day you get back? He probably won't do anything; he only wants control again."

"Jack, that's very sweet of you, but this is my problem. I don't want to involve you in it."

"Maddie, don't be silly. Just say thank you and let me handle it, please?" Jack pleaded.

I thought about it. I didn't want Jack to have to fight my battles, but I was in a bad situation, and I knew it. The Mike I met six years ago was nowhere to be seen, and I disliked the person he had become. I really didn't know what he would do. I finally agreed. "Thank you."

"Good. What day do you leave for New York?"

"Thursday."

"You want to stay until Friday and leave with me? Tom's coming in for a meeting Friday morning, and we are going back on his jet around eleven a.m."

I froze. I wasn't sure if I was ready to share Jack and me with others yet. Everything was so new and I needed to figure out my own personal shit. I hadn't even told anyone at work about my breakup. Plus, we had only known each other for a few days. What if he woke up tomorrow and decided this was a vacation fling?

"Sorry, did I say the wrong thing?" Jack's worry spread throughout his face.

"Come sit with me." I grabbed his hand and led him over to the couch.

A confused Jack glanced nervously at me. I sat on his lap and put my arms around his neck. "I don't want you to take any of this the wrong way."

"Okay…"

"You are the sweetest, kindest person I have met in maybe forever." I stroked his cheek, leaned in, and kissed him.

He pulled away after a bit. "But..."

"I haven't told anyone except you about my breakup with Mike and—"

Jack cut me off. "Because you weren't sure if you really wanted it to be over."

I grabbed his face in my hands. "No! That is not it at all."

Jack released a big puff of air. "Why didn't you then?"

I closed my eyes and focused on my lap. "I felt like I failed.

The longer I'm away, I see that I stayed in that shitty, almost sexless, emotionally abusive relationship because I didn't want to fail. I believed him when he said I wasn't good enough. I held onto the Mike I first met, not the Mike he had become. I just couldn't tell anyone yet. It was too fresh, too raw, too scary, when I didn't even know what my next steps were to find a place, move, and all of that." There. I admitted out loud all the things I hadn't even wanted to admit to myself.

Jack picked up my chin. "I'm so sorry you went through that. You deserve better."

I let out a breath I didn't realize I had been holding in. "I know that now."

Jack started to speak and then stopped.

I waited.

"Maddie, tell me you want to keep seeing me when we leave here and go back to New York." The vulnerability in his voice shot through my heart.

"You really do want this to be more than a vacation fling?"

Jerking his head back, "Have I given you any reason to think otherwise?"

"No, but I don't want to assume anything or make you feel like you're obligated to give me more."

"Maddie, I don't feel obligated. I want to see where this goes and I mean it. I want more with you. But is that what you want? A vacation fling?"

I smiled at him. My insides did a happy dance, and I was surprised how much I wanted to hear that. "No, Jack, I don't want a vacation fling."

"Please, tell me you want to keep seeing me when we get back to New York," he repeated.

I ran my hand through his hair. "Jack, I want to keep seeing you. But I don't think I can get on a plane with Tom and explain my breakup and how we've been together this week. I haven't even told Liv. Can we keep this between us till we get back to the city? I'm not saying I want to hide us, but can you let me tell Liv first? I feel as both my friend and employer, I need to do that. I'll do it first thing Monday or maybe over the weekend."

Relief flooded Jack's face. "I can do that. But that means I have to spend a night here on my own." He gave me a pout and a tickle.

"What will you and your gigantic dick do?"

"You think my dick is gigantic, huh?" He gave me a cocky smirk.

I rolled my eyes and laughed.

"What time do you land in New York?"

"I have an early flight out and I go direct. I think around ten a.m."

Jack thought. "Why don't I have the movers at Mike's by two. Will that give you enough wiggle room?"

"Yes. Thank you again. That's very generous of you."

"Pack up anything you need on a day-to-day basis and your clothes. I'll give you my key and the movers can take it to my place. Stay as long as you need. The rest, put in storage."

My eyes widened, "Jack, that's very sweet but I can't do that."

"Why not?" he frowned.

"I want to be with you, so I don't want you to question that, okay?"

"All right..."

"You've been on your own. I haven't in six years, and even before, I always had a roommate. I need to do this for me."

Jack exhaled. "I get that, but stay at my place when you get back, and this weekend I'll take you around neighborhoods. I'll help you find a place like we discussed. It's only temporary, Maddie."

It made sense, but I didn't want to risk messing anything up between Jack and me. "Don't you think that might be bad for us?"

"You in my bed every night? Nope."

I swatted him. "I'm serious. I don't want my messy baggage in the way of what this might become. I really like you, Jack."

"I really like you too, Maddie. This won't mess anything up. Just think about it."

Fair enough. "I'll think about it."

"Good. Now you fell asleep last night, so I think I need to punish you a bit. You left me with a hard on." Jack gave me his full-dimple smile.

I laughed. "Hmmm...what's my punishment then?"

Jack mischievously ordered me, "Get that t-shirt off, stand in front of the balcony door, and I'll be right back."

I looked at him in question.

"Do it," he commanded.

I gave him a little salute and wondered what he had up his sleeve.

I stood naked in front of the balcony door and waited for Jack, my curiosity in full bloom. My juices began to flow with the anticipation of whatever new skill Jack was going to show me. The air conditioning made my nipples stand erect, and goose-bumps started to form on my skin.

Jack finally came out of the bedroom with a bunch of ties slung over his shoulder, and he carried the bench that was at the end of our bed.

A tiny smile played on my face. I wasn't sure what was about to happen, but I realized I was about to find out.

"Step aside for a minute, Maddie."

I did as Jack instructed, and he set the bench in front of the glass. Then, he looped two ties over the curtain rod. He took my hand and instructed me to step up on the bench and face him.

I stepped up, and he tied one tie around each of my hands and put another tie over my eyes. The ties were made of silk and felt soft around my bare skin. My arms were stretched out with little ability to move.

Suddenly, Jack seized my legs and spread them apart. I felt the silkiness of the ties around my ankles.

If this was a punishment then I needed to get in trouble more often. This was hot and he hadn't even touched me yet. I could feel my body start to bubble.

I couldn't see anything but suddenly felt Jacks lips on mine. I leaned forward to take in more of him, but he backed off. "Ever been tied up before, Maddie?"

I shook my head.

"But you wanted to be?"

I nodded.

"You trust me?"

"Yes," I didn't hesitate.

"Good." I felt his fingers grab my wetness.

I gasped from surprise.

"You're so wet," he praised, as he swirled his fingers around me.

"Ah…"

"Good girl." He stuck his fingers in my mouth and told me to suck.

Jack always talked dirty, something I hadn't experienced before, and I loved that about him. He brought a part of me out that I didn't know existed…and *I liked her.*

I could tell we were almost face to face, as I stood on the bench. I felt his lips on my neck, and it made my nipples stand even straighter. Electric waves ran through my body as he fluttered around my collarbone.

I moaned.

"That's it, baby. Your sounds turn me on so much." He rubbed his dick on my thigh.

My breathing labored as he teased my breasts—one by one, nipple by nipple. He rolled them with his tongue and sucked gently, then hard and gently again. I gasped and moaned in delight.

"I can't figure out what part of your body I love the most, Maddie," Jack mumbled; his hands cupped my ass; his teeth lightly grazed my tits. "Your left breast is more sensitive, isn't it?"

I never thought about it before, but he was right. How was it this man I had known in such a short time seemed to know my body better than I did? "Yes, Jack."

His mouth moved to my ear, and I felt his finger around my anus. "Is anything off limits?"

I inhaled sharply. I hadn't ever done anything anal before, but Jack's finger felt good, and I trusted him. "You can have me however you want," I breathlessly told him, feeling my cheeks flush.

"Have you done anything anal before?" Jack whispered in my ear.

I shook my head and bit my lip.

"But you're okay...if I want to play there? You trust me?" Jack nibbled on my collarbone some more.

"Yes, I trust you."

"Tell me to stop if you don't like anything, okay, Maddie?"

"Okay."

Jack moved closer, I could feel his erection against my sex. I moved my hips to grind my clit into it and moaned out in the process.

"You like my dick?"

"I *love* your dick."

I heard him chuckle a bit. His body moved against mine, and he moved his cock against my nub again. Little ripples of pleasure rolled throughout my body.

I felt his breath on my ear. "I only want you to feel good, Maddie."

"You only feel good to me, Jack," I breathed.

Not able to move, spread out, he wrapped his arms around me, pressing his warm, hard body against mine, destroying any chance I would ever again enjoy kissing any other man, as he urgently claimed my mouth as his own while leaving me breathless.

Stepping back, he trailed his fingers slowly from my hands down my arms to the sides of my chest, then through my stomach and all the way to the outside of my ankles. Swiftly, he moved his fingers inside my legs and made his way back up while he nibbled on my stomach.

"You're so wet, I can smell your sweet sex," he whispered in my ear. "Does anyone else make you this wet?"

I shook my head.

"Tell me."

"Only you, Jack."

Jack moved his lips to my inner thighs, "No one is as delicious as you are."

My breath intensified as his mouth explored my body, drifting lower, creating desperation I never knew existed before him. "Jack," I begged.

He nibbled on my mound, as heat shot through my body, and I arched my back to push closer to his mouth.

A soft laugh echoed the room before his tongue started flickering through my slit, jolting my senses.

"Jack!"

Jack grabbed my ass cheeks with his warm hands and gave me a tiny suck, as I cried out again and bucked my womanhood into him.

"You want me to lick you," Jack licked me once more, "or suck you?" He sucked me a little harder.

I didn't know how to answer that. Did he expect me to? I couldn't see anything. He had me tied up and spread out. My body was at his mercy. Any touch he gave me electrified me. My lip quivered, and he gave me another swipe of his tongue and suck of his lip.

"Oh..."

Jacks lips were suddenly on mine. The taste of my sex filled his tongue, and his strong, warm arms were around my back. He caressed my spine with his fingers, and my body hummed against his touch.

His hard dick slowly grinded against my clit, and I groaned. My nerves stood on edge. I was a bomb, and I wanted to explode.

"Maybe, you want both?" Jack whispered in my ear once more.

"Yes! Please, Jack," I begged. I wanted it all, and I knew all I needed to do was ask, and he'd give it to me.

Jack's finger twisted inside me. He pulled it out and quickly wrapped his hand around my backside, then started swiping it gently around my anus.

I moaned—a new sensation running through my body.

"You like that?" Jack pushed his finger in a bit and then out, gradually pushing more of his finger in me.

"Y—Yes."

"Maybe, you want it all, Maddie?"

I didn't know what he meant. My mind was a hazy fog, and I couldn't comprehend. I didn't answer, I was too busy moaning.

"Tell me you want it all," Jack commanded.

"Jack, I—all."

As soon as the words came out, Jack's tongue licked my pussy, and his finger drove deeper into my ass. His lips started sucking my clit between flicks, and his other finger swiped my sweet spot inside.

Oh, my fucking, God. "J—Jack," I cried out.

The pressure between my vagina and anus was a new welcome feeling and the sensations I felt quickly turned my legs to jello. My back arched, and words I couldn't comprehend flew out of my mouth. I screamed Jack's name, begged him not to stop, whimpered, moaned, and I don't know what else.

I came harder than I ever had before. My body was full of Jack's hands. My senses screamed with ecstasy, and my exhausted body shook like an earthquake against Jack's mouth as he continued to eat me out during my tremor.

When I calmed, my legs were shaky. Jack quickly untied them and put them around his body and entered me, in one swift thrust, before he untied my arms. I held onto him, still blindfolded, as I felt him step over the bench before I felt cold glass against my back.

I was tired, exhausted from my high, but like an addict, I clung to him and wanted another hit. As his manhood filled me up, I nibbled on his neck, sucked him hard, and worked my way from his collarbone to his ear.

"Fuck, Maddie."

He would have marks. I didn't care. My nails scratched at his back. My mouth pressed harder against him. I was a caged animal freed, and he was my prey.

The cool of the glass felt good against our hot, sweaty bodies, and I could hear my body squeak against the glass as Jack pushed me up against it, over and over.

"Faster," I called out, wild with lust, close to my peak, ready to feel the rush again.

Jack moved faster, and I could feel his dick get harder.

I still couldn't see, only feel the intensity of the cold, the warmth, the hardness of Jack's body against mine. I managed to find his lips, kissed him sloppily, desperate for his tongue, and sucked on it a bit when I found it.

Jack pulled back, dove into my neck, and hit the spot he seemed to find so easily that always gave me a new rush of adrenaline.

"So good," escaped my lips.

"Tell me before you cum," Jack commanded.

I didn't say anything.

"Maddie, you understand?" Once again, he was in charge. I mumbled a yes, dug my claws further into his back, and knew that he would have scratch marks, but I couldn't control myself.

"Fucking love your body," Jack muttered into my collarbone and changed up his motion a bit with his hips, as he circled into my body.

"Oh..." I grabbed his ass to push my pussy down on him further.

"You like that, baby?"

I whimpered out, "Yes," and then, "Quicker, Jack."

Jack was in full power, and he knew it. "Why do you want it quicker?" he whispered in my ear.

My labored breath was picking up speed, "I...need...it."

"Tell me before you cum," he reminded me.

I nodded. Anything to make him move quicker and take me to my heavenly space.

"Fuck me harder, Jack."

Jack sped up. His hips danced into my body, his manhood flooded my womanhood, as his tip hit my sweet spot.

And I hit the edge of my ecstasy. "I'm...going...to...cum." I barely got it out.

Jack quickly removed my blindfold and put his forehead up to mine and let himself release in me—his dick pumped hard—as I released all over him and ejaculated my juices everywhere. We were both drenched in my liquids. My wild craze-filled eyes rolled, my back tried to arch, but pressed against the glass. I knew Jack got off more, as he watched my face contort with pleasure only he had ever given me.

We finally slowed from our high. Jack stepped back. My body still clung to his, as he sat on the bench. He grabbed my face and kissed me as though he couldn't get enough of me.

"So delicious," he mumbled between kisses.

This is how a man should make you feel.

When we pulled back, our foreheads butted up against each other—our eyes locked, our breath slowed. I smiled at Jack; he smiled at me. "That was..." I trailed off. "Amazing doesn't seem to be a good enough word."

Jack laughed. “Fucking incredible, Ms. Burns,” and gave me another peck. "Let me get this condom off.”

He carefully pulled me off him and sat me next to him. The window was all fogged up, smeared by my body, and through it, I could see the sun was about to rise. Brilliant pinks and oranges glowed from the sky.

“Sorry.”

His head jerked toward me. “About what?”

“You’re neck and back have some sex scars.” I traced my fingers over the tracks on his back.

Jack laughed. “You don’t ever have to be sorry about that.”

“Yeah? What about that hickey you have on your neck?” I reached up and touched the purple mark that was starting to get darker.

He winced a bit when I touched it. “Don’t worry about it.” He kissed the top of my head and picked me up in his arms. “You go get some sleep, I’m going to get my workout in.”

I laughed. “I guess some things never change. Jack Stevens, endless energy.”

“Something like that.” He winked, carried me to the bedroom, tucked me in, and went for his morning swim.

9

Jack

I didn't waste any time with the movers. "Todd, send a truck with our guys. Then I want you to send over a passenger van with eight additional guys."

"Big job, boss? Lots of packing?"

"No. It needs to be done quickly. I want you guys in and out of there, understand?"

"Sure, no problem, boss."

Every moment I spent with Maddie convinced me more and more that her ex was the biggest asshole on the planet. Anyone who would mistreat her, and then threaten her, was on my dickhead list.

I needed to get her out of there. There was no way I wanted her to have any second thoughts about their breakup. Yes, I wanted her to be with me, but it was blatantly apparent that she was not treated right by him and I didn't want her going back to him.

She stayed for six years, and that concerned me. No doubt he was emotionally and verbally abusive. I wondered if it also included physical or sexual. I asked her, but she insisted he never laid a hand on her.

Maddie had no idea how smart or beautiful she was. I was going to make it my mission to change that.

She questioned whether I wanted her to be a vacation fling. I wanted nothing of the sort. I was beyond relieved she didn't want it to be that either.

I rearranged my schedule so all my meetings were in the morning, and I was back at the hotel early afternoons. I would normally surprise her at the pool. She would be talking to someone new, a smile on her face, and I could always find her from her laugh, which could be heard from hundreds of feet away.

A huge smile would form on her face when I surprised her. Happiness surged through me every time I saw it.

Every day, we lounged at the pool. One night, we dressed up and went out to dinner. The other nights, we ordered room service to snack on between our sex sessions.

The morning after St. Pete, she started packing her suitcase. I crossed my arms over my chest and looked at her. "Maddie, what are you doing?"

Her eyes were wide and innocent. "I thought I would put my stuff back in my room."

"Why?"

"I thought I'd get out of your hair for a little bit."

"You could never be in my hair. Do you feel I'm in your hair?"

"Not at all." She didn't hesitate.

I walked over and grabbed her hands. "Stay."

"Jack, I can come back. I don't expect you to take care of me all week." She bounced back and forth on her heels.

There was nothing I wanted more than to take care of her. I knew she still had some reservations about getting into a relationship too fast. She hadn't admitted it, but I knew it.

And maybe I was going fast, but I didn't care about what would be considered normal behavior. I knew I loved having her around, and I didn't want that to change.

"I know that." I pointed around the room. "I have all these amenities, no point wasting them. Stay. Come and go as you please."

She hesitated.

"What is it?"

"I don't want to be a burden to you, Jack. I really like you. You're already doing so much for me."

I pressed my forehead to hers. "You don't seem to understand that I *want* you here. I *choose* to have you here. It makes me *happy* you're here."

She still looked at me like she didn't know what to do.

"Be honest with me, Maddie. Are you leaving because you think you are bothering me or because you need space?"

"I don't feel like I need space, but I don't want to be a strain on you."

I started taking stuff out of her bag and putting it in drawers.

"What are you doing?"

"It's settled then. If you told me you needed space or wanted to be away from me, then I would tell you to go. But you're only going because you think that is what I want. It's the furthest thing from the truth." I continued to put her stuff away.

She walked over to me, and put her hand on my arm. "Jack."

I turned to her, and my mouth went dry. I was afraid of what she would say.

"I don't want to be away from you either." She pulled me into her, kissed me, caressed me, and made me feel like the most wanted man on earth.

Relief washed over me, "Good. It's settled. I'm putting your suitcase away, and I don't want to see it again until it's time to go back to New York."

"All right, you have a deal. But if you get sick of me..."

I picked her up and put her on the bed and tickled her.

"Jack, stop!" She squealed with laughter.

I kissed her one last time, "I have to get to my meeting. I'll see you tonight." I slapped her ass playfully.

She gave me a little salute. "Yes, sir."

Maddie

The rest of the week flew by fast. I don't know if Jack rescheduled his meetings, but he was out the door early and back by early afternoon everyday. He would join me at the pool, engage in happy hour and take me out to dinner. I never made it back to my room. Jack's penthouse suite became ours, and we had sex in it wherever and whenever we could.

Thursday came fast. It was 5 a.m., and Jack dropped me off at the airport and insisted he walk me in. "You sure I can't convince you to stay till tomorrow? I really don't want you to deal with that asshole on your own." He tried once again to get me to stay.

"Sorry, but I need to go. I have movers coming, remember?"

"I own the company and can rearrange it, remember?"

I laughed, reached up, and put my arms around him to pull him down to me. "I'll see you in New York."

He nodded, slightly defeated, and kissed me passionately. He slapped my ass and sent me off on my way.

God, I love it when he slaps my ass.

At the security gate that led to the terminal, I turned around and blew him a kiss. Jack smiled. I turned back and walked through.

A part of me was sad, and a part of me was flying high. I had the best vacation ever, met the hottest, sweetest man ever, and didn't want to go face what I was sure would be a crappy experience. I hoped that Mike was traveling and wouldn't be home, but I didn't know, and I was afraid if I informed him about the movers, he might do something crazy.

Around 6:30, I sat in the terminal and decided Liv would be up, so I called her.

"Hey, Maddie," Liv answered. "Everything all right?"

I smiled. It was good to hear a friend's voice. I wanted to gush about my time with Jack, but knew now wasn't the time. "Everything is fine, Liv. I want to tell you something and hoped I could ask a favor?"

"Sure! What's up?"

I cut right to it. "I broke up with Mike last week."

“Maddie, I’m so sorry—”

“Liv, it’s been over for a long time. I shouldn’t have stayed with him this long. Anyway, I have movers coming at 2 p.m. today and Mike was threatening to do some crazy stuff the last time I spoke with him. I don’t want to put you in a bad situation, but do you think you could go with me? I’m not sure what I’m going to be walking into...”

“Done. Whatever you need. We can have Gary come, too. I would bring Tom, but he’s flying to Georgia then Tampa tomorrow.”

I pretended to not know anything about that. “Thanks.”

“Maddie, where are you moving to?”

I cleared my throat. “Liv, can we meet for coffee before and talk? I have some things I want to catch you up on.”

Liv hesitated a minute. “Are you moving back to California?”

“No, nothing like that! I promise!”

"Phew! I’m working from home today. Want to meet at my place and we can head to Mike’s from there?”

“Sure.”

“Meg will be here, too. Is that all right?”

I thought about it. Eventually, everyone would know, and

although I didn't know Meg as well as Liv, we had become friends quickly. "Sure, that would be fine."

I hung up, and a few minutes later, I heard my name called. "Ms. Maddie Burns, please come to gate E forty-four."

The flight attendant handed me a new ticket when I arrived at the gate. "You've been upgraded."

"Really?"

"Someone must love you, here's your new ticket."

I looked at her in confusion. *Jack. It had to be Jack.*

I called Jack. "Did you upgrade my ticket?"

"Maybe."

"Jack! It's too much."

"Maddie, get some rest. It's the least I can do for keeping you up all night. Which was pretty awesome, by the way."

My face lit in flames. It was pretty awesome, I had to admit it...like every other night that week. God, how did I go from no sex to sex crazed?

"Jack—"

"Maddie, just say thank you and enjoy it. It's done. And for God's sake, call me, so I know you are safe from that douchebag."

"One, thank you. Two, I called Liv, and she's going to go to the apartment with me, and Gary will be there, so you don't have to worry; I won't be alone."

Jack let out a big sigh. "That's good, but Maddie, still call me?"

I smiled. I secretly enjoyed the fact he worried about me. "I promise."

"And you have my address and key, right?"

"Yes, Father."

"Call me your daddy, not your father."

I burst out laughing. "Ah, your dick is back in control of your brain, I see."

"Did it ever leave?"

"I gotta go. See you in New York."

"Bye, Maddie. Safe travels." Jack hung up.

I boarded the plane soon after and fell asleep in my first class seat all the way to New York. After landing, I quickly hailed a cab to Liv's.

Meg arrived right when I did. Her long red hair blew in the wind, and she was bundled up in a wool coat and scarf. The February wind gusted full force, and I was a little underdressed. I clearly wasn't thinking when I left Florida.

"Damn, girl, you have that fresh sun-kissed look going on!" Meg's green eyes twinkled. "But where are your clothes?"

Meg was one who could always make me laugh. "I just landed..."

"You seem to be glowing. Mike go with you?" She smirked as we got on the elevator.

"Nope. I broke up with him."

"What? I'm so sorry!"

"I'm fine. I should have done it years ago."

Meg quieted for a minute and stared at me.

"What?"

She smirked again. "So if Mike wasn't with you, who was?"

"Let's wait for when Liv's with us."

"EEK!" She clapped her hands.

Just then, Liv opened the door. Her long blonde hair was tied up in a messy bun, and she still wore her pajama bottoms. "What are we clapping about?"

"Maddie has a new man," Meg sang.

Liv's head jolted in my direction. I shrugged my shoulders and laughed. "Does she have a sixth sense?"

"If it's about sex, then yes!" Liv grinned at me.

My face turned scarlet. I thought of all the positions Jack had me in the past week. Liv and Meg grinned at each other. They each grabbed an arm and pulled me into the kitchen and told me to spill it.

I told them I met Jack the first night, and we spent the week together, up in St. Pete, for our first date and Tampa the rest of the time. I admitted I never slept in my own room or even had my clothes there minus a few hours and a cat nap at my arrival. And how much of a connection I felt with him.

"Jack *is* a really awesome guy, Maddie. Tom's known him for a long time. I'm happy for you both."

"Thanks. I was a little worried about the work connection."

Liv and Meg both laughed.

Meg flipped her hair. "I think we've both learned our lesson on that one."

"What do you mean?"

"Well, I used to have a rule..." Liv said.

"And Collin used to have a rule..." Meg rolled her eyes.

"Basically, the stupid rules almost broke both our relationships up," Liv admitted.

"So no more stupid rules. All's fair in love and war," Meg hummed.

I smiled but not for long.

"What is it?" Liv frowned.

"I think I have a war on my hands with Mike. He isn't who I first met, and I realize now how emotionally abusive he was to me. He wants me back, and I just want out."

"Do you think he would get violent?" Meg looked worried.

I shrugged my shoulders. "Jack wanted me to wait until he was back, but I didn't want to put that on him. It's nice enough he's sending his moving company and letting me put my stuff in one of his storage units."

Meg and Liv exchanged a look. "So..." Meg gave me her smirk. "Where are you moving to then?"

"Jack wants me to stay at his place till I find one...but I don't know. Our relationship is so new, and I already feel like I have put a lot of baggage on it."

"Well, you are welcome to stay here," Liv offered.

"Or with me," Meg chimed.

"Thanks." I was grateful for their offers.

"But I have to tell you, if Jack wants you to stay, you aren't putting him out. Jack goes after what he wants, and if he's asking you to stay, then that's what he wants." Liv grinned.

"I think part of me is scared he will try to convince me not to move out. I want to be with him, I do, but I also need to be on my own for a while. I haven't lived on my own in six years, making decisions for myself, without anyone else telling me what to do."

"That makes sense. Did you tell Jack that?" Meg inquired.

"Yes. He offered to show me neighborhoods so I can figure out where I want to live, but wants me to stay with him until I find a new place."

"Jack Stevens is a man of his word. If he told you that, it will happen. I would bet money on it," Liv insisted.

"You're welcome to stay at either of ours, but maybe stay at his and break in every room, if you know what I'm saying." Meg winked at me with a naughty smile on her face.

We all laughed. My face once again burned red. That, no doubt, would happen should I stay with Jack.

"He gave me his key to go stay there tonight. I feel kind of odd staying in his place when I have never been there with him before." I admitted. "But I need to figure this out before the movers arrive because I have to send some stuff wherever I'm staying until I get my new place."

My phone rang. It was Jack.

"Are you still good with two o'clock for the movers?"

"As far as I know, we are all set. I still don't know if Mike is going to be there or not." I pushed my hands through my hair.

"Where are you right now?"

"I'm at Liv's, talking to her and Meg."

"Do they know about us?"

"Yes."

"Good. Do you feel better?"

I smiled. "Yes."

"So I can tell Tom then?"

I glanced at Liv. "Assuming Liv doesn't tell him first."

Jack laughed. "Fair enough. Promise you'll call me if you need anything?"

"Will do. Bye." I hung up.

"That boy has it bad," Meg teased.

"He wanted to make sure two o'clock was still good." I tried not to smile.

Meg laughed, "Sure, whatever you say."

We decided to order in lunch. As soon as we started to eat, Liv's phone rang. "Hey, babe, what's up?"

"Well, we were going to take Gary..." she trailed off.

"You really think it's necessary?"

Meg and I looked at each other.

"What do you mean? Why didn't you tell me this before now?" Liv was irritated.

Meg and I patiently waited to know what was going on.

"Can you tell me a little bit more? I'm not really following this, Tom..."

More silence as Liv listened. Her face turned pissy. "Of course, I trust you, but you're not really giving me a lot of details right now…"

"You know I hate it when you do this."

Liv quieted. "No, you've never been wrong about this type of stuff."

"Promise you'll fill me in later?"

"Love you too. Bye." Liv hung up and turned to us. "Apparently, Tom found out from Jack that you're moving out. He is insisting we take two bodyguards. He claims Mike is involved in some bad stuff and will fill me in later when he gets home. He has to go into a meeting now. Do you know what he's talking about?"

My stomach dropped. I shook my head, but it somehow didn't surprise me. "Mike isn't the same guy I fell in love with. I don't know what it would be, but it must be bad if Tom is insisting that, Liv. I'm sorry. I don't want to put anyone in any danger."

Liv waved her hand at me. "Nonsense. We will take the bodyguards and everything will be fine."

Two o'clock quickly came upon us, and we arrived at the apartment. The movers were outside waiting, right on schedule. One moving van sat on the curb. Another van pulled up with more movers.

"Jeez, your man isn't going to waste any time, is he?" Meg pointed to all the extra bodies. I smiled. Jack definitely didn't want me here long.

The bodyguards led us into the apartment, and I was instantly relieved when I realized Mike was not there, and my stuff hadn't been destroyed.

Liv, Meg, and I quickly decided what to send to storage and what I would need until I found my own place. I decided before I came that I would go to Jack's. It was only temporary, I told myself. I knew I couldn't delay the decision anymore.

The movers worked quickly. Within an hour all my contents were packed up and divided between where they were going. My personal items packed last, so they could be dropped off at Jack's first.

We finished up and I was taking the key off my ring to put on the table when Mike walked in, escorted by one of the bodyguards, the other bodyguard in tow.

"Really, Maddie? This is how you behave after six years?" Mike tried to stand in front of me, but the bodyguard stepped in front of him.

I took a step back in fear. He was so angry.

"Get out of my face. This is my home," Mike spat out.

"We are leaving. Goodbye, Mike."

Liv, Meg, and I walked around him and out the door. "This isn't over, you dumb slut," Mike yelled out at me.

I shuddered as Liv put her arm around me. Mike was definitely not a good guy, and I should have left years ago.

10

Maddie

"EVERYTHING OKAY?" GARY ASKED WHEN WE GOT INTO THE CAR.

Liv nodded as the bodyguards climbed in next to us.

My phone rang. "Hey, Jack."

"The movers called. He showed up? You okay?"

"I'm actually great. Totally free."

"Good. The movers are headed over to my place. Why don't you go grab a drink with the girls at Noreens? It's around the corner from my place. I can call the hostess Jessica and tell her you're coming."

"Oh, aren't you a regular. Jessica...that sounds like a close hostess relationship," I teased.

"Maddie, I own the restaurant," he said quietly.

Okay, now I felt dumb. "Whoops." I laughed nervously.

"No worries. So, should I call her?"

I put the phone down. "Do you both want to go have a drink?"

Liv and Meg looked at each other, and at the same time, replied, "We're in."

I put the phone back to my ear. “Sounds good, Jack.”

"Okay, I’ll call Jessica.”

We quickly pulled up to the curb. After exiting the car, we were ushered right to a VIP booth in the bar where a bottle of Cristal sat in an ice bucket.

Liv snickered at me. “What?”

“Meg’s right. That boy has it bad for you. I never thought I’d see the day Jack Stevens got serious about someone.”

I suddenly realized Liv and Meg could give me more intel on Jack. “Why is that?”

“Don’t take this the wrong way, but Jack usually only does ‘casual.’ But he definitely wants more than that with you by the sound of it.”

My face flushed for the fortieth time that day. “Yes, he told me that.”

Meg and Liv exchanged glances.

“What?” I thought they must read each other’s minds.

“What do you want? I mean, I’m sure that man is an animal in the bedroom, but besides more sex, what do you want with him?” Meg licked her lips.

My face burned hot. "Yes, the sex is...the best...and I want more than that...we have more than that...but I don’t want to rush things. I don’t want to put any expectations on anything.”

“Because you might get hurt again?” Meg tilted her head.

I bit my lip and shrugged my shoulders. It was too much to think about.

“I’m going to tell you what a good friend once told me.” Liv glanced over at Meg. “Men like Jack Stevens don’t come around too often, so don’t be so scared that you push him away.”

“You think I’m pushing him away?” *Jeez, I only met him a week ago.*

Meg shook her head. “Liv isn’t saying that. She’s only saying, don’t let the fact you just broke up with Mike stop you from getting serious with Jack if the connection is there.”

I sipped on my champagne. "I'll keep that in mind," I told the girls as I sat back and thought about my new relationship with Jack. I would never have thought I would be in a relationship again this soon, but I couldn't deny I was. As easy as it would be to go all in, I needed to learn who I was on my own. I felt like Jack was saving me right now with the movers, and staying at his house, and while I was grateful, I also knew I needed to be able to take care of myself.

I needed to avoid falling head over heels too quickly. I still didn't really know Jack, I told myself. Slow was going to have to be good enough.

THE CAR DROPPED ME OFF IN FRONT OF JACK'S. I CHECKED IN WITH the front desk and was escorted to the penthouse. Guess Jack had a thing for penthouses.

I was beyond impressed when I walked in. Jack's place was massive and decorated in modern-day silver and grays. It was stunning. The skyline overlooked New York and lights glowed in the darkness everywhere.

I picked up the phone and called Jack. He answered quickly.

"Hey, not to bug you, but I'm in your place, and I don't want to feel like a snoop. Where do I sleep, and where did you have the movers put my stuff?"

"One, you aren't ever bugging me. Two, you can snoop all you want. Three, I thought you would sleep in my bed, unless you want your own room? Four, I instructed them to put your clothes in my spare closet and your toiletries in my bathroom." He sounded rather authoritative, until that last bit where I heard a bit of nervousness in his voice. "Is that all okay?"

"Perfect. Thanks, Jack."

"Did you get dinner at the restaurant? If not, there is a takeout menu in the drawer by the fridge. Sorry, I probably don't have much there."

"Yes, we ate. I'm all set, Jack. I appreciate this. Thank you."

Jack cleared his throat. "Maddie?"

"What is it?"

Another deep breath. "I have to tell you something that I found out this morning. I have to go into this dinner meeting, and I'm already late. Can I call you later?"

My mind started to race. I wondered what it was. "Sure. Is everything all right?"

"As long as you stay where you are, yes."

"Now you are scaring me Jack." My skin crawled with goosebumps.

"No, don't be. Just promise me you won't leave my penthouse tonight?"

"I won't. You'll call me later?"

"Promise. I gotta go, Maddie. Stay inside."

"Okay."

I hung up and felt a little freaked out. Jack's penthouse had security. I was sure I was safe there, but what was going on? I tried to push my fears out of my head as I toured his place...or should I say palace?

The place really was huge. It had four bedrooms, each with their own bathroom, a gym (not surprising based on Jack's workout schedule), a movie theatre, office, living room, family room, dining room, chef's kitchen and bar/game room. I walked around in awe, from one room to the next.

Jack's master suite was nothing to sneeze at either. A fireplace between the bedroom and bathroom lined the entire wall. There was a sitting area and 'his and her' closets, along with a massive master bathroom.

My clothes hung in the closet, opposite Jack's. My toiletries were put away in drawers and cabinets attached to a vanity that I assumed Jack had no use for. It was going to be hard not to get used to this place.

After a long, hot shower, I brushed my teeth, turned on the fireplace, and crawled into Jack's bed. I wondered again what caused him to stay away so much when he had all this at his fingertips.

Jack's pillow smelled like him, and I curled up to it and realized that I missed him. It had only been half a day, but there was no doubt about it, I missed him. I hadn't been alone in a week, and it occurred to me that I had quickly become attached to Jack.

At some point, I must have fallen asleep. I woke up to my phone ringing. It was Jack.

"Hey, babe, did I wake you?"

I yawned. "I think I fell asleep. What time is it?"

"Eleven thirty."

"Are you just getting in from dinner?"

"Yeah. Back in my hotel room, missing you."

"I fell asleep missing you, too. Your pillow smells like you."

Jack laughed softly. "They washed the sheets today. It smells like bleach here. So, are you naked in my bed?"

I laughed. "Wouldn't you like to know."

"Please, tell me. After the night I've had, I need something else on my mind."

I sat up in bed. "Did something bad happen at your meeting?"

"No, no, just boring. I kept thinking about how I should be making you cum instead of listening to three, greasy, fat guys talk about how great they are."

"Well someone has to do the dirty work."

"Hey Maddie, let me switch to FaceTime." Soon my phone rang and his face popped on the screen.

"There, that's better. Hi."

"Hey, you." I smiled. Jack seemed worn out? Stressed? Worried? Something was a little off.

"So...I have to tell you something. And I don't know how you are going to take this, and some of this I can't go further into until we are together face to face for real."

What is he going to tell me?

"Is this what you found out today?"

"Yes. I only found this out this morning, and I swear I didn't know this, or I would have told you."

"Jack, what is it? You're scaring me."

Jack ran shaky hands through his hair. He closed his eyes, then opened them and carefully chose his words. "I didn't know Maddie...that Michael Dupont was Mike."

I watched him, and didn't quite catch on. "And..." I waited for him to continue.

"He's a business partner in one of Tom and my companies." He let it settle, and I felt like a bomb exploded; I started to grasp the conversation, and my heart started to beat faster as I waited for him to tell me more.

Jack closed his eyes. "That asshole, Jim, he's in thick with Michael...sorry, Mike...sorry, I've never called him Mike before."

My nerves stood on end again, and I remembered how gross I felt when Jim touched me. Jack's words, 'those days are over,' echoed through my mind.

"Something happened, and I can't get into it tonight, but Michael and Jim, they are bad people. *Really* bad, Maddie." Jack ran his hands through his hair. Stress filled his face, and I wanted to reach out and hold him, but I couldn't.

"Say something."

"I don't know what to say. I'm listening right now, so keep talking." I honestly didn't know what to say or think, but I knew there was more.

"The reason Tom is flying in tomorrow is because we are trying to figure out how to get Michael off the company with the other partners. Tom didn't even know the half of what has happened because I was trying to handle it on my own. It's too deep. I couldn't fix it all by myself," he admitted with defeat.

"Jack, I feel like you are talking in code right now. What did Mike do?"

"I can't tell you over the phone. I promise I'll tell you tomorrow in person."

"Is that why Tom made us take the bodyguards today?"

"Yes. I only happened to find out, because when I told Tom about us, he asked if I knew that your ex was Michael Dupont. I never put two and two together. I'm so sorry." Jack's face turned slightly green.

"And whatever Mike did, you didn't tell him until this morning? That is why Tom never warned me?" Parts of the day started to become clear.

"Yes. If I knew, you never would have gone to get your things without me, but it was too late. Tom convinced me you would be safer with the bodyguards."

I bit my lip. "Jack, did you use to party with Jim and Mike?"

"I wouldn't call it a party," Jack gulped.

"But in St. Pete, that was what you told me."

"Look, I never wanted to have to tell you what I will tomorrow night. Once I tell you, you will understand why I choose that route. Please forgive me. I hope you will understand and give me a pass when you find out."

I didn't like being lied to, and I knew that until I heard the entire truth, I wouldn't be able to let Jack off the hook.

Something else occurred to me. "Jack, is Mike a criminal?"

He nodded. "I can't discuss anything over the phone, Maddie." An immense amount of stress and worry loomed on his face.

"Do I need to worry about him coming after me?"

Jack didn't speak right away. "Maddie, whatever you do, don't go near him. I don't want to scare you, but yes, I think he might try to come after you."

I closed my eyes and remembered how he yelled at me earlier in the day.

"Jack, answer this for me. Did you ever see him cheat on me?" It was time to find out for sure what I assumed all those years.

Jack closed his eyes. "Do you really need to know this?"

"Yes. I want to know."

"Yes, I'm sorry to tell you that."

"You were with him when he cheated on me?"

"Maddie..." Jack closed his eyes a bit.

I wasn't going to let him off the hook. "Answer the question, Jack."

"Yes, there were several occasions... I was with him when he cheated on you."

I stared at Jack. All those years, I wondered, but knew in my gut, that he was with other women...and I stayed. But I never did anything about it. What the heck was wrong with me?

Jack assumed my silence was about him. "Maddie, I didn't know about you."

I stared at Jack. It occurred to me that he knew the real Mike better than I did.

I once again felt like a complete doormat.

"Maddie, you okay?"

"No. I need to go, Jack. I want to go to sleep."

"Please, tell me this doesn't change things between us?"

I couldn't answer that. This was a lot to take in. I was sleeping with my ex's partner. My ex was a criminal, but I wasn't sure what kind. I had been cheated on, and apparently my new guy had somehow been a part of it? Or was a part of it really a fair assessment? My mind was spinning. My heart was being shredded once again.

It wasn't really Jack's fault, but I didn't know the role he played in all this. And did whatever Mike do put Jack into harm's way too? Was Jack a criminal? I needed answers, but I wasn't going to get them tonight.

"I don't know, Jack. You're going to have to tell me everything tomorrow and let me process this."

Devastation grew on his face.

I closed my eyes as his sad eyes stared through the screen, then opened them and admitted, "But I don't want it to."

He blinked back tears. "I don't either, Maddie. Get some sleep."

I turned off my phone and cried into the pillow that smelled like Jack, in the bed of my lover who wasn't there to comfort me, who I didn't know if I would ever make love to again.

11

Maddie

After I thrashed around with nightmares all night, dreaming things no one should dream, I decided to get up. I quickly dressed for work and grabbed my phone off the charger.

There was a text from Jack. "I hope you slept well. I forgot to tell you that you shouldn't go anywhere without my driver...he is waiting on standby for you."

I rolled my eyes and texted back, "Is this really necessary?"

"Yes. Be mad at me, but don't try to spite me. Please."

"Fine. You get your way."

"Thank you. I miss you."

I paused for a minute. My anger told me not to respond, but my heart won. I texted him back an emoji heart and left it at that.

Downstairs, his driver waited on standby. His name was Casey. I assumed he was ex-military and had a feeling he was more than a driver.

I arrived to work super early and was surprised to see Liv there already.

"Hey." She glanced up from her desk. "Come on in."

I sat down, unsure where to start.

"What's going on?"

"I don't know." A tear slipped out of my eye. "Did Tom tell you anything last night?"

Liv came and sat next to me and put her arm around my shoulder. "He promised we would talk tonight, but it's bad."

"That's what Jack says."

"Did Jack tell you what's going on?"

"Nothing more than Mike is a criminal, and they are partners. Oh, and Mike cheated on me when he was with Jack."

"Jack told you that?" Liv looked at me in surprise.

"I made him tell me the truth."

"Ah, I see. I'm sorry, Maddie. I dated my fair share of cheaters before Tom."

"Jack was with him several times...when Mike cheated on me. It wasn't a one-off."

Liv rubbed my back and didn't say anything.

Another tear fell from my face. "I don't want Mike back, or have any good feelings left for him, but I wasted so many years on him. Six years, Liv!"

Liv pulled me into a hug and rubbed my back, "I know, girl. But you wouldn't have found Jack!"

"I knew he was cheating on me. I didn't have proof, but I knew it in my gut...and I still stayed. Why did I stay?" I cried harder.

"Shh...you can't go backward. Don't beat yourself up."

I sobbed.

"Hey, what else is this about?"

"Jack asked last night if this changes things between us, and I couldn't tell him no. Until I know the entire story, I can't say either way."

Liv pulled out of the hug. "Hey, listen, I know it's something bad and it's easy to jump to conclusions, but Jack is one of the good guys. So whatever he tells you, I know it'll be okay."

Liv was right about Jack, but I still didn't know where that put us.

"Let him explain when he gets back and take it from there. Relationships aren't perfect."

"Yours and Tom's is."

Liv started laughing, hard. "No, it's not. We have to work on our own crap too. And trust me, we really fought to make it work, in the beginning. But it's totally worth it."

It was hard for me to imagine anything but ease with Tom and Liv's relationship. They were the perfect couple. But I knew she wouldn't lie to me.

I eventually walked down to my office and became lost in my projects when I heard a knock on my door. Jack stood in the doorway, smiling at me, handsome as always, but also tired. His normal energy was drained, and I could tell he probably hadn't slept any better than I had.

My body wanted to go to him, but my mind wasn't going to allow it. I gave him a sad smile, not sure about our status. I had a flashback of yesterday morning, at the airport, when I blew him a final kiss. We both had been oblivious to what was ahead of us. Innocent, naive, and in utter bliss.

Today was a different reality. I wanted to step back in time, but I knew we couldn't.

"Can I come in?" Jack looked at me cautiously.

"Sorry, yes, of course."

He shut the door and sat across from me with his anxious eyes. His normal confidence was nowhere to be seen.

Lost about how to start the conversation, I decided to give him some help. "I need to know the truth."

Jack shook his head. "I know you think you do, Maddie, but I'm going to give you one more chance to forget about this. You aren't going to like what you hear. I really don't want to cause you any pain."

"Get it over with and tell me, Jack."

"I think we should go home and talk about this."

"Why? What does that matter? For God's sake, spit it out, please!" My voice got louder.

"Okay, but I warned you." He blew out some air.

I waited for him to speak.

He sighed, and I could see that his hand was shaking. I realized he was nervous. It threw me for a surprise.

"I met Michael Dupont in Tampa about a year ago. I was working on buying out a marina, and they kept raising their price. It was starting to get really ridiculous, but the potential was too good for me to pass up. I was bidding against him, and every time we bid, the owner would get greedier." Jack rubbed his hands through his hair in frustration.

I waited for him to continue.

"One day, Michael and I were in the same bar. After a few drinks, we decided we should combine forces and become partners or we were both going to lose out. Tom mentioned he knew him, so I didn't vet him like I normally would. I wanted to get this deal done. I was cocky, Maddie, and skipped the crucial step that could have saved us from this mess," he admitted, and looked like he hated himself.

My heart ached, but I wasn't ready to cut him any slack. "Go on."

"We told the owner we were at a final offer and take it or leave it. As we thought, he took it and ran." Jack threw his head back, looking up at the ceiling. Guilt washed over his face.

"Why didn't Tom vet him?"

Jack shook his head. "I was the negotiating arm. I put deals together for all of us. It was my job."

Jack's eyes filled with embarrassment, failure, and regret. It was painful to see. I usually knew him as strong and confident. I also realized I still didn't have a good grip on what he really did.

He continued, "We thought we were buying a marina to save jobs and expand, but that wasn't Michael's plan. The manager of the marina was Jim and as usual, we try to keep the employees in their positions if possible. Michael wanted to take oversight of the staffing and the investors agreed to let him do it."

Jacks face went white. "I didn't know, Maddie, I swear I didn't know."

"Know what?"

"Michael and Jim were trafficking women and children out of the marina," Jack said quietly.

"No," I whispered as my stomach flipped. Mike was a dick, but he wouldn't do that. I couldn't have been sharing a bed with a human trafficker?

"Let's go home and finish this conversation. Please."

"No."

"Then sit on the couch," Jack grabbed my hand and pulled me over to the couch.

I turned toward him. "How did you find out?"

Jack shifted in his seat. "I was in Tampa, working on other deals, and ran into Jim and Michael at the bar. They invited me to an afterparty. We had partied together before, so I didn't think anything of it. But there were all these women and children...up for auction, if you will." Jack stopped, looked queasy, and closed his eyes as if he couldn't get rid of the images.

I grabbed his hand, and realized how hard this must have been for him.

"There was a gun. I didn't know what to do...so I left and was in shock. The next day, I returned, and it was like no one had even been there. I called the FBI, and we started piecing it all together. Michael only wanted to buy the marina to traffic out of it and he and Jim go way back. Our money expanded their operation. I'm the one who put the deal together." Jack quickly wiped a tear away.

I couldn't believe what I heard. How could I have been with someone for six years and not known what kind of a person they were?

"I've been working with the FBI on this for a year now. That's why I was in Tampa. I wasn't able to tell any of my investors, including Tom, the extent of everything. The FBI finally agreed to let me bring Tom into the investigation. I told him as soon as he informed me that your Mike was Michael Dupont. I'm so sorry, Maddie."

I didn't know what to say. Jack went to say something and stopped. "What?" More bad feelings shot through my body.

"Do you remember signing any papers?"

I jerked my head. "What are you talking about?"

"Tom found out yesterday they've been signing all the cargo shipments as Madeline Burns."

My pulse increased, and my mouth went dry. "Jack, you know I don't have anything to do with this."

"I know that, Maddie."

"Does Tom—"

"No way. He knows you have nothing to do with this. The FBI knows, too. We spent the morning with them."

"Why doesn't the FBI arrest them?"

"They didn't have any proof. I should have called as soon as I left that night, but I didn't know what to do. I think I was in shock...I don't even remember driving home. I called the FBI the very next morning, but everything had been wiped clean. If I hadn't seen it with my own eyes, I would think it never happened. We've been tracing their activities over the last year, and they can't seem to get to it in time. The FBI is always a step behind. We are trying to get the next shipment of women and children and find the supplier," Jack shakily ran his hands through his hair.

My head spun. I stared at Jack and tried to process all this. I spent six years of my life with a human trafficker. This was worse than I ever could have imagined. I started to feel sick.

"Maddie, let's go home."

I decided I wasn't going to get any more work done after learning this, so I let him help me into my coat, escort me to the lobby, and into his car. So many thoughts raced through my head. I fell right into Jack's chest, the familiarity of it felt secure in a world I was no longer sure about.

We didn't talk on the way home, and it didn't take long until we were up in Jack's penthouse. He ran a bath. I didn't argue, as I felt emotionally drained and sat in the bath with my mind spinning. When I stepped out, I put on one of Jack's t-shirts and walked into the bedroom. Jack was already lying on the bed, his eyes closed.

"Hey." I rubbed the back of my hand against his cheek.

He opened his eyes and sat up. "I'll go stay in another room so you can be comfortable here."

I grabbed his arm. "No, Jack. I don't want that."

At that moment, I realized he was just as human as I was. He had been manipulated and deceived by Mike, as much as me.

His heart hurt, and I was the one to hurt it with my inability to tell him nothing had changed between us. The man who gave me more pleasure and excitement than anyone, from the moment I met him, who put me first and himself last, didn't deserve to be hurt by me.

It was then and there, I knew no matter what else happened, that I was all in. It didn't matter, because I wouldn't let whatever Mike did, destroy what I could have with Jack.

"You don't hate me?"

"No, Jack, I don't hate you." I leaned in to kiss him, and tried to take all the worry and what ifs and maybes out of his mind and mine.

He pulled me onto him and stroked my hair. "Maddie, I can't believe I put us in this situation. I'm so sorry."

"Jack, you didn't know."

Jack shook his head. "I put together a deal that helped increase human trafficking. I skipped steps. I was arrogant. I'll never forgive myself."

I realized Jack had bottled up a lifetime of pain. Between not being able to tell anyone, and being the one who brokered the deal, guilt ate at him. I sat up and pulled his head to my chest. "It's not your fault."

To my surprise, he started sobbing. The shame of it all too much to bear.

"Shhhh." I rubbed my hands through his hair.

"I can't get the faces of those women and children out of my mind," he sobbed hysterically.

This affected Jack even deeper than I initially thought, and I never thought about the horror he saw that night or the responsibility he felt for it.

Jack sobbed as I tried to comfort him, and I don't know how long I held him. Eventually, Jack lifted his head. His eyes were red, his face tired and swollen.

I realized how exhausted he was. "You need sleep, sweetheart." I removed his clothes and put the covers over him.

"Maddie, lie here with me?"

Not hesitating, I slipped under the covers and snuggled up to his chest.

"Tell me I haven't lost you, Maddie."

I locked my eyes with his. "You haven't lost me, Jack."

Tears of relief swept over his face. I kissed his tears and then lips. "Go to sleep now." I snuggled into his chest, and fell asleep along with him.

12

Maddie

When I woke up, it was dark out. Jack was still asleep. His beautiful face looked peaceful. I moved and tried not to disturb him, but he stirred.

"Hey." He traced my lips with his finger.

"Hey, you." I leaned in to kiss him. He grabbed me and pulled me onto him, and through his kisses, I felt his desire to be mine, a desperation to know that I was still his.

He grabbed the t-shirt I wore, and slid his warm hands underneath, while he caressed my back and pulled me closer to him. My body fell into his familiarity, like a puzzle piece that fits just right.

I wanted to please him. He had been through so much, and he always worked so hard to please me. I wanted to release some of his tension and give him a high to soar on. I began to kiss his pecs, and fondled his already hardening cock in the process. I dipped down to it.

"I want to make you cum, Maddie. Get back up here."

"No, just relax, it's my turn." I took my first lick of his dick and sucked on his cap.

"Fuck, Maddie," he mumbled.

"Mmmm," I responded and pushed his rigid shaft further in my mouth.

"Swing your legs up here, Maddie."

"I want to please you, Jack. Let me."

"Maddie, I want to cum with your pussy on my face. Nothing will please me more. Swing your legs up here," he demanded once again.

I giggled. "If you insist." My inexperienced self once again was trying something new, and I positioned my body on top of his then began to suck his dick again. My body leaped off his when his tongue hit my clit. Jack let out a slight laugh, then grabbed my ass and pulled my body into his face again.

I readjusted myself. I was not going to give Jack bad head because he was giving me head at the same time.

But he felt so good. His big cock was in my mouth, his moans were humming out of his mouth and he licked and sucked, eating me out with expertise.

Jack knew exactly how to play my body, and my nerves fluttered at attention. From time to time, he'd slap my ass and then rub my butt cheek after the slap. My clit would pulse in his face with every slap. My nerves quivered with the sting of his slap and warmth of his hand.

My moans buzzed against his manhood and my chest heaved into his six-pack.

As I squeezed his balls, grazed my teeth along his shaft, and sucked on his tip, his moans became louder. He grabbed my ass and pushed me into his face harder, and I circled my hips into his face. I wanted it...needed it...and knew that only he could give it to me.

A soft laugh and groan vibrated against my throbbing body before he licked and sucked inside my opening. No one had done that to me before, and I inhaled sharply as his warm tongue raged against my walls.

But it didn't last long. Jack's fingers soon were in all my holes. I decided to be in all his. I put saliva on my finger and slowly stuck it up Jack's asshole. Little by little, I inched into him, as I replicated how he gave it to me. I heard him breath harder, and he sucked my pussy with a renewed intensity.

We shoved each other down and pulled each other up, wanting to give the other pleasure but feeling so much ourselves. The sensations overwhelmed me, and a few times, I popped up for air before I could resume my duties.

Jack was ready to explode. I could feel him throb in my mouth. I knew he would only release me when he came. He knew exactly how and when he would give it to me.

His penis started to pulse, and he warned me. I continued to keep him in my mouth and increased my suction. He started spurting his hot liquid in my mouth, and his body vibrated underneath me. With his massive hand, he slapped my ass and sucked on me with so much intensity, I toppled over the edge.

Our bodies ricocheted together. And when we stopped convulsing, my sweaty body laid on top of Jack's, an exhausted yet happy heap of body parts.

I rolled off him as my chest continued to heave, and my eyes tried to refocus from my high. We laid there, and breathed for a few moments, as Jack's fingers trailed my upper thighs.

After I caught my breath and crawled up to him, he flipped me on my back and feasted on my lips, my neck, my collarbone.

"I missed you, Maddie," he whispered in my ear. It was a little over twenty-four hours, but I knew what he meant. I felt an emptiness without him that I didn't wanted to admit.

Our relationship was fast; I knew it was. But we connected: both sexually and emotionally. As much as I tried to tell myself to go slow, I started to think that was impossible with him. I felt wanted, honored, and taken care of with Jack. As much as I needed to figure out my own life, I somehow began to realize that I needed to figure it out with him in it.

"I missed you too," I pulled his face to mine and wanted him to see that how I felt toward him was no less than how he felt toward me.

He closed his eyes briefly, and his eyes were slightly wet when he opened them.

"Hey," I whispered and stroked his cheek.

He closed his eyes again, as if in pain.

"Jack?"

"I don't deserve you, Maddie. But I can't stop myself from wanting you and taking whatever you'll give me."

I was stunned for a moment. My beautiful, confident, normally in charge Jack, was in so much agony. Much more than I realized. I pulled him closer to me. "Don't ever say that again, Jack. I've never wanted anyone more than I want you. You make me feel happy...and alive...and wanted."

A tear slid off his chin. I kissed it off his face, then found his mouth, and I pushed my tongue into his, as I frantically tried to show him that I needed him as much as he needed me.

He made me his number one, but did I make him number two in that process?

The thought crossed my mind, but I couldn't stay there long enough. Jack's body started to respond to mine again, and I rolled over on top of him, sinking onto him as he moaned, and I caught my breath. Bringing my face next to his, I whispered in his ear how beautiful he was and how much I wanted him.

"Maddie, I have to go get a condom."

I grabbed him. "I'm on the pill. I want to feel you, Jack. *All of you.*"

He hesitated, as if he wasn't sure. I moved my hips and he moaned, then he closed his eyes, and struggled to decide.

"You said you'll take what I give you. I'm giving you all of me."

His face registered what I meant, and he found my mouth. He kissed me with a new intensity. It was different than our normal fevered kisses during sex. It was softer, gentler, more intimate, but vulnerable and full of a need not for the high, but only for each other.

Our bodies moved in motion, and melted together as always, but slower, as if they wanted to savor every moment. He didn't make me beg. We didn't play any games. It was just Jack and me, as we made love.

Jack's strong arms held me tight, his hands caressed my naked back and butt. Our lips entwined, and our tongues danced in the dark, as our bodies grew hot and sweaty.

"Maddie, you feel so good," Jack whispered.

I nodded in agreement with my hitched breath. Jack's naked skin slid against mine, filling me up, rippling against my walls, hitting my sweet spot over and over.

Jack sat up and brought me with him. His hands supported my arched back, and his mouth moved to my collarbone. "So delicious," he mumbled.

My knees sank next to the sides of his hips, digging into the bed, as I tried to push all of him into my body, and his warm tongue sent new tingles through my nipples.

"I need you, Jack," I whispered to him.

Hands grazed my cheeks, and his heavenly lips were once again worshipping mine, as our hips moved together in a slow, almost lazy rhythm.

"I only want you," he whispered between kisses.

Sweat dripped from our bodies, while moans and breath reverberated through the room in a new quiet compared to our usual louder selves.

My hips sank deeper, his arms gripped me tighter, and his heat melted into mine, coursing through my body. And as he drove me to the gates of paradise, he murmured, "Maddie, I don't think I can go much longer."

I put my forehead to his, then let myself go, as I felt the slow tremble of my euphoria, that started to speed up.

"Jack," I cried out as he pumped hard against my bundle of nerves and violently began to shake, igniting more tremors throughout my body.

We held each other tight. I felt his heartbeat through his chest, and Jack found my lips again, feverishly kissing me, thanking me...just loving me.

Something changed with us. It was no longer just sex. We had made love. And as I laid in Jack's arms, with my head on his chest, he stroked my hair, quietly, from time to time, kissing the top of my head.

And I knew there was nowhere I wanted to be but in his arms.

I don't know how long we laid there, but suddenly, my stomach started to rumble.

Jack laughed. "Hungry?"

"Guess so." I realized I hadn't eaten all day.

Jack turned on his side, his elbow on the bed, hand on his face. "Want to shower and then walk to Noreens?"

"Sure, but the last one in the shower has to scrub the other person clean!" I jumped off the bed and ran to the bathroom.

Jack laughed and called out, "I'm going to enjoy being the loser of this one."

A LONG, HOT, STEAMY SHOWER LATER, WE STARTED TO GET READY to go to dinner. After I dried my hair, I sat at the vanity and put on my makeup. Jack stood at the counter and shaved. I could feel his gaze.

"What?"

"Nothing." His dimples popped out.

"What?"

"That red lipstick on you is going to make me horny all night."

I laughed. "And your dick is back in your brain!"

He shrugged and kissed the top of my head.

A few minutes later, we walked hand in hand. It didn't take us long to get to Noreens. We were quickly ushered to the same table I sat at the day before with Liv and Meg.

"Is this your table?" I teased.

"They open it up when I'm out of town."

"So you come here a lot?"

"I'm not really in New York that often, remember," he reminded me of our conversation in St. Pete. I decided to dig a bit deeper and hoped he would be more open than the last time.

I peered at him.

Jack raised his brow, "Go ahead."

"What do you mean?"

"You're going to ask me why I'm never in New York."

I laughed. "Reading my mind now?"

"Maybe..."

"So? Why aren't you in New York? You have an amazing home, what's the point of having it if you don't get to enjoy it?

Jack beamed with pride. "You like my home?"

I tilted my head to the side and squinted at him slightly. "Do you seriously have to ask me that? Your home is gorgeous. It has everything. Why don't you want to be here?"

Jacks face dropped a bit. Sadness once again entered his eyes. "It reminds me of what I don't have."

I didn't understand. "I'm not following. What don't you have?"

"You're going to make me spell it out, aren't you?"

"Jack, I'm really not following you."

His finger started to tap the table, as if he was a bit nervous. I put my hand over his. "Look, Maddie, I had a plan for my life. I put everything into it and when it exploded, I…I shut off..."

I waited and stroked his hand some more.

"I thought I was going to be a husband and a dad. When we lost the baby," Jack paused and closed his eyes as if the pain was still fresh, "everything changed. It didn't matter what I did, I couldn't bring us back."

"That's not your fault. It happens sometimes. It takes two people to be in a relationship."

He shook his head, "I decided work would be it for me. No more relationships. It just...hurt too bad. I jumped in full force, started to make a lot of money, and decided to buy the penthouse. I became obsessed with it, and made sure every detail was perfect."

"It is perfect. That's why I don't understand why you aren't enjoying it."

"You're missing the point, Maddie."

"Tell me then."

He swallowed hard. "It's empty."

I sat back. Slowly, I realized that Jack was lonely, and the penthouse reminded him of the relationship and family he didn't have.

"So I travel. I told myself so many lies over the years. I have to be gone. I have it all. I don't need to really get to know anyone else." Jack's vulnerability ripped through me.

"But you made it clear from the start that you wanted more with me. Why?" It didn't make sense that he wanted more from me if he really didn't want to get to know anyone else.

Jack sat back a bit, took his hand, and rubbed it through his hair. "When I saw those women and children being auctioned off, I realized that while I never paid for sex, all I did was use women for my pleasure, and I was no better than Michael and Jim."

"Surely, you don't believe that? Anyone you had sex with was a willing participant."

"You don't think many of them wanted more?"

"I'm sure, but that isn't the same thing, Jack."

"Maybe not the same thing, but it's still heartless. It's still selfish."

He paused, and I waited for him to continue.

"Maddie, I've used *a lot* of women. I took what I wanted and threw them to the curb. *Nice* women. Women who deserved better than that."

I didn't speak. I wasn't surprised Jack had a thriving sex life before me, but I hadn't thought of him as a womanizer.

"Now you know. I don't blame you if you want to get up and walk out of here." His eyes were full of shame.

He thinks I want to leave him now?

"Don't be silly. We've all done things we aren't proud of."

Jack snorted. "Oh yeah? Maddie, tell me one thing you have done that you aren't proud of."

"That's easy."

Jack raised his eyebrows at me and waited.

"I lived the last few years as a doormat. I stayed with someone who had no respect or true love for me."

"Like I said the first night I met you: dumb guy."

I stared at him. "Do you know what it's like to be someone's doormat? To base your entire world around someone who doesn't want you? To be rejected, over and over, and still want that person to love you? To stay with someone who criticizes you in every conversation you have?"

Jack scooted over in the booth and put his arm around me. "Maddie, you have nothing to be ashamed of. It's not disgraceful to want to be loved."

"I stayed six years, Jack. *Six.*"

"At least you didn't use people."

I rolled my eyes and laughed. "Don't give yourself so much credit. Those women *wanted* to sleep with you, and I'm pretty sure you gave them a good time. If we only had a one-night stand, and I never saw you again, sure, if I am honest with myself, a part of me would have been disappointed. But you would have been the guy I always remembered who brought me back to life."

Jack smiled. "You were never dead, Maddie."

"But wasn't I?"

Jack shook his head.

"Look, am I saying that you didn't hurt a lot of hearts? No. You probably did. Disappointed a lot who wanted more? Sure. Jeez, Jack, I didn't expect anything, and after a night with you, I would have been disappointed. But it takes two people to consent. They *wanted* what you gave them as much as you wanted to take what they gave you. Life isn't fair. There are worse things you can claim to have done."

"Still doesn't make it right."

I sipped my drink. "No, it doesn't make it right, but it doesn't put you anywhere close to the type of men Mike and Jim are."

Jack didn't say anything; he tapped the table with his index finger.

"So, after the night when you saw those women and children, you decided you weren't going to casually date anymore? Only look for something serious?"

Jacks head snapped. "No."

I tilted my head in confusion.

"I wasn't going to date or sleep with anyone. I haven't had sex since before that night."

I sat in stunned silence. Jack hadn't had sex in close to a year? How was that possible? It took me a minute to get over my shock. "Why me?"

Jack clasped my hand and stroked it with him thumb. "I couldn't help myself. When I met you outside the bathroom…I was only in the bar to use the restroom. I didn't plan on being there. I stopped frequenting bars after everything happened. I stopped partying. I stopped being *that* guy."

I held my breath and waited for him to finish.

"You ran into me and I had to know more about you. I *needed* to meet you. It was like I was drawn to you. I tried to talk myself out of it, but I couldn't force myself to walk out of the bar. I saw you sitting by yourself and had to at least try."

"Try to sleep with me?"

Jack shook his head, hard. "No, Maddie. I told myself I wasn't going to sleep with you, I would only learn more about you. Then when everything happened with the hotel, I honestly only brought you to my room to keep you safe. I was happy that you were there, but I gave myself a talk while I changed my clothes. Told myself not to touch you again, because I didn't want to make you uncomfortable or ruin any chance I might have with you. I was serious about my promise to be a gentleman. When I walked out on the balcony and you stood there in your bra and panties...I couldn't help it."

I smiled, then I started slowly to laugh.

"What's so funny?"

"Thank God I stripped then, because we would have missed out on a pretty good night."

Jack softly laughed. "How are you so cool about all this, Maddie?"

"I like you Jack...I like *us*. I'm glad you shared this with me, but I've spent six years wanting a fraction of what I think you and I have. So, I see you as the man you are now, and that other man you were, well, I don't think he's as bad as you do." I leaned in and kissed him.

The waitress came up and inquired if we were ready to order. We placed our orders, and she left. Jack trailed his fingers on my hand. "You still want to go visit neighborhoods tomorrow?"

I had forgotten about that. "Sure. Do you still have time?"

"Yes. I promised you, so I cleared my day. But to be crystal clear, you can stay at my place for as long as you want. I like you there."

Liv's words about Jack being a man of his word flew back to me. She had been right. It would be so easy to stay at Jack's forever, but no matter how much I wanted to, I knew I needed to also spend some time living on my own.

"I like being there with you too. And thank you for being my knight in shining armor, because you fixed my huge mess." I leaned in and stole another kiss.

Jack pulled back, "I'm glad I could help. Maddie, we really do need to make sure that monster never comes near you again."

I closed my eyes briefly and took a deep breath. Now that I knew who Mike really was, I couldn't agree more. I hoped that Mike would never hurt me, but I feared he wouldn't think twice, now that I had gone against his wishes.

"I think you need to make sure wherever you decide to live has security."

He was right. I needed to feel safe, and that would at least give me some protection against Mike, should he ever find out my address and come after me.

"I had my real estate agent send over some listings, to give you an idea of what's out there with security. We can go in some of the lobbies tomorrow to check them out if you wish. Then, if you like what you see, we can schedule a time with the real estate agent to go view the actual apartments." Jack pulled up a list on his phone.

I glanced at the list on Jack's phone. There were hundreds of listings, all throughout different parts of New York.

"This is overwhelming." I started to scroll and stopped.

Jack put his arm around me. "What's wrong?"

"I honestly don't even know what to do with that list. There are so many...how do I even know which ones to start with?"

"Why don't we filter the listings to places nearest your work, how many bedrooms, etc. and start from there?"

That sounded like a good idea. "I only need one bedroom."

Jack hit a few buttons on his phone and the list reduced to a few dozen. "Better?"

"Yes!"

Jack changed the list to a map view. He zoomed in and pointed out, “Here’s your work, and here’s my place.”

“Is that your way of saying ‘don’t go far’?”

Jack held up his hands in defense, a big cocky grin on his face. “I’m only showing you, that’s all...but, wherever you decide to move to, I don’t have a problem traveling to break it in.”

13

Jack

I WANTED HER TO STAY FOREVER, BUT I KNEW HOW IMPORTANT IT was to her to have her own place. So I wouldn't stand in her way. No, I would do everything in my power to make sure she was safe and happy.

Then I told her my darkest demons, and she still wanted me in her life. I didn't know what she saw in me, but I was thankful for whatever it was.

When I discovered her Mike was Michael Dupont, I couldn't believe it. Tom didn't know it, but I would be introducing him to our FBI contacts. The FBI finally agreed to let me get Tom involved. And he flew to Tampa under different assumptions.

Like an excited schoolboy, I called Tom to tell him about Maddie and me, and because I wanted to find out if he knew anything else about her ex, Mike. I didn't get the reaction I expected.

Tom sighed. "This is going to be tricky, Jack. Have you told Mike yet?"

"Tom, what are you talking about? She broke up with Mike before we met."

"Okay. But have you told him that you're sleeping with his ex? It does make things a little awkward sometimes in business relationships."

"Tom, I'm not following you. What does Mike have to do with business?"

"Jack, do you not know that Maddie's Mike is Michael Duponte?"

My blood drained in my body; my stomach flipped. No. It couldn't be.

"Jack, you still there?"

My mouth went dry. "Tom, I was going to tell you this when you landed. We have to stop the girls from going to Michael's today."

"The girls? What are you talking about?"

"Liv is going with Maddie to meet the movers. Michael is running a human trafficking ring out of the Marina with Jim. I can't get into it all till you're here tomorrow, but we can't let them go."

Within minutes, Tom sorted out bodyguards, called Liv, and was back on the phone with me.

"Why the hell didn't you tell me this was going on?" Tom's angry voice flew out of my phone.

"The FBI wouldn't let me. I wanted to."

I could hear Tom breathe as he tried to calm down.

"I need to fly back. I can't let Maddie near him."

"Jack, you need to stay put. The bodyguards are safer than you going. If he does show up, it's better he doesn't know you're with Maddie."

My heart raced, and I realized my hands were in tight fists.

"You know I'm right," Tom said.

I closed my eyes and sighed. I knew he was right, but it didn't feel good. "Okay."

"Stay in Tampa. I'll see you tomorrow. And Jack?"

"Yeah?"

"Don't do anything stupid. Lay low."

He knew me well. I hung up and sat in shock. The thought that Maddie was with him for six years made my skin crawl. *What did he do to her over all those years?*

I knew I needed to tell her. I didn't want to, but I had to. I thought for sure she would leave me and never want me again. But like always, Maddie surprised me. She still wanted me and claimed she needed me. My prayers were answered.

But I knew that until Michael Duponte was in jail, he wouldn't just let Maddie peacefully go. No, he would be angry because she left him. I needed to do everything to make sure that he never got near her again.

Maddie

THE NEXT DAY, JACK AND I WALKED ALL OVER DIFFERENT neighborhoods. It was the first week of March, and the weather was surprisingly kind.

Each neighborhood had its own charm. We drank coffee at a neighborhood cafe, saw too many lobbies to count, ate lunch at a bistro, and continued to make our way through the list Jack printed off. At each place, he would cross it off if I wasn't interested, or circle it if I wanted to look into it further. By the time evening approached, my head was spinning. My legs were exhausted. It had been a perfect day. Exactly what I always envisioned I would have done with Mike when we decided to move.

It's so much better because I'm with Jack.

The night air became chilly. Jack pulled me into his warm body as we made our way back to his building. We quickly rode up the elevator. I walked into Jack's penthouse and pulled off my shoes. As I sat on the couch, I started to rub my feet.

"Feet hurt?" Jack asked.

"More like cold."

"Hold on." Jack left the room. I sat on the couch, rubbed my feet some more, and wondered what he was up to.

About ten minutes later, he came back out, grabbed my hand, and pulled me through his bedroom and into the bathroom.

Jack had lit candles everywhere. The lights of the city danced through the window. Soft music played, the fireplace flickered, and warm bubbles filled the tub. Jack grabbed my shirt and pulled it over my head, released my bra, and threw it all on the floor before he grabbed my pants and shoved them off me.

I stepped out of my pants and stood naked.

"Get in." Jack pointed.

I gave him a sly grin. "Only if you come with me."

Jack's dimple popped out. "I won't make you ask twice." He quickly removed his clothes.

We laid in the tub, opposite one another. Jack grabbed my foot and gave me a foot massage, then worked his fingers up through my calf. I leaned back, closed my eyes, and let him take over, as I melted into the feel of Jack's hands on my body.

We didn't speak for a while. Jack started to work on my other leg. "Hey, Maddie?"

"Hmm," I opened my eyes and could see Jack's mind working, hesitating, almost conflicted.

"I don't want you to take this the wrong way or feel rushed, because I mean it when I say you can stay here as long as you want. But in New York, you can't wait long if you want an apartment. If you are interested in any of those places, you need to grab it quickly." I saw a flicker of sadness in his eyes.

I slowly nodded. Being with Jack was easy. I don't know how, but it was. I felt alive and wanted and treasured. It was exactly why I needed to secure a place soon, because if I didn't do it now, I could easily stay at his place forever.

And I was pretty sure Jack would let me.

"I'm not taking it the wrong way. I appreciate you telling me. I feel rather naive about all this." I felt the heat, creep up my face.

Jack saw it and sat up. He grabbed my waist and pulled me over on top of him, so I laid on his chest. My leg grazed his hard-on. "You're new to New York; that's all. Don't be so tough on yourself."

I leaned in and kissed him. Like always, his kisses made me feel like I was the only thing on earth that mattered to him.

He pulled away. "I can have my real estate agent show you the ones you are interested in tomorrow if you want?"

"That would be great. Thanks."

"Do you want me to go with you? I can change my schedule..." he said absentmindedly.

I thought about it. As much as I loved having Jack as my crutch, I didn't want him to have to rearrange his schedule all the time to keep bailing me out of my problems. I locked eyes with him, "I don't want you to take this the wrong way."

"Every time you say that, my stomach drops..."

"Sorry." I kissed him and smiled. "I think I need to do this one on my own. Don't get me wrong, I love how helpful you've been, but you have things to do, and I don't want you always having to bail me out of my problems."

"Maddie, I'm not—"

I put my finger over his lips. "Shhh. You're amazing. But I need to do this part on my own, all right?"

His Adam's apple throbbed. I could feel his heart thump in his chest and saw his mind spin. He slowly nodded.

I leaned in and kissed him. Our tongues quickly found the other, as if they were lovers who searched forever and finally reunited. I moved on top of Jack, as my naked breasts pushed against his warm chest, his arms wrapped around my back, and my body easily slid onto his girth.

Our bodies glided to the rhythm. Our skin easily slid over each other's, as Jack moved from my mouth and pulled my chest to his face.

My head fell back, and my back arched when Jack's lips hummed gently onto my breasts. I sank deeper onto his throbbing manhood. My hands pulled at his hair.

"So perfect," Jack mumbled against my breasts.

Tiny volts of electricity shot through me as Jack ever so diligently gave equal attention to both of my nipples. He swirled, sucked, and caressed me with his tongue. My oh's and ah's tumbled out of my mouth, as he owned my body once more.

At that moment, I knew I would do whatever this man wanted—to feel how no other man could ever make me feel. I would be his slave if necessary.

Jack moved from my chest and up my neck, then moved his forehead to mine and stared into my eyes. Both our breaths were labored, and his lips slightly shook as his jawline hardened. My arms wrapped around his shoulders and his hands moved on the sides of my head.

"Whatever you want," I mumbled under my breath.

Jack scanned my eyes for an explanation.

"You can do anything you want to me, Jack." I didn't know why I felt the need to disclose that to him.

Jack whispered, "I'll never hurt you, Maddie. I only want to be good to you."

I'm not sure what made him think I didn't know that, or at what part of our quick time together I so willingly gave my complete trust over to him, but I knew in my heart if there was anyone in the world I believed in and trusted, it was Jack.

The realization that I didn't only trust him to do illicit things to my body, but I quickly handed over my heart to him, rushed to me. But I wasn't alone, because I knew from Jack's eyes, if I wanted his heart, he would give it to me.

"I know that," I whispered back.

I leaned in and found his mouth.

He seized my hips and urgently pushed them quicker. "Let me make you feel good."

"Jack, no one has ever made me feel good except you."

His eyes gazed at mine as if he was surprised by my admission. Why? I didn't know.

Does he think anyone else in the world even compares?

Jack thrust against me quicker and pushed into me farther as he drove me to my place of worship. My insides were on fire again, and I wanted to explode.

"You're so good to me.... So fucking good, Jack," I blurted out as his body bulged into mine.

His fingers started to rub my clit, and I cried out, as my body continued to rise and fall on him.

"Let me give you everything, Maddie," he whispered in my ear.

Everything... It crossed my mind he wasn't only talking about ways to make me orgasm anymore. We had quickly crossed those borders in the last few days.

"Everything," he repeated.

It was as I suspected. He was declaring to me that whatever I wanted from him I could take, but I didn't want to take. "What can I give you?" I whispered back.

"Just you, Maddie, just you."

"I'm yours, Jack." I closed my eyes, not sure how much longer I could last, as he intensified the pressure on my clit, his penis began to hit my sweet spot repeatedly, and my walls began to clench him over and over.

Jack blurted out, "Oh fuck, Maddie," started to release in me, and sent me over the edge. We held each other close, and he continued to release into me, as we ricocheted together into a sea of moans and labored breath.

We cried out each other's names, with Jack's face in my neck and my hands gripping his hair.

As we started to come down from our high, Jack grabbed my head and pulled me into his mouth. In his kisses, I felt his need for me and his desire to claim me as his. And I felt the promise that I was his everything.

After his kisses, I laid on his chest and traced his pec muscles. I put my ear on his heart and listened to the beat slowing down as Jack cupped my butt.

"Hey, Maddie."

I tilted my head up and smiled at him. "Yeah?"

"You sure you're okay not using a condom? Don't get me wrong, I've always had safe sex except with one person, and I've been tested and am clean, but are you sure?"

It occurred to me that Jack's one was Kelly, and he got her pregnant. I never thought about how that must have affected him when I didn't make him use a condom.

"I haven't had sex with Mike since before moving to New York. I'm on the pill. I had a test about five months ago and am clean too. If you aren't comfortable though, we can go back to using condoms."

Jack didn't say anything for a minute. "I prefer not to, but I want to make sure you are really okay with it."

I reached up and stroked his cheek. "Jack, you haven't made me do anything I haven't wanted to. You never will. I know that. I'm good with it if you are."

"Okay."

I rolled into him more, and my tongue lazily explored his mouth. Then I snuggled back into his chest.

We laid there for a while. I'm not sure how long, but Jack was lost in his thoughts. I figured it was memories of Kelly and the baby he lost. As much as I wanted to ask, I figured if he wanted to talk about it, he would, so I laid on his chest and listened to his heartbeat.

We were in the tub for so long that my fingers started to resemble raisins. I glanced up at Jack. "Let's get out."

He kissed my forehead. "Okay."

Jack dried me off, wrapped a towel around me and then himself, and slapped my ass playfully. The deep-in-thought Jack was gone, and back was the fun-loving, confident guy.

"The last one to bed has to make breakfast in bed in the morning." He took off and ran out of the bathroom.

I laughed, in tow, and wondered if he had any whipped cream...

14

Maddie

MORNING CAME QUICKLY. AS JACK PROMISED, HE CALLED HIS REAL estate agent to set up showings on different apartments. He made his driver available and insisted I didn't go out alone.

"Jack, I'm going to be on my own, eventually. You can't keep security on me twenty-four seven."

"But can't I?" He gave me a cocky, challenging stare.

I cocked my head to the side. "No, you can't."

He stepped up to me and kissed me on the head. "Take the driver. We can discuss this later." He slapped me on the ass and walked away.

"Jack," I called after him.

He kept walking, put his hand in the air with his back to me and waved, "Bye, Maddie."

I shook my head at Jack's cockiness. He had it wrong if he thought he was going to keep me under his security when I moved out. Besides, once things were sorted out with the FBI and Mike, hopefully, he would be in prison and out of our lives for good. In the car, I wondered, again, how I could have been so stupid to be with someone for six years without really knowing who they were?

And then anxiety popped up about Jack. We were moving fast. I knew it but was unsure how to take it slow. The fact was, I really didn't know him. If I was such a lousy judge of character for six years, how could I be sure about Jack?

Every fiber of my being told me that Jack was special, not only a good guy but an amazing man. But I needed to figure out what was wrong with my radar on Mike. Then, it occurred to me, it wasn't my radar on Mike because I felt for a long time he was no longer a good man.

If my radar told me he turned bad, why did I stay?

I couldn't risk getting into that situation ever again, and if Jack and I had any chance, I needed to figure that out about myself.

Casey dropped me off at the first building. I walked into the lobby and saw a stunning, blonde-haired, model-type, woman. She sat in the lobby, fidgeting with her nails. When she noticed me, she smiled at me and stood up. "Maddie?"

I smiled at her. "You must be Evelyn?"

She put her hand out. "And you're Jack's new girl?" She spoke like there was a secret she knew that I didn't.

I peered at her, not quite sure how to respond to that. *Am I Jack's girl? Yes, I guess I am.* But why did I feel that she didn't like the fact I was with Jack? And her tone suggested that I wouldn't be a permanent fixture in his life, and that there had been many before me.

Did Jack help all the women in his life find apartments?

I decided not to answer her question, as I felt like she didn't expect a response. "Are we able to go see the apartment?" I stared at her confidently.

"Sure, Maddie." She laughed and threw her head back and enunciated my name like I was a child.

The hairs on the back of my neck stood up.

The elevator door shut. "So, how is Jack doing?"

"He's great, thanks for asking." I hoped to leave it at that.

"Yes. I'm sure Jack is." Her eyes scanned over me.

Even her saying his name made me feel gross. But it was official. Evelyn definitely didn't like the fact I was with Jack.

Is there a history between them or something? My stomach flipped at the thought.

We quickly reached our floor and went into the first apartment. It was a small space, typical for New York, with good light. I walked through it quickly while she tried to point out different features. I turned my back to her and rolled my eyes. Like I couldn't see those features with my own two eyes, I thought.

After the first showing, she jumped into the car with me. The smell of her perfume filled the car, and I felt slightly suffocated. She directed Casey where to take us next then sat back.

"So how long have you and Jack been seeing each other?"

I debated about what to tell her. I counted the days in my head. Ten days…I realized how pathetic that would sound. I should have told her that it was none of her business, but I found myself blurting out, "Not long."

She sneered, "Of course not, darling. Jack Stevens is not a long-term strategy."

Anger flooded my eyes. "Long-term strategy? He's not a piece of meat."

"Tsk, tsk, tsk...so innocent you are. I see why he's into you at the moment. But isn't he?" She licked her lips.

"What do you know about Jack Stevens?" I hissed.

She played with her nails. "Don't get your panties in a twist. Save that for Jack while you have him."

We pulled up to the next building. I jumped out of the car and walked away from her as fast as I could.

"Hey, where are you going? We have a full day of places to visit!"

No way would I spend another moment with her. My face was red with rage. My insides quivered. Another moment with her, and I would end up in jail for assault. I couldn't believe the nerve of that woman.

Once again, the thought that Jack may have a closer relationship than just a professional one with her punctured my heart. My stomach flopped between anger and disgust, as the smell of her perfume still filtered my nose.

"Ms. Burns," Casey called out the window as he followed me. "Please, get back in the car."

"I need some air, Casey, you can go now."

"But Mr. Stevens—"

I turned and angrily shouted, "You can tell Mr. Stevens that I am not his property, and you are not on my payroll." I spun around and felt a tad guilty that I yelled at Casey but continued to walk away.

It didn't matter how many blocks I walked. Nothing calmed me down. I wished for my insides to stop shaking, but I couldn't stop thinking about all the nasty things Evelyn snarled at me. "Jack Stevens is not a long-term strategy," and "I see why he's into you at the moment," replayed in my head, over and over again. Tears started to gush out of my eyes.

How naive did I have to be? Jack was honest regarding his history with other women, but to have it thrown in my face like that hurt. And how could Jack change so easily from one night stands to a serious relationship? Granted, he was affected by what he witnessed, but to put it into practice, well, it couldn't be easy for him only because he thought he needed it. What if he thought that is what he needed, but realized in a few weeks or months that it wasn't?

I turned the corner, not able to wipe the tears away fast enough. I didn't want to be Jack's for the moment. It had only been ten days, but I knew I didn't want only to be a blip on his radar. Evelyn was nasty, no doubt about it, but it occurred to me that she had known Jack longer than I had.

Does that mean she knows him better? Once again, the thought of her and Jack together made me feel sick.

I walked several more blocks, not sure where I was, and wiped more tears off my face. I cursed myself that I fell for Jack at first sight, when I shouldn't have fallen for anyone until I figured out who I was and what I wanted.

Our relationship had been intense from the start, and Jack and I hadn't spent much time apart. My bad judgment about Mike resulted in years of unhappiness, and I began to think about how Jack was partners with him. I couldn't blame him. Jack was swindled as much as I was, but what happened during all those nights they partied together? Thoughts of all the things they could have done with women together flew into my mind.

As a wave of nausea hit me, I crouched on the sidewalk. I held my nausea in and slowly stood up, then continued to walk to the corner, lost deep in thought, as I tried to remove images of Jack and Mike together. I didn't hear the door of the taxi slam, or when he shouted my name.

Suddenly, Jack was at my side. He grabbed my waist and pulled me up against the side of the building. "Maddie!" His face was red and full of emotions I couldn't even decipher. His hands tilted my chin up as his thumbs brushed away my tears.

"Let me go, Jack," I hissed.

He gazed at me in confusion. "What happened? Tell me what happened so I can make it right."

I laughed, a little bit of hysteria or delirium, not sure which. I blasted him, "There goes Jack Stevens, thinking you can just make everything right, but you can't."

His head jerked back in panic. Was it panic because I was closer to the truth or because he really did want me for the long term?

"Maddie, tell me," he pleaded.

I pointed in his face. "How could you set me up with that...that woman."

"What did she say?"

"What do you have to hide?"

"With Evelyn? Nothing. I don't understand what's happening here."

"What's your relationship with her, Jack?"

Jack stayed calm. "She's my real estate agent. I own a lot of properties. She finds good deals for me, we view them, and I decide if I want to buy it or not. When it's time to sell she lists them. That's it."

"What's your past with her? Tell me the truth."

"I *am* telling you the truth. It's never been and never will be anything but professional with her."

"I don't believe you." I tried to shrug his hands off me and walk away, but he moved his body closer to mine and trapped me against the wall.

"Let go of me!"

"Not until we sort this out. I don't know what Evelyn told you or why she would lead you to believe anything other than she is just my real estate agent, but that's the truth."

"So how many of your 'casual' girls has she found places for?"

His head jerked back in shock. "No one. Just you, and you know you aren't casual to me. Why?"

"Why don't you ask Evelyn." I tried again to leave, but he had me cornered and wouldn't let me go.

Jack's voice rose and began to match the anger of mine. "I don't want to ask Evelyn. I'm asking you."

"Then why would she say the things she said to me and insinuate what she did?" I fired at him.

Jack grabbed my face in his hands. "I don't know, Maddie, but if you think I would ever intentionally put you in a situation like that, you really don't know me."

"You're right, I don't," I snapped back.

He inhaled sharply and took a small step back. Hurt, insult, and disappointment all shot through his face. I don't know how long he stared at me, but the longer he stared, the more my anger turned into panic.

Pictures of Jack flew into my mind. When he grabbed me and escorted me to safety the first night in the bar and then assured me I didn't have to do anything I didn't want to. When he pulled me away from Jim, then, when Jack stopped to ask for my permission the first time we had sex. He wouldn't ever do that, and I knew that about him. "I'm sorry. I know you wouldn't ever intentionally put me in a bad situation."

"You sure about that?"

"Yes. I'm sorry I said that."

It started to snow. Tiny snowflakes covered his hair and shoulders. Jack stepped closer to me, grabbed my face, and pulled my lips to him. When he pulled back, he said, "I don't know what Evelyn is up to, but I'll get to the bottom of it."

"She wants you for herself."

"I assure you that will never happen. Come on, let's go home." He led me to the car where Casey waited.

Embarrassment surged through me, as I remembered that I yelled at Casey earlier. "Casey, I'm sorry—"

He put his hand up to stop me, and he opened the door for me to get in. "No worries ma'am. Glad you're safe."

15

Jack

CASEY CALLED ME. "WE HAVE A PROBLEM. EVELYN DID SOMETHING. Maddie is very upset and walking down the street. She is refusing to get in the car."

"Casey, don't let her out of your sight. I'm jumping in a cab." I stood up and was out the door, immediately hopping into a cab, as panic seized me.

Grabbing my phone, I pulled up the tracker on Maddie's phone I had secretly installed when I found out who her ex was. I didn't tell her because I knew she was already scared, but I didn't trust that Michael wouldn't try to come after her.

The tracker showed me what street she was on, and I instructed the cabbie to go quickly.

I called Evelyn. "Jack," she purred.

"Evelyn, what the fuck is going on?"

"Your girl took off. I have no idea what happened."

"Something obviously happened. What?"

"Honestly, Jack, I have no idea."

She was lying. I don't know what happened, but I would deal with her later. I didn't have the time or patience for her games. I hung up.

Then I saw her. Maddie was bent over like she was going to get sick, then stood up and started to walk again.

I threw money at the cabbie and jumped out of the cab. I ran over to her and shouted her name. When I pulled her face to mine, I could tell I surprised her.

I saw her tears, anger, and pain. I didn't know what Evelyn had done to cause this, but I needed to find out.

When I got Maddie back in the car, she didn't say anything. I just pulled her close and held her.

After we got back to the penthouse, Maddie told me she had work to do. I had a lot of work to do too. So we set up our work spots in the living room. I sat on the couch, and Maddie sat at the table. But I only pretended to work. From time to time, I snuck glances at her and continued to curse myself.

It was my job to protect her, and it included her emotional well-being. The fact that I put her in that situation made me more disgusted with myself.

She had been disrespected and not properly taken care of for the last six years, and I didn't want her ever to feel that again. And now one of my contacts had disrespected her. I didn't know what Evelyn thought she was accomplishing, but she was going to learn what messing with Maddie would do for her career.

I gazed over at Maddie, her black hair was twisted up in a claw clip, and her fingers quickly typed. I walked over to her and nuzzled her neck.

She laughed. "Jack, I need to finish this."

I smiled at her and kissed her lips. "I'll go make us dinner."

Her head jolted up. "You cook?"

"I'm a thirty-six-year-old man. I can cook a few things."

"TV dinner?"

"Ha, ha, very funny." I gave her a quick tickle, then turned to walk away, as she smacked my ass.

I walked into the kitchen so she could finish her work.

I wasn't in the kitchen long before she came in. "Jack, we're okay, right?" Her eyes were wide, and her fingers fidgeted.

My heart throbbed. "Maddie, as long as you are okay, we are okay."

She shifted uncomfortably. "I shouldn't have insinuated that I ever thought you would put me in harm's way."

I walked over to kiss her. "Already forgotten."

"I don't want to cause problems in your business relationships."

I put her face in my hands. "You've caused no problems."

"But—"

I put my finger over her mouth. "Shhh."

But she wasn't convinced. Her eyes were full of worry, and her concern was only for me. It drove into me like a knife—that she was worried she had caused any disruption in my life.

I sternly repeated to her, "You've caused no problems."

Maddie bit her lip. She continued to be worried. I grabbed her and set her on top of the counter, so she was almost eye to eye with me. Again, I repeated, "You've caused no problems. She is replaceable. You aren't."

"Jack, you don't have to—"

I put my finger over her mouth again. "Stop. No one will disrespect you. I won't have it. Do you understand me?"

She stared at me with wide eyes.

"Maddie, do you understand me?" I needed her to tell me that she understood...because I wouldn't tolerate it from anyone.

She nodded slowly. "Yes, Jack."

"Good. Now I hope you like spaghetti."

Maddie

We spent the rest of Sunday mostly in the penthouse; both of us worked a bit and tried to avoid the topic of Evelyn. I was worried that I caused problems for Jack with his business. After everything he had done for me, it was the last thing I wanted to do.

It was like we both walked on eggshells, and the only thing that got us past it was late-night and early morning sex.

I woke up the next morning and turned over to see Jack wasn't in bed. *Probably working out,* I thought and threw on a robe then walked out of the bedroom.

"What the fuck was that all about, Evelyn?" I heard him bark as he paced over to the window and stared out at the morning light. His body still had sweat on it—definitely post-workout.

Jack put his hands through his hair. "No, she isn't just some girl, not that it's any of your concern."

There was silence as Evelyn was talking. *If only I could hear what she was saying.*

"All the years of business I've given you, and this is what you do? I don't understand."

I watched as Jack's shoulders tensed.

Jack shook his head. "It's not just a bit of fun, and it's not just a misunderstanding. You're fired, Evelyn. I'm taking my business elsewhere. You'll be getting a letter from my attorney today severing you from all my listings."

I winced. I guiltily thought, *how much extra work did I just put on Jack's plate?*

"Yes, I am serious. I'm sorry, but no one is going to disrespect Maddie. Take care, Evelyn. And if you ever come close to Maddie again, I'll make sure your relationships with any investor I know is severed," Jack threatened and hung up.

He stood at the window and stared out. His shoulder muscles

were outlined in his sweaty workout shirt, and I could see the tension. I walked over to him and put my arms around his waist. "You all right?"

Jack turned around. "Did you hear all that?"

"Yes."

"I don't know why she did that, but I won't be dealing with her again. I'm sorry you had to go through that."

"Jack, it's not your fault. Let's forget about it."

He stroked my cheek, "Okay. So…as much as I'd love to start your Monday morning with a lazy day in bed, I have to get ready. I have a flight to catch."

"Oh?" He hadn't mentioned it.

"I just found out I need to be in North Carolina for a few days. I'll be back Thursday night. Dinner when I get back?"

My heart dropped. The thought of not seeing Jack for three days felt like a punishment.

"Sure."

He tilted my chin back up, "It's the quickest I could get in and out."

"It's okay. I'll miss you, but I know you still have to run your business."

He started to talk, then stopped as if he wasn't sure if he should say something or not.

Then, "Maddie, please don't argue with me about this, but I don't want you going anywhere unless Casey drives you."

I rolled my eyes.

"Stop," he said to me sternly. "This isn't a joking matter."

"Is there something you aren't telling me?"

"You underestimate Michael. I've seen him in action. We need to take precautions for your safety."

"What did you see him do?"

Jack closed his eyes briefly. "I can't get into that now. Please, do as I ask?"

I knew I had already caused enough stress on him for one day. "All right."

"Thank you." He kissed me, and I felt him start to harden. He pulled back and viewed the time on his phone.

I licked my lips at him.

Jack's dimples popped out. He picked me up and slung me over his shoulder, then gave me a playful swat on the butt. I giggled as he carried me into the bathroom. "I'll give you a reward in the shower."

JACK

I CALLED MY REAL ESTATE ATTORNEY. "I NEED YOU TO SEND A letter to Evelyn and revoke all my listings from her."

"Jeez, Jack. What did she do?" Bill questioned.

I sighed. "I don't want to get into it. Just do it, please?"

Evelyn and I had worked together for years. She made a few passes at me at the start of our relationship, but I wasn't into her. Even though I rejected her, she still brought me great real estate deals, and I hadn't thought much about it again. I didn't realize she still harbored feelings for me.

She was an excellent real estate agent and had done well for me over the years, but no one was going to disrespect Maddie.

"But Jack, it was only a little fun," she purred into the phone.

My stomach flipped at the thought that she saw disrespecting Maddie as fun.

There were lots of women, with good reasons to hate or cause me trouble. Never in a million years would I have guessed Evelyn would try to mess with my life.

Once I arrived at the airport, it wasn't that long before it was time to board. I quickly found my seat, put my carry-on in the overhead bin, sat down, and sighed.

That morning, I woke up to the FBI phone call. They required me to meet them in Tampa. Like usual, I had no idea why they needed me there.

The reason I told Maddie I was going to North Carolina was that I didn't want her to worry. There were many things I couldn't tell her regarding the investigation. I hated lying to her, but I couldn't bear the thought that she would worry about me while I was gone.

Casey had photos of both Michael and Jim, just in case. Maddie wasn't taking security as seriously as I wanted her to, but it occurred to me that maybe it was a good thing. Casey would watch her, and she wouldn't have that extra stress on her.

Relief surged through me when she didn't argue about living in a building with security. I thought she would possibly fight me on it, but she surprised me and agreed.

Besides not being able to be with her for several days, the security issue had my worries in overdrive. I hated the fact I had to leave her. What usually was something I did with no thought was now a nuisance.

"Mr. Stevens, do you want something to drink?" The flight attendant gave me a smile that suggested she was interested in more than just serving me a drink.

I shook my head. "No thanks."

The flight attendant moved on. A girl rushed onto the plane and sat down next to me. I gave her a quick nod and opened my laptop. I could feel her eyes on me. She was attractive, but like the flight attendant, I wasn't interested.

My previous self would have had her in the bathroom, and my hands would have covered her mouth up to contain her cries and moans. Even in the last year, when I swore off women, her attention would have still given my ego a big boost. Now, it was an annoyance.

Maddie was the only person who mattered to me. In fact, she was the only thing on my mind. I closed my eyes again.

The last year of my life had been spent with the FBI. I was ready for all this to be over, and now that I had Maddie in my life, it was even more important to finish this. The quicker Michael and Jim were in jail, the better.

Maddie

It was lunchtime on Monday. I was at Delaney's with Liv and Meg. I recited my story about what happened with Evelyn. Once again, Meg and Liv exchanged glances, like they could read each other's minds.

"What?"

Meg gave me an uncomfortable glance. "We've known Evelyn for a long time. Last year, at the Field Canes Ball, she was pretty drunk and trapped Liv and me in the bathroom."

I waited for them to continue. "And?"

Liv cleared her throat. "She went on and on about how fine Jack Stevens was and made comments about his ass and how she wanted to lick it."

"Evelyn mentioned that Jack was the bachelor to snatch, then spouted off about all his properties and the millions she made off him over the last eight years." Meg shifted in her seat.

"What did Jack say when you told him?"

Meg and Liv eyed each other. Meg shook her head. "We didn't."

"Why not?"

"We figured she was super drunk. We felt bad for her that she had it that bad for Jack when he obviously had no interest in her.

I'm sorry, Maddie, we didn't realize she would be vicious like that," Liv apologized.

"I know you didn't. But now I need to find a new real estate agent and start from scratch," I sighed.

"Hey, I think Tom has a place in Chelsea almost ready to rent. The last tenant destroyed the place, and we had to remodel the entire unit." Liv rolled her eyes in disgust.

"Why do renters trash places? I don't get it!"

"No idea. Do you want to go check it out?"

"Really? That would be great! Does it have security? Jack thinks I need it."

Liv picked up the phone. "Yes, it does. I think that's a smart move. Let me call our agent to see if she can meet you over there after work."

A few hours later, I met with Tom and Liv's agent Carol.

"They painted today, so don't touch any walls," she warned, as I stepped into the front door.

The apartment was an open floor plan with a nice master, full kitchen, and family room. The windows were almost floor to ceiling, and let in a ton of light.

"What do you think?"

It was perfect. "I'll take it!"

"Great. Let me send the contract over to the office tomorrow?"

"That is perfect. Thanks, Carol, I appreciate you showing it to me so quickly."

"That's my job. If you know anyone else who needs a real estate agent, I'd love to help them out."

"Give me your card. I might know someone."

16

Jack

I SPENT THREE AND A HALF GRUELING DAYS WITH THE FBI, MISSING Maddie and just wanting to go home.

Apparently, a new shipment was scheduled, and the party would be bigger than ever. One of the agents found the invite on the dark web. Michael and Jim were getting greedy because the starting bid levels were higher than ever.

The whole thing made me sick. For three and a half days, my stomach was in a constant state of nausea.

I received a text from Maddie. She wanted me to meet her at a dinner party. I didn't even ask who's party it was. The last thing I wanted to do was share her with anyone after being gone for three and a half days. I wanted to spend the night making her shake beneath me, call out my name, and listen to her beg me to give her the high she craved.

But if she wanted me at a dinner party, then I would go. I wouldn't be the guy who didn't support what she wanted to do. I dropped my suitcase off at the penthouse and grabbed a quick shower.

The good news was that it wasn't far from the penthouse. Any extra minutes I could have with her, I would take. A quick walk home and we could be alone.

I took a deep breath and texted her that I was there.

Maddie

The week flew by fast. Besides some quick text messages and a few short phone calls, I didn't get to talk to Jack a lot. I signed my lease and got the key to my new apartment. I kept it a secret from Jack, and I wanted to surprise him when he returned.

I sent him a text, "Have to go to a dinner party at six near your penthouse. Meet me there?"

"Sad to share you, but yes. Send me the address."

I smiled. I could only imagine how sad Jack was and guessed he was ready to have me naked all night.

I didn't have any furniture in my new place yet, but I brought a few blankets and pillows, some candles, a mini speaker for music, and ordered some take-out.

Jack texted me right at six. "I'm standing outside. Are you inside yet?"

"Yes, come up, I gave your name to the security desk. Tell them you are here for eight-zero-two."

Jack soon was knocking on my door. I opened it up wearing red high heels, black fishnets, and a red bra and garter belt. My black hair was curled long, and the red lipstick I knew drove Jack crazy was on my lips.

"Holy shit!" His wide-eyed, dimpled grin flooded his face. He stepped in and drew me into a long kiss. He pulled back and glanced around. "Tell me there isn't a dinner party in the other room?"

"It's a secret sex club."

He cocked his head to the side, not sure if I was serious or not.

"I'm joking. This is my new place!" I beamed.

He picked me up, twirled me around, and gave me another quick kiss. "Looks perfect! How did you find it? It wasn't on our list."

"Tom owns it. They were about to relist it. They remodeled it after the last tenant trashed it."

Jack peered around some more and smiled. "Congratulations, Maddie. You did it!"

I grabbed his hand and led him over to my picnic. I unbuttoned a few of his top buttons and pointed. "Sit."

"You don't have to tell me twice dressed like that."

I opened a bottle of wine and handed him a glass. "Tell me about your trip."

"No offense, Maddie, but the last thing I want to talk about is business right now." He put the glass on the floor and crawled over on top of me, so my back was bent to the ground underneath my legs.

"Why not?" I giggled, as his mouth found mine in an urgent kiss.

"I missed you," he mumbled, and took his finger and swirled it on my torso.

"I missed you too."

"I'm glad you didn't torture me with a dinner party full of people after not touching you for three and a half days."

I giggled. "Don't forget that half-day!"

Jack smiled, and his dimple popped back out. "The half-day was extra torture."

I giggled again.

His long fingers traced the outside of my womanhood.

"So...you aren't hungry?"

"Oh, I'm hungry all right." He leaned in and took a nibble on my neck. His already hard dick grazed my body.

"In fact, this meal is all I've been thinking about." He took his hand and pushed my bra strap over my shoulder.

I slid my feet from under my butt and put them in front of me. Then, I took my foot and slowly moved it on Jack's leg. I batted my eyes at him. "But I brought sushi."

"Sushi can wait." Jack grabbed under my shoulders and rolled over while he pulled me on top of him.

I put my face right next to his. "What about my bag of tricks? Do you want to see those?"

He gave me a sly look. "Bag of tricks?"

"Oh, you know. Just a few things I thought you might enjoy..."

Jack's eyes were wide with curiosity and amusement, "What's that, Ms. Burns?" His hand pulled me in for another passion-filled kiss, as he grabbed my ass with his other hand and squeezed it gently.

I mischievously leaned over to his ear. "I have a gift for your cock."

Jack let out a roar, "Really? Now you have me curious."

"Have you been a good boy or a bad boy?" I kissed his collarbone and opened his shirt up more.

He let out a small moan and squeezed my ass harder. "I was a very good boy when I was gone, but I plan on being very naughty tonight."

Little bursts of adrenaline shot through my veins as he started to slap my ass and rub it after.

My junkie was back. And she was ready to get high.

I let out a little moan as he slapped my ass again and drove my clit up against his pulsating dick. "You like it when I slap your ass?" he whispered.

I nodded.

"Tell me," he ordered as he slapped it again. My clit once again felt the hardness of his manhood through his pants.

"I love it when you slap my ass, Jack, but I prefer your dick to hit my clit naked, so take off your fucking pants."

Jack's head jerked in surprise at my dirty talk. Once again, his dimples popped out. "Yes, ma'am!"

I pushed my body off him, knelt on both sides, and unzipped his pants. I slid them off and made my way to his massive erection, then I took him in my mouth all the way and grazed it up with my teeth.

"Maddie," Jack gasped and grabbed my hair to lower my head.

I gave him a few more rounds and tasted his precum. I sucked his cap a bit then crawled back up on top of him. I teased, "What do you want me to give you, Jack?"

"Whatever you want, I'm not picky." He grabbed my head and pulled my face toward him, then found my tongue quickly.

"Close your eyes then." He quickly shut his eyes and humored me. "Don't open them until I tell you, or you won't get your present for your cock."

I grabbed the cock ring I had bought and a lubricant that was supposed to enhance our sensations. I rubbed the lube on Jack's cock. "Jesus, Maddie," he muttered, as my hands slid over his cock with the lube a few times to heat it up.

"You like it?"

"Mm-hmm."

I stopped. "Say it out loud, Jack." He always made me tell him things out loud, so I decided it was his turn to tell me.

"Feels amazing."

"You want more?"

"Yes! I want more!" His schoolboy grin was on his face, and his eyes were still closed.

I positioned my body over him, with my back to his face and my knees on both sides of his body. His hands found my back, and he rubbed his warmth into my body. I grabbed the cock ring and slipped it over his shaft.

"What's that?" Jack still had his eyes shut.

I didn't respond and turned the vibrator on, and in one swoop slid fully onto his big, hard cock.

"Fuck, Maddie," he bellowed out.

I gathered my senses and started to grind on him backward, while the vibrator slapped at my nub.

Jack must have opened his eyes. He sat up, and started to kiss my back, then moved all my hair to one side.

I moaned.

"You're so hot in this outfit," Jack mumbled, between muffled kisses.

I grabbed the back of his neck with my bent arm and hoisted myself on him some more.

"You drive me crazy." Jack unhooked my bra and threw it to the side. His big hands wrapped around me, and he started to play with my nipples.

"Mmm."

Jack slowly started to massage my nipples. His kisses fluttered across my neck as he nibbled and gently bit my skin.

"Ah..."

"So delicious," he murmured, as I arched my back in response to his touch.

I ground down on him harder as the bullet sent volts through my nub.

He grabbed me and pushed me off him. "Kneel forward on your hands, Maddie."

I did as I was told, and got on my hands and knees. Jack re-entered me, grabbed my shoulders, and pulled me into him.

"Did you get this outfit for me?"

The new position made the vibration of the cock ring hit my ass over and over, as he grabbed my hips and thrust faster.

"Yes, Jack."

"Did you think about my cock all week?"

I was out of breath, slightly dizzy, and quickly moved to the top of the rollercoaster, "Yes, all week."

The lube I put on Jack before the cock ring started to heat up, and the tingles were hot. Jack slapped my ass, hard. He quickly brought it back to my body and rubbed his hand on my cheek.

It about sent me over the edge. "Oh, God, Jack!"

"I thought of all the ways I wanted to make you cum, while I was gone. I couldn't decide which one I wanted the most." Jack's hands moved back to my nipples, and he massaged them between his warm fingers and thumbs before he grabbed my hips and pulled my body into him more.

My body was so hot now. My outsides and insides had a steady heat, and Jack's words were setting me on fire even more. He kissed the top of my shoulder. "Did you think about me making you cum when I was gone?"

"Y...yes." My voice sounded hoarse, and my chest heaved with heavy breath.

Jack continued to whisper. "Did you think about me licking your pussy or sucking your clit?"

"Oh, God," I moaned not sure how much longer I could hold out, as I got more turned on by Jack's dirty talk.

Jack wasn't done yet. He thrust hard in me. "Did you think about my cock hitting your sweet spot over and over?"

"God, yes!"

"I thought about you and all the ways I wanted to make you call out my name. How I wanted to make you fly higher than before. Do you want to fly, baby?"

I was going to explode. My vagina started to contract around his penis involuntarily. "Please, Jack."

"Not yet, baby. I want to keep you high like this." My drug dealer knew his role.

My entire body was on edge, my eyes wild with lust, and my

nerves crazy with the heat and vibrations. Jack's girth and length filled me and crashed over and over against my walls.

"I...I...oh shit!" I closed my eyes and panted as Jack grabbed me around my waist and pulled me into him.

"Want me to cum with you baby?" Jack knew full well that I wanted nothing more.

I nodded.

"Tell me."

"Please. I want to cum."

He slipped the bullet off the cock ring, wrapped his hand around me and pushed it against my clit. He ruptured me into my high and sent me into oblivion. Jack exploded in me with a powerful force, and his body forcefully convulsed behind mine.

I soared, I'm sure to the stars, as Jack's arm around my waist stopped me from crashing into the floor. "Easy, baby." He rolled me over and onto his chest, then ferociously kissed me like we hadn't yet climaxed.

As he cradled me into his chest, I grabbed a blanket and pulled it over our sweaty bodies. His head rested on a pillow, and his fingers grazed my back. He grabbed the cock ring with his other hand and brought the bullet out from under the blankets. "How do I turn this off?"

I laughed, grabbed it, then expertly flipped it off.

Jack laughed, "That was a nice surprise."

"I'm glad it fit around your gigantic dick."

Jack's face gushed with pride. "Maddie Burns, you're always full of surprises."

"Someone has to keep your scheduled self in suspense."

Jack pulled me closer to him. "I really did miss you this week. I hated being away."

I turned over to face him better. "I really missed you, Jack. Are you in New York for a while now?" I made a wish he was here to stay for a bit.

"I'm here till Tuesday. I'll cram all my meetings back to back so that I can return by Wednesday night."

I clapped my hands together.

Jack looked at me slyly. "You're excited I'm leaving?"

I laughed. "No, but I'm glad it's not longer!"

Jack kissed me and then his stomach growled.

"Hey, I forgot we have sushi!"

He laughed. We sat up and grabbed the bag of food. Jack put the blanket around his shoulders and told me to sit between his legs. My back rested against his chest, and he put another blanket over my lap.

We fed each other sushi rolls. Jack's eyes scanned my apartment. "This is a nice place, Maddie."

I glowed. "Thanks! It's my first place on my own. I was always too afraid to live on my own."

"Really?"

"Yes."

"How much longer do I get to keep you at my place?" Jack's eyes registered a hint of sadness, but he put on a good face.

"Depends on when I can schedule your movers? I want to pay them though."

"Absolutely not."

"Jack—"

"Don't fight me on this, Maddie. Just say thank you and let me make you cum again later tonight."

I laughed, shook my head, and rolled my eyes. Oh, what was the point of arguing? I knew he would only get his way. I turned to face him. "Thank you." I popped a piece of sushi in his mouth.

"You know what the great part about your new place is?"

"No, what?"

"Breaking in all your furniture." He grinned at me.

I stuffed another piece of sushi in his mouth. "Hey, that reminds me. I need to buy a bed. Want to go shopping with me this weekend?"

Jack gave me a sly grin. "That depends. Do we get to try them all out?"

I swatted his arm. "Ha ha."

"Yes, count me in. I'm especially pleased you didn't take your old bed. I would have thrown it out the window."

The thought of Mike entered my mind. "Hey, Jack, I need to ask you something about Mike. I want you to be honest."

"Why do I get the feeling I'm not going to like this question?"

"You probably aren't, but I need to know."

Jack took a deep breath, exhaling slowly. "Go on."

I licked my lips and thought about how to word my question. "What did Mike do the night you discovered they were trafficking women and children?"

Jack turned a bit white. "Maddie, you don't want to know that."

"I need to know."

"No, you don't."

"Jack, I have to know."

"Why? What exactly will you accomplish if you make me relive all that?"

I sat for a minute and thought about what Jack was asking me. While I didn't want him to have to relive things, I needed to know. "I don't know, Jack, but I feel like I need to know. Why won't you tell me?"

"So you can have a permanent image of what he did in your mind, like I do? Sorry, but I won't do that to you. You can be mad at me all you want, but I will never put those images in your head. It's probably best if you remember any good parts you can of your relationship with him because if I tell you what he did, you aren't going to be able to come back from it. It will always haunt you."

I turned away from Jack for a bit, then gazed back at him and met his eyes. "Answer this then. I know Mike was selling the women and children. Did he partake in raping them too?"

Jack closed his eyes as if in pain. “Why do you need to know this? Why can’t you let it be?”

“Six years, Jack. I needed to know. The fact that you won’t say yes or no already gives me my answer.”

Jack opened up his eyes. They were wet. “Did he ever hurt you, Maddie? Force you to do anything you didn’t want to?”

“No. Besides berate me, he honestly didn’t pay that much attention to me the last few years. I guess I should be thankful for that right now.”

Jack shifted, paused, then again, “He never physically hurt you?”

My head jerked. “No. Honestly, Jack. It was only words, that’s all. No biggie.”

Jack exhaled, hard. He pulled me closer, “Maddie, don’t say it’s no biggie.”

“It’s okay. You more than make up for it, Jack.”

“I can’t make up for someone hurting you. Words or otherwise.”

“But you do. You make me feel special…like I’m the most important person on earth…like you want me around.” I concentrated on my fidgeting fingers.

Jack tilted my chin up, his eyes full of emotion. “You are special. You are the most important person on earth to me. I always want you around me.”

I blinked back a few tears and kissed him.

“But that doesn’t make up for how he talked to you. And it burns me that he is still walking around the streets.”

“Are you any closer to trapping him?”

“Look, I want to tell you everything, I do, but there are things I can’t. It’s not only because of the FBI. It’s for your safety. Please, trust me on this.”

"Jack, I do trust you. Just tell me when the bastard is locked up.”

Jack pulled me close to him. "I will. Let's change the subject, please?"

I nodded and kissed him. If Jack wanted me to drop it, I was going to have to let it go.

I gave him a naughty grin. "What room do you want to break in next?"

17

Maddie

IT WAS SATURDAY NIGHT. JACK AND I WERE AT TOM AND LIV'S, along with Meg and Collin. We ate dinner and were enjoying some drinks when Jack's phone rang a strange ring. I sat next to him and felt him freeze.

He glanced over at Tom. "Excuse me." Jack stood up and left the room.

"Do you know what's going on?" I looked at Tom. My guess was that Jack's call had to do with Mike.

"You'll have to ask Jack."

Collin cleared his throat and tried to change the subject. "Meg, did you tell everyone our news?"

Meg's face lit up. "We finally decided on Bermuda for our wedding. We still have to figure out the date, but probably after season when Collin's contract negotiations are over."

"That's awesome! I was there years ago, and it's amazing! Lucky us you picked such an awesome place!" Liv gushed.

"Maddie, we hope you and Jack can come too," Collin invited.

"That sounds amazing! Count us in!"

"Now that we know where you're going, let me know when you figure out the date, and we'll get the flight plan ready for the jet. The new FAA rules are driving my pilot crazy. Anything they can do with notice they are appreciative of," Tom said.

Collin nodded. "Will do."

Jack walked back into the room. "What did I miss?"

He acted like nothing happened, but I could tell something was up. Tom and Jack exchanged another look. I thought I saw Collin exchange one too, but as quickly as it crossed his face, it was gone.

"Meg and Collin decided on Bermuda for their wedding location," Liv reported.

"Congratulations, man," Jack patted Collin on the back. "I haven't been there before. Is it true the sand is pink?"

"I think Liv is the only one who's been there before," Meg chimed.

Liv nodded. "It really is pink!"

"Can't wait to see it." Jack pushed a smile on his face. To everyone else, he seemed fine, but I knew something was up.

I saw Tom and Jack exchange a glance once more. Jack wanted to talk with Tom in the bar area, so, together, they left the room.

"What the heck is going on?" Meg wanted to know.

I shrugged my shoulders. "I honestly have no clue."

Collin laughed. "Meg, not our business."

"Well, Meg only asked what the rest of us want to know." Liv wasn't happy she was left out of the conversation either.

"Agreed!" I jumped in.

Collin laughed again and shook his head. "I'm outnumbered here, huh?"

Meg reached over and gave Collin a peck on the lips. "At least you know when to give up."

Collin snorted. He was, after all, known all over New York as the negotiator. He leaned over and whispered something in Meg's ear. Her face blushed, and she giggled. Liv and I exchanged glances. It definitely had to be something dirty.

"Time to go. Liv, Maddie, give your men our regards." Meg jumped up and grabbed Collin's hand.

Liv rolled her eyes. "All right, love birds."

Collin leaned over to give Liv and me pecks on our cheeks. "Ladies, it was great seeing you. Give the guys my regards as well."

They left, and it was only Liv and me.

"Did Tom say anything about Mike?" I tried to figure out if she knew something I didn't.

She hesitated.

"What?'

"He told me that Mike is involved in human trafficking? Somehow Jack found out, and the FBI is now involved."

My face went red with embarrassment. "Yes, that's right. I can't believe I was with him for six years."

"You couldn't have known. Try not to beat yourself up."

Jack and Tom walked back into the room.

"Where did Collin and Meg go?" Tom looked around.

Liv laughed. "Home to play sex games is my guess."

Everyone laughed.

"They sent their regards to you guys." I smirked.

"Aw, isn't that sweet?" Jack teased.

"Now, are you going to tell us what's going on?" Liv was ready to get down to business.

Tom and Jack both hesitated.

My stomach dropped. "What?"

Jack grabbed my hand. "Maddie, they've signed more papers in your name. This time, the FBI traced it to a shipment of drugs they raided in the harbor."

My stomach flipped. I forgot all about the papers Jack told me were signed in my name. "But I haven't signed anything, I swear!"

"We know that. So does the FBI," Tom tried to assure me.

"Why is he trying to frame me? How long has he been doing this?"

Jack gazed uneasily at Tom. Tom started to say something and stopped. He looked back at Jack.

"Tell me!"

Jack put his arm around me, rubbed my back, and tried to find words. "We don't know exactly why, other than you're an innocent person to pin crimes on."

I realized Jack was holding back. "How long, Jack?"

He glanced nervously at Tom.

I knew this wasn't going to be good. "Jack, how long?"

"Four years."

I was stunned. Four years. How was that possible? "You guys bought the marina four years ago?"

Jack shook his head.

"We believe he's been working with Jim, trafficking women and children, for at least four years. The FBI also believes he is hiding money in accounts in your name in the Cayman Islands," Tom informed me.

"The FBI needs to question you, Maddie," Jack quietly informed me.

All the blood must have drained from my face. "They think I knew about this?" I cried out.

"No!" Jack and Tom said in unison.

"I don't understand then."

"They want to question you so you can tell them more about Michael. His family life, background, anything he is an expert in, your relationship..." Jack trailed off.

"It's only to help them," Tom jumped in. "They know you aren't involved in anything criminal."

I tried to comprehend all this. "When do they want to see me?"

"Tomorrow morning. They are coming to my place at ten a.m." Jack pulled me in a bit closer.

Tom added, "We are going to have our attorney there, just in case."

"In case of what? Am I a suspect?" My stomach started to flip.

Tom and Jack both shook their heads. Jack hugged me into his chest. "No, you aren't. But we aren't going to take any risks. Our attorney will be present...for an extra layer of protection."

"I really don't understand this. If they don't think I'm guilty of anything, then why the extra layer of protection?"

Jack grabbed my face, "Because we aren't going to take any chances. It's only a precaution."

"But I didn't do anything or know about anything!" I cried out.

"We all know that. The FBI knows that too, but I wouldn't send Liv in there without an attorney."

"And I'm sure as hell not sending you in there without one," Jack proclaimed.

Liv put her hand on mine. "Trust Tom and Jack. They wouldn't do anything to harm you, Maddie."

Did I even have a choice?

Jack

The FBI needed more intel. They lost the ability to trap and arrest Michael and Jim, and they needed more ammo. They called to say they wanted to interview Maddie.

I paced the room, "You know she doesn't have anything to do with this."

"Yes, Jack, but she was with Duponte for six years. She has to know something or someone we don't," Agent Piper insisted.

"She didn't know anything until I told her," I spat at him.

Piper sighed. "Jack, this is merely for us to learn more about him. She knows him best."

"She doesn't know him best. She didn't know anything until I told her," I repeated, as my stomach curled at the thought of Maddie being with him.

"She may know someone that is connected and doesn't even realize it. We need to talk to her. We can either do it in our office or your place, so take your pick. Jack, this is happening." Piper informed me.

I closed my eyes and didn't say anything.

"Jack, we know she's innocent. We need more intel on him. We all want the same thing here."

I wasn't going to win. "Fine, you can question her at my place, but I'm bringing my attorney."

"Jack, she isn't a suspect. We only want to know more about Duponte."

"I don't care. If you're going to question her, I'm bringing my attorney."

Piper let out a sigh. "Fine. Have it your way, Jack."

Maddie

We returned to Jack's penthouse. I changed my clothes, brushed my teeth, washed my face, and hopped into bed. Jack watched my every move. He came over and sat next to me on the bed and stroked my cheek.

"Hey." He knew I was upset.

I didn't respond.

"Hey," he repeated. He wiped the tear off my cheek. "It's all going to be okay, Maddie. I promise."

"This is bullshit, Jack."

Jack climbed in bed next to me and brought me into his arms. "I know, but honestly, everything is going to be fine, I promise you."

"You don't know that." I turned away from him.

I heard Jack sigh, then he walked over to my side of the bed and knelt, so he was face to face with me. "I do know that, Maddie. You have to trust me."

"This is the FBI. I'm being framed. You're having a lawyer go with me. There is a lot more you aren't telling me. I know it. I can feel it. You want me to trust you, but you can't trust me to tell me what the hell is going on and this is my life."

"I would do anything to protect you. I know this is your life. Do you think I would do anything to put that in jeopardy?"

"Not intentionally, but you aren't the FBI. You know something, and you're hiding it from me."

"I have to protect you, and I'm going to ask you again to please trust me," Jack pleaded with me.

I sat up. "I'm going to stay in the other room tonight. Until you can tell me what you're keeping from me, I don't want to see you."

"Maddie—"

"No, Jack! I'm done with the 'trust me but don't ever tell me what I need to know.' It's late, I'm being questioned tomorrow by the FBI, in case you forgot, and I want you to leave me alone," I hurled at him.

"Maddie, please!" Jack tried to grab my hand.

"No. I'm done with you tonight." I walked out of the room, as a river of tears fell from my face. I went to the closest bedroom and slammed the door.

I laid in bed and cried on and off. A few hours later, I heard the door open. I blew my nose from another wave of tears, and Jack was suddenly in bed next to me. His body spooned me, and his fingers wiped my tears away, which made me cry harder.

"Shhh." Jack tried to soothe me and moved the hair off my face. I turned to face him and cried into his chest.

"I'm scared, Jack," I sobbed.

"I know, baby, I know."

"This is my fault. If I hadn't stayed with him for six years…"

"Shh. You didn't know. And I won't let anything happen to you. I promise. I won't do anything to put you at risk, but please trust that whatever I'm not telling you is for your protection. Please believe me. It kills me that you hate me over this."

I rolled over. "I don't hate you, Jack. I could never hate you. Don't you know that by now?"

He leaned into me. Our lips found each other. My body molded into Jack's as it so easily always did, and my womanhood pulsated at the touch of his manhood next to me.

We quietly made love. There was no pleading, no games, no commands, or dirty talk. Just Jack and me, as our bodies melted into each other.

Jack's hands were magic on my body and played me like a familiar instrument. He worked my insides and outsides as his mouth worshiped every inch of me.

He didn't make me wait, as if he knew how much I needed it. In his typical way, he made me number one. He swiftly moved to my sex and threw my legs over his shoulders while he ate me out with voracity. My hands gathered in his hair and pushed him into me, as my moans told him exactly how to send me over the edge quickly.

And after my high, he stayed there, kissed my thighs, and let me catch my breath. To my surprise, he started pleasuring me again. He glided his fingers into me, and gently wrapped my already exhausted clit with his lips, as he once again flew me to the heavens.

I was exhausted, yet Jack wasn't done with me. He feasted some more on my body, as he made his way up. I bucked my pelvis into him and wrapped my legs around him tightly, as I pushed him into me, because I still needed more.

With passionate kisses, he stated how delicious I was, and my previous orgasms danced on his tongue. His moans escaped his mouth as we made our journey together to the place that only he and I could take each other.

We violently climaxed together. Jack was on top of me, our foreheads were together, and our eyes watched the others. From time to time, our lips would meet with heat.

When we finished, I fell asleep in Jack's arms; exhausted, content, and not thinking about anything except him.

18

Maddie

AT 9 A.M., JACK AND TOM'S ATTORNEY, CLAIRE WHITFIELD, WAS IN the living room, asking me tons of questions about Mike. Many of them I couldn't answer. It was another sad indication of how much of a doormat I had been in our relationship.

The question, *why did you allow that,* haunted me for the millionth time since I left Mike.

"Maddie?" Claire prompted.

"Sorry, what was the question?"

Claire smiled gently. "I know this is hard, but the FBI is only trying to find out more information about Mike."

I sighed, still not sure they didn't think I was a suspect.

Claire put her pen on top of her notebook. She had questioned me for about an hour. "Maddie, there are going to be a lot of questions they will ask. I don't know exactly what, but at any time, if you need clarification or don't know how to answer something, say my name as a question, okay?"

"Okay." *I need a code word with the attorney? What the hell?* My stomach was officially a pool of anxiety.

Jack came over with more coffee, refilled our cups, and put a fresh pot on the serving tray. The doorbell rang. Jack rubbed my leg and kissed me on the lips. "Don't worry, babe. It will be fine." He stood up to let the two FBI agents in.

Agents Piper and Creedie were both men, probably in their forties. They seemed nice enough, but it was hard for me to relax. Piper put a recorder on the table and turned it on. "Please state your full name."

Claire piped in and smiled at them. "Gentlemen, I thought this was an informal questioning?"

I caught Agent Creedie as he glanced at her. A small flush crept up his neck.

Yep, he's interested in Claire, went through my mind.

"You're correct. This is an informal questioning," Creedie assured us.

Smiling some more, and wagging her finger in a slightly flirtatious way, Claire directed at Creedie, "Pull out your notebooks then; the recorder goes off."

Creedie's flush deepened. Piper was about to talk when Creedie held up his hand and stopped him. He leaned in and turned the recorder off, then put it in his briefcase.

"Thank you!" Claire flipped her hair, drilling her eyes straight at Creedie, then gave him another flirtatious smile. "Now what questions do you have for Maddie?"

Oh, she is good, I thought, and I watched her uncross, then cross her legs again, as Creedie's eyes nearly popped out of his head.

Suddenly, I wanted to laugh. Claire Whitfield knew the law, but she also knew how to make men putty in her hand. My anxiety started to leave. I gazed over at Jack, who was standing off to the side, and he winked at me.

Piper spoke up, "So Maddie, as you know, we are investigating your ex-boyfriend, Michael Duponte. I believe you call him Mike?"

"Yes."

He continued. "Mr. Duponte is being investigated by the FBI for human and drug trafficking, along with fraud, embezzlement, money laundering, rape, and murder. We want your help to lock him up."

I think my jaw hit the floor when I heard the FBI rattle off all of Mike's crimes. It hit me like a shock wave, and nausea raced through me. I think my face turned green because Jack grabbed the garbage can near the desk and brought it over to me, then rubbed my back.

I tried to breathe through it and willed myself to not throw up in front of all these people.

"Ms. Burns, are you able to continue?" Agent Creedie gave me a sympathetic gaze.

I looked up from the trash can. "I'm fine." No way I wanted to have to do this at a later date.

"My client doesn't know about any of Mr. Duponte's criminal activities. She wasn't a part of them, so what can we do for you, gentlemen?" Claire sweetly but sternly told them.

Piper and Creedie both nodded in unison. "Yes, we do believe Ms. Burns isn't involved, but we are hoping she can give us something, anything, to help lock him up," Piper repeated again.

"I don't know what I can tell you. I didn't know about any of this. My relationship with Mike was almost non-existent over the last few years. He was never home, constantly canceled plans, or stood me up. We rarely shared a bed he was gone so much."

Jack shifted uncomfortably on the couch next to me.

"Ms. Burns, when did you start dating Mr. Duponte?" Creedie inquired.

"June eighteenth, 2013."

"And you lived in Anaheim, California, and met there?" Creedie queried.

"Yes."

"Can you give us a timeline of your relationship. When was it really sexual, when did you feel a shift in your relationship, etc.?" Piper's pen was on the paper, all ready to write down my sexual history.

I turned toward Claire. *Why were they asking me this? Was it really necessary to make me spill all my personal details?* "Claire?"

"Could you be more specific as to why you need these intimate details of my client's life?"

Piper cleared his throat. "We tend to find that there is normally a change in behavior in the bedroom when someone enters the criminal world. From what we have gathered, Mr. Duponte was not a criminal at the time he met Ms. Burns. It was during the relationship when the criminal activity started, and if we can pinpoint the time, with Ms. Burns' help, we might be able to find others involved."

"Go ahead, Maddie." Claire motioned her hands for me to continue.

My head was spinning. "I'm not sure how to answer that."

"How was your sex life at the beginning?" Piper asked.

"My sex life with Mike was...I was young." I fidgeted with my fingers, and my face burned red hot. "I wasn't very experienced..."

God, this is so embarrassing.

"You were a virgin?" Creedie blurted out.

My head snapped up. "No!"

"Now that isn't any of your concern. Besides Michael Duponte, Ms. Burn's previous lovers don't have anything to do with your investigation," Claire scolded him.

"Sorry..." Creedie's face turned purple as he looked at Claire and cleared his throat. Out of the corner of my eye, I saw Jack drum his fingers on his upper thigh.

Piper continued, "And was there ever a point in your relationship where you remember the sex increasing? A time when he wanted more, and it was out of his character? Or a time when the sex changed? Maybe a normal style to rougher or gentler?"

"Claire?" I assumed Claire would step in, but she motioned for me to answer the questions.

You have to be kidding me. I wanted to die from embarrassment. I shifted in my seat. Then I spun toward Jack. "Can you leave the room?"

He rubbed my back again. "It's okay...I'm okay."

"No, Jack. I need you to leave the room."

His face dropped, wounded. "Why?"

"I don't want you to hear this, Jack."

"Maddie—"

Claire cut him off. "Jack, why don't you go to the coffee shop? I'll call you when we are done."

Jack glared at her. He was a man used to getting his way.

I fidgeted with my fingers. I could feel Jack's stare before he stood up and quietly left.

I took a deep breath, "There was a period where my sex life with Mike changed. Probably eighteen months into our relationship."

"Can you expand on that?" Piper pushed for more.

"Is this necessary?"

"Unfortunately, we believe it is. Please, go on, Ms. Burns." Piper motioned for me to continue.

I once again hoped Claire would help me out. I turned to look at her, but she gave me her nod to answer the question.

I thought back to my relationship with Mike during that period. "I thought Mike was cheating on me because he started coming home late at night. He would take a shower and then get in bed with me. Anytime I questioned him, he would go down on me, which was something he didn't do prior. But he wouldn't have intercourse with me." My face was in flames.

I would fake an orgasm so he would get off me. I left that part out.

"The morning after, I would wake up with him on top of me,

as he pounded into me, almost frantically. I hated it," I admitted it out loud. It was the first time I ever spoke about it.

Piper cocked his head to the side. "Did you tell him to stop?"

I bit my lip. "No."

"Why not?" Piper questioned.

"I don't know. I was young? I didn't want what I suspected to be true? I wanted him to be happy? I don't know," I repeated, not sure myself, as shame ran through every cell of my body.

"How long did this last?" Piper tapped his pen on the notepad.

I thought for a minute. "About two months. As quickly as it came, it passed. Our sex life became less and less, typically only on a special occasion like an anniversary or birthday. That was the time he started to travel a lot more."

Creedie leaned toward me, "Do you remember anyone new entering his life? Business or personal?"

My head snapped up. "Bo Crumo."

"Who is Bo Crumo?" Piper wrote the name down on his notebook.

My stomach did a flip when I thought of Bo. "He started coming around the house. Mike and Bo would go out in the garage and have long conversations. I don't know what about, but he always gave me the creeps. One day, Mike wasn't home, and Bo came over. I had a car full of groceries, and he grabbed some bags and came in. I insisted I didn't need help, but he wouldn't listen."

I stopped, as I remembered Bo shoving his way past me and into my house.

"Please, go on, Ms. Burns." Creedie motioned.

I closed my eyes, flooded by memories I had tried to forget. "Bo wouldn't leave and insisted he would wait for Mike. I texted Mike that Bo was over and he needed to come home because he wouldn't leave. I repeatedly told him to leave, but he sneered at me and wouldn't go. I grabbed my keys to leave myself, but he blocked me and pushed me up against the sink..."

I stopped. I bit my lip as the fear I felt that day crashed through me.

"Maddie, do you need a break?" Claire gave me a concerned glance.

I shook my head. "He pushed up my skirt and had just ripped my underwear off right when Mike walked in."

"What did Mr. Duponte do?" Piper inquired.

"That was the worst part. Mike stood at the door, said in a strict voice, 'Bo,' and Bo laughed and let go of me. Then, Bo walked over to Mike and said, 'Party later,' and walked out."

I paused and took a sip of water. The agents and Claire waited for me to continue.

"Mike told me to put my underwear back on and walked out of the room." Fresh tears bubbled in my eyes.

"Why didn't you leave after that?" Creedie questioned.

Why didn't I leave? The big question that I've asked myself over and over again. "I was stupid. Mike took me out that night. We made love, and he said things I wanted to hear. I loved Mike. I wanted him to love me. He was attentive toward me for about a month, and then things slowly went back to old ways."

"This Bo Crumo, when did you see him last?" Piper wanted to know.

"I never saw him after that day. Mike promised me I wouldn't have to see him again, and he kept his word on that."

Creedie piped in, "Did you ever sign any papers Mike gave you?"

I shook my head. I had already thought long and hard about that, and I knew I never had. "I've never signed anything. Anything with my name on it has been forged."

"We believe that, Ms. Burns." Creedie nodded.

Claire piped up, "Gentlemen, are there any other questions?"

Piper and Creedie glanced at each other. "I think that will be all for now, Ms. Burns. We appreciate your time and would like to be able to ask you more questions in the future if needed."

"Okay." *Did I even have a choice?*

We walked them out. Claire picked up her phone. "Jack, you can come back now."

I had forgotten about Jack. He would be pissed. Well, he was going to have to be pissed because there was no way I wanted him to know that. It wasn't a secret that I felt shame for the years I spent with Mike. But, as I listened to myself telling the story of what Bo tried to do to me, and that I still stayed with Mike, a fresh layer of shame wrapped around me.

Claire packed up her bag.

"Is what I said confidential?"

Claire looked up. "Don't worry, Maddie. Jack won't ever find out what was discussed today unless you disclose it."

I gave her a grateful smile. "Thank you."

"I'm not sure if this helps, or not, but we've all dated shitty boyfriends and made decisions we regret."

"I appreciate you being here today. I think Creedie did too," I teased. I really liked Claire.

She laughed. "He makes it too easy, huh?"

"Did you see his neck flush?"

"Yep. Well, tell Jack goodbye for me, and call if you need anything."

"Thanks, Claire." I walked her to the front door, and she left.

Walking over to the window, I gazed out at the New York skyline. The city hustled as usual. I thought about how much of my life I spent trying to make someone love me, who was incapable of love. Those two months, when I would wake up, and Mike would be on top of me, I didn't want or enjoy it, but I never told him no because I desperately wanted him to love me.

How desperate was I to want someone like Mike to love me? How low was my self-esteem that I stayed in a one-sided relationship?

Disgust filled me, and I wanted to erase all the years I spent with him, make different decisions, and be a different person. But I knew I couldn't.

I didn't hear the door open. I was staring out into the city, beating myself up, lost in thought when I felt Jack's arms around me, and his lips on my neck. "Maddie, are you okay?"

I shook my head. The truth was, I wasn't okay. What kind of person was I to allow myself to be mistreated and for so long? To feel unsafe but stay? The lies I told myself, over the years, played on repeat in my mind. My shame morphed into anger, and disappointment in myself deluged my soul.

"Tell me what's wrong, Maddie."

"You deserve someone better than me."

"Shh, nonsense." Jack wiped away my tears and held me tighter. "What did he do to you?"

"It's not about what he did to me. It's about what I didn't do for myself."

Jack pulled me in tighter. "Help me understand, Maddie."

"I can't, Jack...I stayed. I don't understand it myself. All I know is you deserve someone better. Someone stronger who doesn't need to be rescued every time you turn around."

"Stop. You're not being fair to yourself right now. We all do things we wish we could go back and change. Decisions we wish we could have a do-over on. All we can do is move forward."

I didn't say anything. Jack held me for a bit. "Come on. Get your coat on. I have something to show you."

I didn't move.

"Come on." Jack grabbed my hand and pulled me to the coat closet.

I put my coat and boots on, and he led me out the door. We rode down the elevator and soon walked down the street. Jack put his arms around my shoulders and guided me through the city.

"Where are we going?" We had walked several blocks.

"You'll see."

We walked in silence. About ten minutes later, he led me into a huge building that was under construction. I gave him a quizzical stare.

"This is a building I bought."

"Congratulations." I tilted my head and squinted at him, not understanding why he brought me here.

Jack laughed and continued, "I bought this building after it was destroyed in a fire. Almost every wall in the place was burned to ashes, and only the steel shell remained. The electric caused the fire. It was old and outdated. If the landlord had repaired it, then the fire wouldn't have occurred. But the landlord was too cheap and instead, put the lives of all his tenants at risk."

Chills ran through my body. "Did anyone die?"

"Luckily, no."

"That's good."

He continued, "I bought this about eight months ago. It'll be a safe place for victims of human trafficking. They will have a safe place to live, get intensive therapy, and be able to get their education or learn new skills so they can support themselves."

I looked at Jack in awe. "You did all this?"

"The nonprofits I'm working with will run it. I only bought the building and coordinated it." He shrugged.

"Jack, this is amazing!"

He held up his hand. "Maddie, I'm only showing this to you because I will always be haunted by that night. But at least I can try to play a role in helping those who have been victimized." He stepped forward, grabbed my face, and tilted it toward his. "You aren't a victim. I'm not a victim. We have the ability to move forward. Some people don't."

I let Jack's words sink in. He was right. I made my own choices. I needed to figure out how to move forward from them.

"I'm trying to move forward, in a good way. You're part of that. You're good in my life. You're moving forward in yours.

Hopefully, you see me as a good part of that, no matter what my past is?"

"Yes, Jack, you're a good part of it."

"Don't ever tell me again that I deserve someone better than you, I won't have it." His voice was authoritative, and he raised his eyebrows at me.

I bit my lip.

"I'm choosing to move forward with you. I know it's quick, but I'm a man who knows what he wants, and what I want is you. So you can live on your own as long as you want and figure out your shit, but at the end of the day, don't ever question your worthiness or the type of person you are. I can give you time, space, whatever you need, but make sure I'm part of whatever you figure out, okay?" There was confidence, yet vulnerability, in his eyes.

I reached up to grab his neck and pulled his face to mine. "Okay, Jack. I understand." I kissed him. He was mine, and he wouldn't let me forget it. And he was right. I needed to figure out how to move forward and put the past behind me.

Jack drew back from my kiss and grabbed my hand. "Come on, Maddie."

"Where are we going now?"

He laughed and gave me his schoolboy, full-dimpled grin. "To try out all those beds!"

19

Jack

I don't know what he did to her. The FBI, Claire, no one would tell me...and especially not Maddie. It drove me crazy, but I wouldn't push her, because I knew she was already close to a breaking point.

When she mentioned she shared a bed with him, my stomach flipped. Yes, I knew they had, but I still didn't like to think about it. When I heard the words flow out of her mouth, I swallowed hard not to have the contents of my stomach come up.

They kicked me out of the penthouse, and that upset me. As much as I didn't want to think about Maddie and Michael together, I also felt like I needed to know what he had done, so I could help make it better.

I sulked my way to the lobby and out into the street, where I ran into Collin.

"Hey, where you off to?" Collin must have been out for his run because he was sweaty and wore his running gear.

"Did Tom fill you in about the FBI questioning Maddie?"

"He called me this morning to fill me in. Today, right?"

"Right now. She kicked me out."

He gave a low whistle. "Why did she kick you out?"

"They inquired about Maddie and Michael's sex life, and she made me leave." New anger started to boil in my blood.

Collin put his hand on my shoulder. "Listen, I know this isn't easy, but don't push her to talk to you about it when you go back up there. Give her time, and she'll eventually tell you when she's ready. One thing I've learned from Meg is that there is a lot of shame involved in any abusive relationship. I don't know if she was abused, but if she was in any way—"

I cut him off. "I don't know what happened, but he was emotionally and verbally abusive to her, but I'm not sure if it went past that."

"Then take it from me, Jack. Let her know you are there, but allow her to process and deal with it a bit. If you know everything right now, it isn't going to fix it, and it could make her feel worse."

"Noted," I told Collin.

"Give her some time. She will eventually tell you."

I nodded. "Any progress with the other investors?"

Collin shook his head. "They are stuck on no proof, no clause."

I rolled my eyes in frustration. I wanted this to be over. "Well, I appreciate all you're doing."

"Hey, I'm always here for you, man."

I patted Collin on the back. He was secretly working with Tom and me to try and get the investors to revoke Michael's shares of the marina.

"I'll see you soon. If I don't get back, Meg will kill me. We've got a full day ahead of us."

"Okay, thanks for the advice."

I thought about what he said. I definitely didn't want to make

Maddie feel any worse than she already did. That's why I decided to let it go and not press her.

And I know I pressured her to make sure she figured out her life with me in it, but I couldn't help myself. I needed her to know I wanted her. Now and in the future.

We went bed shopping. Then I made the hard phone call I didn't want to.

Maddie wanted to move into her own place. I was sad, but I tried not to show her. I knew how important this was to her, and I wouldn't be the guy who made her feel bad or guilty.

No, I would be happy for her. So, I called the movers and scheduled her move.

I was concerned about the security though. The day shift had been there forever, but the night shift seemed to have a lot of turnover. That was a red flag to me, but there hadn't been any security issues in the building ever, according to Tom.

The day she moved her stuff out of my place, reminded me once again how empty my penthouse was. When Maddie was there, it felt like a home. I would walk into my house and feel life inside it. But once she moved out, it felt like before.

Empty.

And now that I was with Maddie, I couldn't run from it anymore. I couldn't fly off somewhere and stay away to avoid it. I needed to be in New York for her, so I would have to deal with it.

She left a few items at my house for sleepovers, but my heart dropped the day I walked into her closet and found it almost empty. I knew that it was important to her to live on her own, but it still stung.

I would stay at her place or mine. I didn't care where we were, as long as she was with me, but I longed for the day she would come back to me permanently. I would give her the time and space I promised her.

I prayed it wasn't too long.

Maddie

A week later, I fully moved into my apartment. My new bed arrived, and Jack's movers quickly filled my apartment with all my stuff. I woke up in Jack's arms when I heard his alarm.

"No, stay in bed where it's warm." I grabbed him when he tried to get up.

He chuckled softly, "Time for my run, babe. You can come with me if you want."

"No chance!"

He shook his head and stood up naked.

I grabbed his semi and licked my lips. "You sure you don't want to stay?"

A small but cocky grin came on his face, "The five orgasms I gave you last night wasn't enough?"

"Nope." I bit my lip, and he quickly swooped in and tickled me.

"Jack, stop," I giggled, as he straddled me. His knees were on both sides of my rib cage, his butt was on my stomach, and his dick was near my cleavage.

He stopped and gave me another cocky grin. "What now, Maddie? What should I do to you?"

Quickly, I leaned up and licked the tip of his dick, then rubbed my spit all over it before I put my lips around his cap. I gently sucked before I slid his shaft between my breasts.

"Fucking, beautiful dirty girl!" Jack's eyes lit up, and his dimples popped out.

I gave him my innocent eyes and continued to rub him as I grabbed his balls and massaged them.

Jack groaned, hard.

I took more of him in my mouth and kept him positioned between my breasts.

"Jesus, Maddie," Jack muttered, as he gazed down at me and enjoyed his view.

His hands played with my nipples, and I started to moan while he was in my mouth. "That's my girl," he whispered as I moaned. "Now squeeze your beautiful pussy for me, baby."

I squeezed and sucked his cock as he continued to play with my nipples. I closed my eyes, surprised at how good it felt.

"Pretend you're squeezing my big cock."

I did as Jack commanded, and my lower region began to drip.

"Does it feel good?"

I nodded as Jack started to pull on my nipples gently.

I gasped and sucked him harder.

"Shit, Maddie!" He closed his eyes and opened them back up quickly, as he pushed my breasts together and thrust his dick through them.

"Are you wet for me, baby?" Jack gazed into my eyes, on his power high.

Loudly moaning, I tried to nod, while I kept control of my mouth on his cock. I had no idea how he knew what to tell me to do, but it didn't take long for my body to respond. My body was on fire, as my chest heaved from my labored breath. Jack continued to thrust through my breasts, and I savagely sucked any part of his cock I could get.

"Move your hand and play with yourself while you keep squeezing," Jack commanded me.

I hadn't touched myself in front of anyone ever, but I did as I was told, once again, without reservation. It never mattered what Jack told me to do, I always did it without hesitation or question. I moved my hand from his balls to my clit then took my other hand and put it back on his balls.

I grabbed my wetness and made circular motions on my sex, as I continued to squeeze and release.

"Rub harder, Maddie."

I did as Jack wanted and knew I wouldn't be able to last long. Loud moans started to fly out of me.

"Your so delicious, Maddie," he whispered to me for the thousandth time since the night we first met.

Like an injection of heroin, my lower region sped into Neverland, and my back arched with Jack on top of me. My nipples grew harder, as Jack continued to manipulate them, with his big, beautiful cock in my mouth.

"Let me taste you, baby," Jack demanded.

My hands left my body and pushed into Jack's mouth. He sucked on my fingers as I felt his girth pulse against my breasts. I knew I needed to cum, but he wasn't far behind me.

I grazed my teeth on him, and he groaned, as his chest heaved. I shut my eyes for a minute.

He released my fingers. "Touch yourself again."

I put my hand back on my clit and instantly started to whimper, as my body responded, and I brought myself back up to the edge.

"Open your eyes, Maddie, and make yourself cum," Jack ordered, with his eyes full of the same wild-and-craziness I felt.

Ready for my apex, I moved my hand quicker and let myself go. My body lifted further into Jack's. My eyes rolled as I continued to suck his dick. He started to throb, and I released his balls and grabbed his hips to push him further into my mouth as he erupted all over me. I continued to shake and moan, as I drank his hot juice, and he cried out my name in ecstasy.

In the aftermath, he rolled off me and grabbed my hand. He stroked my fingers with his, as we both lay on our backs and tried to catch our breath. I looked over to see his schoolboy grin on his face as he stared at me.

"What?"

"I think you just made every dirty fantasy I ever had come true."

I laughed. He leaned over me and kissed me, "Don't freak out, but I love you, Maddie."

I grinned and kissed him. "Not freaked out. I love you too, Jack."

He kissed me harder, jumped off the bed, and swatted my ass. "Okay, time for my run."

JACK

I LOVED MADDIE MORE THAN I EVER LOVED ANYONE. I THOUGHT she would freak out when I told her, but she didn't, and she loved me, too.

As I ran through Central Park, my thoughts in the clouds, I didn't realize it, but I ran straight toward Michael Duponte. I froze.

My time with Michael over the last year had all been calculated. I wasn't prepared to bump into him on my run, and especially in New York City.

"Jack." He stopped.

"Michael, I thought you would be in Tampa?" I quickly recovered as my blood began to boil—just like every other time I spent in his presence.

Something seemed off, but I couldn't put my finger on it. *It must be because I'm not prepared to see him.*

He snickered. "You like to keep me there, don't you?"

The hair on my neck stood up. "Sorry?"

He shook his head. "Nothing."

I wasn't sure what to say. Finally, I asked, "You going back soon?"

He paused, then nodded. "Yep. See you around, Jack." He ran off.

My body went colder. *Something is off.*

I picked my phone out of my pocket and called Creedie. “I just ran into Duponte. What’s he doing in New York? I thought he was in Tampa?”

“He left last night.”

“What do you think he’s doing here? Shouldn’t he be in town if a shipment is coming in?”

“We would assume.”

I kicked a leaf on the ground. “Assumptions aren’t enough. Don’t tell me you guys aren’t going to nail them this time.”

“Jack, calm down. We’re doing the best we can.”

I grunted. “Really? It’s been over a year, and we aren’t any closer. If he’s in town, something is off with your intel. He isn’t going to miss a party.”

Creedie sighed. “Look, Jack, we’re on it. You need to have a little more patience.”

I sneered, “Patience? It’s been over a year!”

“I know. We need more time. Trust me. We will get them.”

“In the meantime, he’s running around New York in the same city as Maddie. Creedie, you either take care of this or I will.”

“Jack, don’t do anything stupid. You’ll put yourself and Maddie in more danger,” Creedie warned.

I knew he was right, but I still wanted to go over to his place and cripple him.

“Jack?”

I kicked the ground again. “Yeah, I hear you.” I hung up.

Duponte needed to get out of the city and as far away from Maddie as possible.

I called Casey. “Put a trail on Maddie. Don’t let her know. Duponte is here.”

I closed my eyes. This thing really needed to end.

20

Maddie

The weeks turned into months. Jack and I only became closer. We traded nights at each other's places. We didn't care where we were, as long as we were with each other. Our clothes and other personal items were at both places, and we traded keys.

The investigation with the FBI continued, but I stopped asking Jack about it because I realized that I couldn't make it happen any faster. Our prior conversations weren't positive, so it was easier for me to ignore it. I knew Jack was still heavily involved and stressed out by it, so I made it my mission to do whatever I could to make him happy and laugh when we were together.

The winter turned into summer. Jack was out of town again, and I was outside my work building when I saw him. As I grabbed my lunch from the street vendor, I spotted a man with a long lens camera, taking pictures of me.

At first, I thought maybe I was wrong. I went and sat on a bench. Sure enough, the man from far away took more pictures. I quickly pulled out my phone and pretended I was FaceTiming someone. I zoomed in and snapped a photo of him.

My insides quivered but I told myself to hold it together. I didn't want to worry Jack while he was away, so I walked back inside and directly to Liv's office. She and Meg were meeting at her desk.

"Hey, Maddie, what's wrong?" Liv wrinkled her brows at me.

"I can come back." I turned to leave.

Liv called my name and told me to come back in. "Maddie, what's going on?"

I showed the picture to Liv and Meg and told them he photographed me. I tried to zoom in on the photo I took, but it was too far for a clear shot.

"Crap, Maddie." Meg walked over to the window and pointed. "Look, he's still there."

Liv and I both joined Meg at the window. Liv snapped photos, but like my phone, it was too far away.

Meg picked up her phone. "Collin, are you here yet or on your way for our meeting?"

She paced. "I need you to do something. Some crazy guy is taking pictures of Maddie. I'm going to text you where he's located. Can you get a better picture?"

Quiet filled the room as Meg listened.

"No, we're inside Liv's office, safe and sound. I can see him from Liv's office window." Meg listened as Collin spoke. "I'm texting you a picture now," Meg hung up and sent him a picture, then told me to airdrop her my pic so she could send it as well.

Liv glanced at me. "Have you called Jack?"

"He's out of town. I don't want to worry him. It could be nothing. I could have imagined it."

Liv gave me a serious look. "You need to call Jack."

I shook my head. "I don't want to worry him."

Within a few minutes, Collin sent us a picture. The guy wore sunglasses and a hat, but there was no doubt who he was. My knees buckled, and I sank into the chair.

"Maddie? Do you know him?" Meg questioned me.

"It's Bo Crumo, Mike's friend from California." I shuddered.

Within minutes, Jack texted me the same picture Collin sent us. My Facetime rang as Liv's phone rang as well. She stepped outside before I heard her say, "Hey, Tom."

"Maddie, what's going on?" Jack demanded to know.

"I was outside grabbing lunch and saw him taking pictures of me. I couldn't get close enough to see who it was, so Meg called Collin to get a picture."

"Do you know who he is?"

I quietly nodded.

"Maddie, for God's sake, who is he?"

"Bo Crumo, from California. Inform the FBI…they know about him." I turned away from the phone and knew Jack would ask questions.

Jack's voice was very stern. "What are you not telling me?"

"He's an old friend of Mike's. Just tell the FBI."

"Tom and I are heading out as soon as this storm is over and we can get in the air. It's not supposed to let up until around four o'clock. I don't want you going anywhere except with the bodyguards and Casey. Go right to my place."

"Okay." I wouldn't argue this one.

Collin walked into Liv's office.

"Maddie, stay close to the bodyguards. I've already sent the photo to the FBI and will call them now."

"Okay."

"I have to go. I'll call you as soon as I know we can leave. I love you."

"I love you too, Jack." The screen went blank.

"Maddie, did he approach you?" Collin sat down next to me.

"No. Thanks for taking that picture." I gave Collin a grateful smile.

"I don't want to scare you, but whatever you do, don't get a false sense of security with the bodyguards. If you are out of the office or penthouse, make sure you keep your eyes open and wait for them to make the first move."

I nodded and remembered how Meg told me how Collin got shot by her ex-boyfriend.

Liv walked in with six bodyguards. "Tom thinks all of us need bodyguards tonight."

"What else did Tom say?" I felt like there was more.

"Nothing, but I know something has to be serious for Tom to take these precautions."

"Why do we need bodyguards?" Meg inquired.

Collin put on his negotiator's face.

"Collin, you better spill it now!" Meg stood right in front of his face and glared at him.

"I've been negotiating, behind Jim and Mike's back, with the other investors. We're trying to get them to pull the morality clause, but they are worried about being sued without proof of anything. We don't know that one or several haven't talked with Michael or Jim."

Meg seethed at Collin. "Why didn't you tell me this?"

"You didn't need to know. Now you need to know, so I'm telling you." Collin didn't show any emotion.

Meg's face turned as red as the color of her hair. Collin stood up and put his arms around her. "Everything will be fine." He kissed her.

Within seconds, her face resumed its normal shade. When she pulled out of the kiss, she gave Collin a smirk and glare. I had a feeling they would be having some mad makeup sex.

Liv turned to me. "Do you want to come over to my place till the guys get home?"

"I better not, Liv. Jack told me to go to his place. I should follow the plan."

"Understand."

The rest of the day crawled by. It was 4:30 when Jack called. I was still in the office. "We should be able to take off soon. The lightning has cleared."

"I'm finishing up and about to leave."

Jack reminded me to go straight to his house.

"I will."

"Maddie, when I get home, you need to tell me everything."

I sighed. "Jack, it's a friend of Mike's. About two years into our relationship, he tried to rape me. Bo had ripped my underwear off and had me bent over the kitchen sink. Then Mike walked in. That's the story, now you know, can we not talk about it ever again?"

"Oh my God, Maddie!"

"Jack, stop. Please. Just like you don't want to relive stuff, I don't either. It could have been a lot worse."

Jack became silent. Then calmly, "I'm going to fucking kill him when I get my hands on him."

"Jack, no! Please," I cried out, afraid he would do it. "We need to move forward, not backward, remember?"

"Maddie, you told me nothing happened, this isn't nothing."

"Nothing did happen! Mike came home."

"Did he beat the shit out of him?"

Silence hung between us.

"That fucking bastard. I'm going to kill Michael first, then Bo's next," Jack seethed through clenched teeth. He quickly became an angry ball of rage.

A cold chill went through my body, and I started to cry. "Jack, don't! I don't need you in jail. Please, come home and be with me. You're scaring me right now."

I heard Jack inhale and exhale slowly. "Maddie, go home, do not stop anywhere. I'll see you after I take care of these assholes." Before I could respond, he hung up the phone.

Cold chills coursed through me. I ran to Liv's office.

Liv sat at her desk and looked up when I flew into the room. "Maddie, what's wrong?"

"I think Jack is going to do something stupid. You have to get Tom on the phone."

She picked up the phone and put it on speaker.

"Hey, Gorgeous," Tom answered the phone.

"Tom, it's Liv and Maddie. Is Jack with you?" Liv urgently asked.

"He forgot something at the hotel. He will be back soon. Why?"

"Tom, you have to go find him. He's going to do something stupid and get hurt! Please stop him," I cried out.

"I'm already on my feet. Let me call security and have him stopped. Call you soon." Tom hung up.

Liv pointed to her chair. "Sit, Maddie. Tom will find him. Tell me what happened."

I told Liv that I told Jack about Bo and Mike. "Jack's going after Mike. I shouldn't have told him. This is my fault."

"It's not your fault. Don't worry. Tom will find him and talk some sense into him."

My stomach flipped with thoughts of Jack behind bars or possibly murdered.

It felt like forever, but within five minutes, Tom texted Liv.

"Security has Jack. I'll get him on the plane and text you when we take off."

"See! Tom will talk sense into him. Everything will be fine, I promise."

"Liv, what if it's not? What if this never ends?"

Liv put her hand on mine. "Look, I know how you feel. When I found out about Tom's secret, I had the same feeling. But this will end, I promise. You have to keep Jack's head straight though."

I closed my eyes.

"Maddie, you can't do anything here. Go to Jack's, take a warm bath, and have a glass of wine. Call me if you need to talk."

She was right. Unfortunately, I would have to wait.

JACK

MY STRESS LEVEL WAS THROUGH THE ROOF. IT HAD BEEN OVER A year since I began to work with the FBI, and they couldn't seem to take care of this. I felt like I would never be free, and now Maddie was involved and being threatened.

The FBI couldn't seem to do their job, and Michael was rumored to be in Tampa, waiting for a new shipment. I wasn't getting back on that plane until he was in a body bag.

I didn't know who Bo Crumo was, but once I finished with Michael, I would take care of him too.

Security stopped me as I was about to walk out of the main doors. "Mr. Stevens, come with us, please."

I jerked my head back. "Why?"

"We need you to come with us," the officer repeated.

Angrily, I shook my head. I didn't know what this was about, but how much more did I have to take?

They led me back to Tom's jet, which sat on the runway. "What is this about?"

"Mr. Stevens, you need to get on the jet. This isn't a choice."

I laughed. "Is this a joke?"

The security officer shook his head. "No, sir, you must get on the jet now."

"And if I refuse?"

"Then you will be detained."

Tom popped his head out of the jet's front door. "Jack, get in."

"Tom, what's this about?"

"Get in, and I'll tell you," Tom sternly replied.

"I have something I need to take care of first."

"*No, you don't.* Get your ass in here, Jack." He turned and went back into the jet.

The security guard glared at me. "This is your last warning, Mr. Stevens. If you don't get on the jet, we will arrest you."

Not able to win, I threw my hands in the air and stormed to the back of Tom's jet, where he was seated. "What the fuck is happening, Tom?"

"Sit your ass down, Jack." He pointed to the seat.

The beep of the machinery from outside rang loudly, and I saw the stairs back away from the jet. I knew that the jet door was shut and locked. I scowled at Tom. He grabbed his phone and sent someone a text message.

He pointed to the beer that sat in the cupholder. "Sit. Have a drink and relax, Jack."

"You had security come after me? That's pretty low, Tom." I snarled at him.

Tom's leg started to twitch, but his face went calm. "Listen, I get your pissed off, and you want to kill the guy, but you need to use your head. You do something stupid, and the investigation goes up in smoke. Maddie ends up what, visiting you in prison? Who will protect her then? Come on, be smarter than that."

Defeated, I put my head in my hands. I was so tired and stressed over this whole thing. It had been too long, and it just seemed to get worse.

Frustrated, I looked up at Tom. "This is never going to be over, is it?"

He sighed. "Listen, I can only imagine what this last year has been like for you, but we are close. You need to hang in there a bit longer. Maddie needs you. She doesn't need you going all crazy and going off the deep end."

I swallowed a big swig of beer and closed my eyes. "I'm so tired."

"I know, but we get one chance to fry these guys. Let's not screw it up."

"The FBI isn't getting shit done. It's been over a year. If they aren't going to take him down, I will."

"Listen, if anyone knows what you're going through, and how ready you are for this to be over, it's me."

It was true, if anyone could understand how tired I was, it was him.

He continued. "When Kylo assaulted Liv, I almost killed him. I wanted to kill him. I'm lucky D was there to pull me off. As pissed as I was at D, I'm grateful he did, because I'd be in jail right now, sharing a bunk with God knows who, instead of coming home to Liv every night. Just take a breather, have a beer, and use your head. You want to share a bunk, or go home to Maddie every night when this is over?"

I leaned back in my seat. He was right. I knew he was.

"Jack, trust me on this. They are going to get what's coming to them."

I sighed. "You better be right."

21

Maddie

BACK AT JACK'S, CASEY CAME UP WITH THE BODYGUARDS AND stood with me in the hallway while they did a sweep of the place.

"You aren't just a driver, are you, Casey?"

He hesitated. "No, ma'am."

"Do you have a gun?"

He searched my eyes. "Yes, ma'am."

"Do you know if Jack has a gun?"

He wouldn't answer the question. Once again, silence gave me answers.

"Would I find this gun in the house, should I need it?"

Casey peered at me. "Ma'am, have you ever shot a gun?"

"No."

He pulled out his gun. My heart raced. I had never been in front of a gun before. "I'm going to show you one thing because, as I'm sure you are aware, guns are not to be taken lightly. However, should you be in a situation where you have to use one, you need to know this."

I leaned in and watched him handle the gun.

"This is the safety. You cannot shoot without the safety off. Flip it like this if you need to shoot before you pull the trigger."

I nodded.

"But I don't recommend you start playing with guns, ma'am. Please leave that to us." He gave me a serious but kind smile.

I smiled back. "Thank you, Casey."

He put the gun away as the bodyguards came out. "Place is clear. You are all set to go in, Ms. Burns. We will be out here in the hallway should you need anything."

"Thank you." I walked in.

The penthouse was shining brightly with the light of the summer sky as if everything in the world was normal. Inside, I felt everything but normal.

I was tempted to call Jack, but Tom assured Liv that they were in the air and I knew he couldn't go anywhere. I prayed that Tom would talk some sense into him, and he wouldn't do something stupid once he landed.

But I couldn't guarantee that. So, I started to search Jack's house for his gun. I didn't want to do anything with it, but I needed to know that he didn't have it on him.

I hunted everywhere. My former sentiments to not be a snoop never once came into my mind as my hands and eyes frantically tried to find for what I prayed was still there. I entered Jack's office and found a safe inside the drawer of his desk. I wondered how I could open it.

I don't know how long I tried different combinations. It became dark. I continued to punch in codes, one after another, but none of the codes worked.

I put my hands on my face and finally resorted to the fact I did not know the code.

Then it came to me. There was one set of numbers I hadn't tried yet. It was a long shot, but I hit zero-two-two-three: the day we met. The safe opened up.

The gun was in the box, and I said a prayer of thanks that it wasn't on Jack. I don't know why I did it, but I picked it up. I found the safety like Casey showed me, and I flipped it back and forth. I was engrossed in it, and held it in my hand and imagined what I would do to Mike, Bo, or even Jim if I saw them again.

"Maddie, what the fuck?" Jack stood in the doorway.

I dropped the gun by accident. It made a massive clank as it hit the ground.

I ran to Jack. I threw myself on him and showered him with kisses.

He wrapped his arms around me, then carried me to the couch in his office. "Maddie, what are you doing with my gun?"

"I needed to make sure you didn't have it on you." I started to cry. "I was so scared, Jack. I thought you were going to do something foolish."

Jack grabbed my face, pushed my hair away, and shushed me. "I'm sorry. I was so angry. I was on my way to find Michael. I know he's in Tampa right now. Tom had the security stop me, and he talked some sense into me on the flight home."

"Jack, you can't do anything to put our future in danger."

"I know, Maddie, I'm sorry I scared you. The thought of what they did to you..."

I pulled his forehead to mine. "Jack, nothing happened. It's why I made you leave when the FBI was here questioning me. Please, let's forget about it?"

He closed his eyes, then opened them. "Maddie, have you shot a gun before?"

"No."

"You shouldn't be messing around with a gun then."

"I know. Casey told me about the safety."

Jack's head about spun off. "What!?"

Oh shit, now I did it. "Jack, calm down. I asked him."

"Why?"

"Why do you have a gun?" I threw it back at him.

Jack stared at me then stood up, grabbed my hand, and pulled me up. "Come on."

"Where are we going?"

He grabbed the gun off the ground, made sure the safety was on, and stuck it in the back of his pants.

"Jack?" My hand shook as it grabbed his arm.

He spun, then put his hands on my shoulders. "Maddie, if you're going to play around with guns, then I'm going to teach you how to shoot them properly. Let's go."

He pulled me down the hall and through the penthouse. At the end of the hall, there was a bookshelf. Jack pushed one of the books, and a number panel appeared. He pushed 0223, and the wall opened up. My mouth fell open as he pulled me into the room and pushed a button so the wall closed again.

"Jack?"

Jack flipped the light switch. An entire part of the penthouse I didn't know existed was there.

My mouth gaped open. "What is this place?" I finally mustered.

"Sit, Maddie." He pointed to the couch.

I sat and surveyed the room. There was a kitchen, living area, bedroom, bathroom, and something else I couldn't see further back.

He sat down next to me, ran his hands through his hair, then took a deep breath. His tongue slowly licked his lips, and he fidgeted with his fingers. I sat and waited.

"Kelly was five months pregnant when our house was broken into. The robbers smacked her around, and she fell, and that was how we lost the baby. I was there, tied up to a chair, and watched it all. I wasn't able to protect her or our baby." Jack closed his eyes in agony.

Stunned and in shock, my heart broke in two for the pain Jack must have gone through and still carried with him today. I put my hand on his leg.

He opened his eyes. "That is why I have a gun. It's why I have this room. When the robbers broke in, we were asleep and heard a noise. I told Kelly to stay upstairs. When I went downstairs, they hit me in the head and tied me to the chair. We had no gun, no safe place for Kelly, or even for both of us to go."

The horror of the story slowly sank in. I heard and saw the guilt Jack carried with him.

Jack put his hands on my shoulders. "I built this room so I would have a safe place for my family to go to if needed. I have a gun because if anyone tries to break into my house and hurt someone I love, I will not hesitate to shoot. Do you understand me?"

His eyes bore into mine. "Yes."

"Good, come on." He stood up again and grabbed my hand.

He pulled me to the back of the room and turned on another light. It lit up a shooting range. There was a table with drawers, and he pulled two sets of ear protectors out. He put one around his neck and one around mine.

"Step up to the wall, Maddie."

I stepped up. He stood next to me and snatched the gun out of his back pants and pointed it straight at the target.

"This is unloaded right now, but you flip this switch and squeeze the trigger. Try it," he ordered me, as he took one arm away from the gun then wrapped it around me. He pulled me tight to him, in front of his body. Then, he grabbed my hand and put it around the gun before he put his hands over mine and showed me how to release the safety and pull the trigger. After a few times, he put the safety back on and set the gun on the table.

"Never point the gun, even when you think it's empty, at anyone, understand?"

I nodded.

"Tell me you understand, Maddie."

"I understand, Jack."

"Good. Now I'm going to show you how to load it with

bullets." He opened a drawer and pulled out six bullets. I watched as he put in two and then he made me put the other four in.

We put our ear protectors on, and he stood behind me once more. With his hands on top of mine, he flipped the safety and prodded me to squeeze the trigger. The gun fired and shot me back a bit into Jack, who stood firmly planted.

He put the safety on, set the gun back down, and uncovered our ears. "Did you feel how you bounced back?"

"Yes."

"That's the gun kicking back. You need to plant yourself into the ground." He showed me how.

"Okay, Jack." I put my ear covers back on and stepped in front of him.

We stood back in position, and I fired. Then again. And again. And again. The last bullet, Jack stepped away from me, and I fired on my own.

Jack's face was serious. He pulled our ear protectors off and put the safety back on the gun. "There are bullets in my desk drawer, the opposite drawer where this gun is. You figured out the code, so if you ever get stuck and can't get to this room, you remember where I have this, okay?"

"I understand. But Jack, we have security in the lobby and right now bodyguards outside our door. Nothing is going to happen."

"Probably not, but I won't take my chances with you."

There was still so much I didn't know about Jack. But I felt like I had just learned the most important piece. His need to protect me I could always feel, but now I knew it ran deeper than I realized. I thought back to his immediate flight mode the first night we met in the bar.

I glanced around the room, and then at Jack, and I saw so much sadness in his eyes. This room was extreme, and it represented what he blamed himself for. I realized that he thought it was his fault they lost the baby, and I grabbed his face and pulled it to mine. "It wasn't your fault, Jack."

His eyes welled up. "It was. I couldn't protect them," he whispered.

I shook my head. *"No. It wasn't."*

Tears began to fall. An ocean of guilt, a lifetime of self-hatred, a never-ending stream of pain fell in those tears, as I pulled him into me.

I let him cry. I don't know how long it was. I finally grabbed his hand and the gun. "Come on, Jack, let's get out of here."

We turned off the lights and locked up the room. I walked into the office and locked the gun in the safe.

Jack stood in the doorway and observed me. "Maddie, we have to find out what Bo wants with you."

"I'm assuming he is working for Mike."

"But what are they planning?"

Shivers whipped through my body, as I had a flashback of Bo when he ripped off my underwear and pushed me up against the sink. "I don't know. What did the FBI say when you called them today?"

Jack sighed. "Not much. They said they would put a trail on him, but other than that, they couldn't disclose anything to me." He paused.

"What is it?".

"A new shipment came in today." Disgust filled his face. "One of the agents got wind of 'the party.'"

"What else aren't you telling me?"

Jack took a big breath and ran his hands through his hair. He didn't say anything at first.

"What?"

"The FBI doesn't understand why they are so interested in you. Another account was opened today in your name. It was one thing to use your name to have you be the fall person, but they feel it's more personal...more like revenge."

My mind spun. "Revenge for what?"

Jack shrugged his shoulders. "We don't know. I hoped maybe you could think of something?"

There wasn't anything I could think of. "Jack, I swear, I don't know why they involved me in this!"

Jack came over to me. "Maddie, I know that. Everyone knows that. Don't think for one minute that anyone thinks you're involved in this."

"I feel like I need to defend myself or something."

Jack pulled me close. "No one thinks you are involved, Maddie. And you never have to defend yourself to me."

I closed my eyes. *When would this nightmare end?* It felt like we were in a never-ending trap that we couldn't get out of, and until we did, we would never be free.

"Hey, I don't think all this worrying is helping us. Why don't we do something to take our minds off this?" Jack gave me his boyish grin. It was the look that always made my insides turn to jello.

I laughed softly. "And what would you have us do?"

He whispered in my ear, "I brought you a gift."

My insides instantly woke up. I gave him a sly look. "Yeah? What kind of gift?"

"I can't tell you. I can only show you." He gave me a cocky grin while he trailed his fingers over my collarbone.

He didn't have to ask me twice. "Well, show me then."

Jack didn't need any more encouragement. He stuck his fingers in my pants and traced the back of my thong. My body pulsed and knew it would soon be soaring. He clutched my butt cheeks and picked me up as my legs automatically wrapped around his hips. He set me on the desk.

Jack put his face next to mine. His lips and tongue explored my mouth and quickly lit the fire within me.

"Stay here. I'll be right back." Jack left and returned with a bag. He set it next to me and drew me to his body.

My underwear sat against his hard cock. His pants were still on, but it teased me and made me wet through our clothes. As I pulled Jack closer, I felt it expand, which turned me on further. It was a power trip I always felt every time we had sex—that my body could do that to his, and that his dick was mine and mine alone.

I ground into him and shoved my heels into his buttocks to get his manhood closer to my body. With a swift yank, Jack ripped my thong off me. I gasped with pleasure at the quick moment of pain.

He wadded my dress up further and grabbed a handful of my wetness. "God, I love how wet you get for me," he praised me as he rubbed my nub and made me moan.

I reached out and unzipped Jack's pants and unbuckled his belt. His pants fell to the ground, and I forced his boxers along with them.

"Little feisty today, are we?" He raised his eyebrows along with his cocky grin.

I didn't respond. Instead, I reached up and hungrily kissed him, as I claimed him as mine. His naked skin melted against me.

His hands bunched up my dress, and he whipped it over my head and tossed it aside and leaned back into my mouth.

As Jack's large hands stroked my back, he removed my bra. He nibbled on my ear and whispered, "I'm going to make you cum harder tonight, Maddie, than ever before."

My vagina started to spasm at his promise. "Ah, God Jack, yes," I moaned and threw my neck back so he could feast on it.

"Do you want your present, Maddie?"

"Yes, Jack."

"Lay down then."

My hot skin laid back on the cold, hard wood. Jack grabbed my feet and planted them at the end of the desk. "Close your eyes, Maddie."

I closed my eyes. I could hear the shuffle of a bag, a box being ripped open, and the squirt of something...but I didn't know what he was doing. He didn't take long and began to rub his fingers over my clit.

"You can open your eyes." Jack leaned over me and kissed me.

My eyelids fluttered open.

"Maddie, tell me to stop at any time, okay?"

"Okay, Jack."

He started to suck on my breasts, and his fingers played with my ass and vagina.

He stuck what I thought was a finger up my asshole. I sucked in a deep breath. "This feels okay, Maddie?"

"Yes," I breathed, enjoying the pressure. Jack's lips fluttered on my mound and sent tiny volts through my body. I loved it, but I wanted him in my pussy, and I shoved his head there.

He quietly chuckled, moved his mouth to where I wanted him and gave me a few sucks as his finger went deeper into my anus.

With hitched breath, I mumbled, "Oh..oh..oh..."

Jack's soft hands teased my areolas, as his mouth pulled more of me into him. One hand caressed my left breast, and I felt his finger go deeper in my ass. Then, both hands found my breasts again.

Jack sucked me hard, and I cried out, "Oh, God!" I pulled his hair and pushed his head back on me and then pulled his hair again.

"You're so wild today," Jack rubbed my butt cheek with his warm hands, then I felt something twist deeper in my backside.

Okay, it now was apparent; it wasn't Jack's finger but something else that filled me up. "Mmm," I moaned.

Jack's mouth left my clit and made its way up my stomach. Both of his hands grabbed my face as he kissed me. I grabbed onto his neck. "I think I'm going to make you wait for your high."

I shook my head feverishly. I felt full of whatever was inside me, but I wanted my high. "Please, Jack, suck me," I begged.

His warm breath whispered in my ear, "I know what you need, baby. Just trust me."

Jack pushed in me with his cock. Slowly, he gave it to me inch by inch.

I was so full; between his dick and whatever was in my ass, I had never felt so filled.

He pushed into me all the way. "Oh...fuck, Jack," I cried out with hitched breath.

Jack stopped. "You okay? Want me to stop or keep going?"

"Don't stop, Jack. It's good. Please, don't stop."

"Hold on then, Maddie." Suddenly, I felt a slow vibration in my anus.

As my mouth contorted in a big O, I gasped. My breath shallow, my eyes met Jack's, as he intently watched my face for my every reaction.

"Fuck you turn me on." He started to thrust in and out of me.

Every cell in my body vibrated, and I couldn't think. The slow vibration suddenly went faster, and ripples of pleasure coursed throughout my body like never before.

I couldn't speak—only gasp out ah's and oh's.

Jack felt it too. A grunt came out of him as his eyes closed, and his neck moved back slightly.

My body quivered from the vibrations, and my vagina gripped Jacks' penis like never before as I dug my nails into the back of his waist while he thrust into me faster.

Jack's finger started to rub my nub, and I flew over the edge. "Jack, I..." I couldn't finish my sentence. Heat flowed through my body, and the lava erupted from the volcano.

Jack nodded, red-faced, hardly able to speak.

Oh, fuck. Oh, fuck. Oh, fuck! I clawed my nails across his back.

With one last rub of my clit, he pulled something out of my ass and pumped himself into me as I climaxed like never before. My back arched off the desk, and my juices squirted out all over him, as our bodies spasmed uncontrollably.

I laid on the desk and tried to catch my breath. Our body fluids were everywhere. Jack leaned over me, with his elbows and forearms on both sides of my chest. His breathing was labored, and sweat dripped off both of us.

He shoved his tongue in my mouth and once again, claimed me as his and made me feel like no one else on earth existed...like I was his prize...as if nothing else in life mattered but me.

I wondered if I was more breathless from the intense orgasm or his kisses? When he pulled back, I asked him, "What was that?"

He grinned. "Vibrating anal beads."

I laughed. "That was crazy."

Jack moved his hands between the desk and my back and pulled me up, then massaged my thighs and slowly released my legs straight out. Once my legs hung over the desk, I sat up, and he put his palms next to each side of my thigh and kissed me some more. Then he picked me up, threw me over his shoulder, and slapped my ass.

"Jack," I giggled. "Where are you taking me?"

"We're due for a bath." And he slapped my ass again.

22

Jack

When I walked in and saw Maddie with my gun, I about lost it. I realized we were at the point of no return. If she wanted to play with my gun, then she needed to know how to use it.

I knew I would eventually tell her the entire truth about my past, but I wasn't ready. I was tired, stressed, and holding onto a thread. But it couldn't be avoided. We were in a situation that may require her to be able to protect herself, and now that she had opened Pandora's box, there was no going back.

When I took her into my safe room, I realized I probably looked like a crazy person and had a lot of explaining to do. But now she knew my full story. She could now understand why I would do anything to protect her.

It had been twenty-four hours since then. I chewed Casey out for showing Maddie his gun, I was on constant phone calls with the FBI, and the word was that they would raid the next party, which was that night.

I prayed that it would be over soon as I was a man on the edge of a breakdown, and my demons came out all day long.

The flashbacks. The night terrors. The sounds of the women and children's screams ran in my mind, along with Kelly's the night of the break-in. It was all just too much.

The only thing that kept me sane was Maddie. She had gone to work for the day. I had been cooped up in the penthouse all day, and it suddenly hit me that it was summer. With everything going on, I hadn't even noticed the change of the season.

When Maddie returned from work, I led her over to the stairs.

She turned her head at me, confused. "Where does this go?"

"You'll see." The thought crossed my mind that she probably thought I would lead her to another safe room.

At the top of the stairs, I opened the door, and sunlight flooded in. She stepped out and gave me a huge smile. "Jack, this is amazing!"

I had converted the rooftop of the penthouse into an outdoor paradise, complete with a swimming pool and hot tub. It was my favorite aspect of the penthouse. The flowers were in full bloom, and I realized that I hadn't been here since before the incident occurred. I had missed it all last summer.

Maddie quickly stripped out of her clothes. I grinned at her. My carefree girl, full of adventure, ran and yelled, "The last one in the pool cooks dinner naked."

I threw my head back, laughing, then quickly stripped my clothes off and ran after her. It was exactly what I needed.

I dove in after her, swam to the other side where she was, and pulled her naked body to mine.

"You're going to have to cook me dinner naked now."

"Yeah, what do you want me to make?"

"Hmmm." She pointed over to the outdoor kitchen. "You can grill for me whatever you want, and you can wear an apron."

I let out a big roar. "You're serious?"

"Actually, I think chicken takes longer to cook. Yes, cook chicken," she smirked.

"Anything else?" I asked her, amused at her request.

She put her arms around my neck. "I want dessert first."

Maddie

It had been three days. I went to work and back to Jack's with no stops between. The bodyguards would take me to work and meet me in the lobby on my way out of the building. Jack worked closely with the FBI, and they busted Jim and Bo in Tampa, the night before, with the new shipment of women and children. Mike had escaped off the grid, and the FBI was on the hunt.

Liv, Meg, and I ate lunch in the building cafe. My phone rang. "Hey, Jack."

"Maddie, I have to take a dinner meeting tonight. I'm so sorry, but I can't put it off."

Jack came home early from Tampa. He had only taken meetings while I was at work since the Bo incident.

"Jack, go take your meeting. I'll be fine."

Jack hesitated. "I hate to leave you by yourself tonight."

"You'll be home later, right?"

"Yes, but it will be late. You probably shouldn't wait up."

"No worries. Do what you need to do. I'll be fine."

Meg and Liv listened and waited for me to update them.

"Jack has a dinner meeting tonight. I told him last night that we can't hide out forever. This is getting a bit ridiculous." I rolled my eyes.

"I think we all know what it's like to be cooped up," Meg said, and Liv nodded.

"Now that Jim and Bo have been caught, surely it won't be long before they find Mike," Liv declared.

I shook my head. "At least it's summer, and Jack has the rooftop. It's been nice for us to be able to get outside still and the nighttime weather has been nice this week." I omitted the details that Jack and I had fucked like rabbits on his rooftop patio the last few nights.

We finished our lunch and started to head back to the office.

"I'll meet you upstairs. I need to use the restroom," I told them.

The restroom was quiet, and I was the only one there. I entered a stall and went about my business.

"Sorry, this restroom is closed for cleaning," a muffled deep voice said. The sound of the big, white bin wheels turning, and the door locking creeped me out a bit, but it was standard throughout the day.

I could hear them open all the stall doors, and they tried to open mine.

"Just a minute," I called out.

No one responded.

They tried to open my door again.

"I'll be a minute," I puffed out, slightly irritated, finished up, flushed the toilet, and pulled my pencil skirt over my butt. I unlocked the door and stepped out of the stall.

When I turned to look around, I didn't see anyone and assumed the cleaner must have left or been in one of the stalls, so I made my way to the sink to wash my hands. I gazed up in the mirror and saw him.

He stood behind me and wore a hat pulled low over his eyes. "Hello, Maddie."

My eyes locked with Mike's. Panic gripped my body. I tried to scream, but he quickly grabbed me and pressed something over my mouth and nose. I tried to get out of his grasp, but I wasn't strong enough.

The last thing I remember was him saying, "It's time to teach you a lesson."

EVERYTHING WAS PITCH BLACK, I FELL IN AND OUT OF consciousness and could feel that I was moving. My head hurt, and my lungs felt like I inhaled a bottle of bleach. Disoriented, I tried to get up, but I could hardly move. Something was over my mouth so that I couldn't talk.

Mike's face came into my mind as I tried to remember what happened. The bathroom incident flooded back. "It's time to show you a lesson," flew into my mind before I lost consciousness again.

Whatever I was being transported in hit a bump, and my head hit the ground, which woke me up again. I opened my eyes and saw stars.

Jack. I need to get a hold of Jack, I thought. Jack's face came into my mind. His eyes, smile, and dimples. Thoughts of fucking Jack under the stars on his rooftop and him saying, "You're so delicious, Maddie." I tried to say his name, but something was stuffed in my mouth and prevented me. I lost consciousness again.

When I opened my eyes, I couldn't see anything. I think I laid on cement. It was smooth and cold and smelled fresh like it had just been poured. I tried to move my head, and I winced. A moan stifled in my throat because of whatever was stuck in my mouth.

I needed some water. My mouth was dry. My body trembled from the cold of the ground. I tried to move my arms and slowly realized that both my hands and ankles were tied with a thick rope.

Dizziness and nausea overpowered me, as I tried to sit up. I lost consciousness again.

The next time I woke, I was in a bed. The sun was shining in through the window, and I thought I must have dreamed it all because my eyes registered that I was in my own bedroom. Disoriented and groggy, I closed my eyes again, as my head continued to pound.

Do I have a hangover? I tried to remember if I drank the night before but couldn't remember. *Is Jack with me?*

I slowly opened my eyes again and realized I was tied to my bedposts. My arms were stretched out, along with my legs, and I laid in bed in the outfit I wore when I showed Jack my apartment: fishnet tights, a red garter, and a bra.

Why does Jack have me tied up like this? It didn't feel like the silk of Jack's ties. My wrists and ankles hurt and felt raw. I realized I was tied up with rope—something Jack never tied me up with in the past.

I tried to tell Jack it hurt, but I couldn't speak and realized once more that my mouth was stuffed with something.

Why does Jack have something in my mouth?

That's when I knew I wasn't with Jack. My skin grew clammy; the hairs on my neck stood up. I opened my eyes, turned my head, and saw Mike. He sat in my chair and tapped his fingers together.

Hoping it was a nightmare, I closed my eyes, then opened them again and realized it wasn't.

Mike stood up and walked over to me, stared at me with crazed eyes, then took his fingers, and roughly put them on my breast.

His sinister laugh echoed in my ears as he put his fingers on my trembling lips, and I wiggled my body and tried to escape.

"It seems you didn't appreciate how well I treated you, Madeline," he sneered at me in a sinister voice.

I tried to speak.

"What's that? Do you have something you want to say?"

Scared, I stopped, not sure what to do. To my surprise, he removed my gag and pulled the wadded cloth out of my mouth. I started to cough.

Mike laughed deeper. He got close to my face and whispered, "Smile for the camera."

Camera?

"Oh, Maddie dear, you should have been grateful for what I gave you. All you had to do was sit there and be your dumb self. I gave you the world, and you spit it back in my face. All those men that wanted you, I kept from you so you would be mine. But now..." he started to laugh, "...now I want you to smile at everyone watching." He pointed to a camera attached to my ceiling, with a green light that blinked.

Horror filled me. I rapidly blinked, tried to hold back my tears, as my heart beat so hard I was sure he could hear it.

"What? Nothing to say?" Mike hissed in my ear. The stale odor of his body filled my nostrils and sent a new wave of nausea throughout me.

I turned my head to avoid looking at him. I quickly learned that it was the wrong thing to do.

He roughly jammed his fingers in my crotch. I cried out in pain as he stuck four fingers up me, and jabbed me, over and over. "Mike, please, stop," I cried out, not able to hold back the tears that fell on the bed.

He took his fingers out and put them up to my face. "Suck it."

I shook my head.

He pinched my cheeks to open my mouth and shoved his fingers in, then yelled at me to suck it. I shut my eyes, trembled, and almost bit him, but I was afraid it would provoke him more.

"Open your eyes, you bitch," he shouted at me.

Painfully, I opened them.

"We have guests, Maddie." He pointed to the camera. "People are bidding on you right now."

People are bidding on me?

New panic surged through me. I grabbed hard onto the ropes my wrists were tied to and tried to get out of the restraints, but all it did was dig them further into my already raw skin.

My outburst excited him. "That's it, fight, you dumb whore!"

I stopped moving. My insides quivered, and I wondered what he would do to me next.

Grabbing a bottle of whiskey on my nightstand, Mike downed a big swig and then put it in my mouth. He told me to drink and made me drink several ounces.

While I gagged, he yelled at me that I better not throw up.

My cough finally stopped. "Mike, what do you want from me?"

He laughed again, loud and crazy. "Why don't I show you?"

He walked over to my desk and grabbed my open laptop.

"Have you ever heard of the black net, Maddie?" He put the laptop on my chest, so the screen was in my face.

My eyes went wide.

Mike put his face right next to mine, his breath full of whiskey. A huge smile grew on his lips, "The black net is where I get to auction you off. I'm going to give our bidders a show. Whatever they pay me to do to you, I'll do. After that, I'll sell you off to the highest bidder. Don't worry. I'll let them have their way with you too."

My eyes grew wider. I tried to yank my hands and legs free and lifted my head off the bed, but I was trapped. Mike just sat there and laughed, then pointed out to me how my bidding numbers skyrocketed from my outburst.

"The people I deal with, they like a fighter. I didn't think you had it in you, Maddie. I wish I would have known you were a fighter all those years I was with you." Mike trailed his finger on my jawline.

I glared at him.

"We could have had a lot more fun," he whispered.

An ocean of tears appeared, "Mike, please, let me go."

"I told you that you were mine. You disobeyed me, Maddie. I was so good to you all those years. It's time to give me what is mine."

More tears fell.

He walked right in front of the camera, spread out his arms, and yelled, “Start the bidding! Highest bidders get the first choice of how I take her! You have four hours to bid. The show starts at exactly six p.m.!” He walked out of the room.

My body convulsed in fear, tears streamed down my face. I tried not to look at the computer screen as numbers started to go up with all kinds of foul things to do to me.

I needed to escape. But I didn’t see how.

23

Jack

"WHAT DO YOU MEAN YOU STILL DON'T KNOW WHERE SHE IS? You're the God damn FBI," I screamed at Agents Piper and Creedie.

Tom walked over and put his hand on me. "Let's take a walk, Jack. You have to calm down. This won't help find Maddie."

It was a little over twenty-four hours since Maddie walked into the bathroom, and I felt crazy. We knew from the security footage it was Michael. It was clear he wheeled her out in the janitor bin. We also knew what van he drove, but after that, they vanished.

I looked at Tom. "It's been too long, Tom. He could have done anything to her by now."

"Jack, we're going to find her. I need you to stay in the game with me." He patted me on the back.

I nodded. As scared as I was, I knew he was right.

My penthouse turned into an FBI war zone. Agents were everywhere on computers and phones. I hadn't slept all night, nor had Tom, Collin, Liv, or Meg, who were all over at my place.

Liv and Meg walked in and brought a fresh set of coffee for everyone.

"Any news?" Meg looked at Collin.

Collin shook his head. I saw Meg's eyes drop.

Panic, anger, and fear were all I had felt since about 4 p.m. the day before when the girls realized that no one had seen Maddie since their lunch. How Michael passed the office building security was an issue in itself, but how he managed to get Maddie alone and out of the building seemed nearly impossible. *But he had.*

"We think we have something," one of the agents who worked on the black net called out.

We all raced over to see what he pointed to on his computer.

"What is that?" I stared at a countdown clock.

"There seems to be an auction going on. The deadline is six tonight, and the woman has Maddie's features listed. We are trying to get into the auction room right now."

"Why can't you get in it?" Liv put her arms across her chest.

Piper spoke up."These things are like clubs. You have to have secret codes and passwords to get in, so people like us can't."

Meg quietly asked Collin, "What does he mean by auction?"

My stomach flipped at the thought of my precious Maddie being auctioned off. Flashbacks of the night in Tampa, where I witnessed Michael and Jim's auction, raced into my mind.

"We're running out of time. Once this auction ends, she will disappear forever. You know that." I slammed my fist on the table Creedie worked at.

Creedie looked up. "Jack, I need your head here. This isn't helping. Think of where he might have taken her to."

"You don't think that's all I've been thinking of?" I spat out.

Liv put her hand on me. I spun. "Jack," she softly looked at my eyes.

Completely losing it, I started sobbing as Liv pulled me into her arms.

I cannot not lose her. She is my life. What is that bastard doing to her?

"This auction has the characteristics of Michael Duponte," the agent said and snapped me out of it. "We don't have the right password yet to enter."

As I paced the room, Collin came up to me. "Jack, what was the password for the auction Michael and Jim took you to?"

"Meatpacking,"

"Try meatpacking," Collin told the agent.

He shook his head. "That's not working."

Collin burrowed his eyebrows. "He used meatpacking before, why?"

"That's where he and Maddie lived."

Collin snapped his fingers. "Try Chelsea," he told the agent.

The agent entered Chelsea. "Something is happening."

The computer flashed, and doors opened. A picture of Maddie on a bed, in fishnet tights, a red garter and bra, popped up. My gut flipped, as I remembered Maddie when she greeted me in that outfit at her apartment.

The picture switched to the rules. A man's voice started to read off the rules. Nausea passed through me as I listened. It was a two-part auction—one for Michael to violate Maddie, and one to own Maddie after. Fifteen minutes later, the rules were all read, and the window finally opened.

Maddie laid on a bed, in the outfit in the original picture, her hands, and ankles tied with ropes. Then, Michael walked up to her and roughly stabbed his fingers in her as she screamed and cried out. My heart shattered into millions of pieces.

"I'm going to kill that bastard."

Placing his body on hers, he made her suck his fingers.

My stomach flipped as I watched the footage with helplessness, rage, and fear running through me at lightning speed. My body turned clammy, and the room was silent as everyone watched in horror.

Michael proceeded to show Maddie how she was up for auction. I watched the numbers on the agent's computer fly up, with bids already in the seven-figure range for Maddie to have the vilest of things done to her.

Nausea rippled through me again, and I had to turn away. I put my hands through my hair. "Where is this at? Can't you trace the location?"

The agent shook his head. “It’s too locked up, and it’s zoomed in on Maddie, so we don’t have any clues about the room. It could be anywhere.”

I became fixated on the screen. My poor Maddie laid there terrified and helpless.

I needed to figure out where she was, but the video didn’t give me any clues.

Regardless, I had this nagging feeling that I was missing something. I peered closer at the screen. All you could see was Maddie, the ropes around her ankles and wrists tied to something.

Think, Jack.

“They think they found the van,” an agent called out. I ran over to the computer screen in front of him.

“I know where that is.” Hope grew inside me. “I own that building.”

“That’s your new center for human trafficking, isn’t it?” Tom looked at me.

“Yes. Let’s go.”

24

Maddie

My mind was racing as I tried to avoid the countdown clock on the computer, or reading the bids that popped up so fast on the screen it made my head spin. But I could see the bids were now up to $2 million.

I closed my eyes and tried to think of what would make Mike come to his senses. The problem was, he lost his senses and sold his soul, maybe even before I met him.

The bid was now $2.3 million, and I saw the words 'plastic over face.' It was more of a reaction maybe, but I moved my hips to the side of the computer with all my force, and the computer screen slid off the bed, crashed on the floor, and banged loudly.

Mike ran into the room. He saw the laptop on the floor and laughed. "What's wrong, Maddie? Don't you want to know what people want to see me do to you?"

"You're sick," I hissed. I was angry now. "A worthless piece of shit you've become."

It was the wrong thing to say. Mike came up and slapped me

across the face, hard. I yelled out in pain as blood started to drip out of my nose. I could feel the warm blood dripping off my face.

"You have anything else to say?" Mike sneered, as I whimpered in pain. I shook my head. Fresh tears mixed in with my pool of blood.

Mike picked up the laptop. He walked up to the camera, and laughed hysterically, "Oh, you all liked that, huh? Tell you what, once we hit $3 million I'll give you a little mini-show."

My insides shook harder. My mind raced to Jack. Did he know I was missing? Surely he would be searching for me?

Jack, please find me.

"You guys are frisky tonight! That was quick!" Mike exclaimed, and my gut dropped further, as I didn't know what was in store for me.

Mike went into the bathroom. I laid there, scared of what he planned next for me. My heart raced in fear, and I tried to figure out how to get out of there but wasn't sure how. I tried to move my limbs again, but there was no use. It cut further into my skin, and my wrist started to bleed from the ropes.

Mike came out of my bathroom, a washcloth in his hand.

I stared at him, not sure what he was up to. He started to clean the blood from my nose. "People are paying good money for you. You're a dirty whore, but you don't have to look like one."

"Six years, how can you do this to me?" I blurted out.

He became enraged. "Six years and you disrespect me!" He jumped on top of me so I was underneath him. His body completely laid on top of mine, and his hard-on grew through his anger.

I tried to move my body. "Get off me," I yelled.

He laughed. "Tell me," he seethed, "does Jack play with your breasts like this?" He squeezed my breasts hard.

I froze. *How does he know about Jack and me?*

"Ah, you didn't know I knew, did you? You cheating whore," he slapped me on the other side of the cheek.

"Mike, please!" I sobbed as I felt his dick get harder, right next to my crotch.

He took the washcloth, wiped away the new blood, then started to move my bra strap off me. I tried to get away from him again, but I was stuck.

His hands roughly grabbed my breasts. I winced, but he laughed again and sneered, "I think we should give Jack a show, shouldn't we?"

My head jerked in confusion.

Jack can see me? Why isn't he rescuing me?

He leaped off me, picked up the laptop, and started to type something. I heard a phone ring. Then, I heard Jack's voice.

"Dupont, you piece of shit, where is she?" Jack's voice demanded to know, as my heart soared at the sound of his voice.

Mike's smile widened. "Why, Jack, is that any way to greet an old friend?"

"Jack," I cried.

"Maddie!" Jack's distraught voice filled the air.

Mike laughed. "I thought you might want to watch a bit, eh? For old times' sake?" He put the computer on my desk, where I could see Jack's face.

"Jack, help me," I sobbed, as a new, never-ending supply of tears streamed down my face.

"Maddie." His face was a wall of pain and fear.

Mike came over to me, grabbed my bra, and ripped it off me. It hurt and tore into my back when he ripped it.

"You piece of shit," Jack yelled through the computer.

He came over to me and bit my breast. I cried out in pain. Blood started to form on my breast. "Why are you doing this to me?" I sobbed.

"Dupont! Stop! What do you want? I'll give you anything, just leave her alone!" Jack cried out through the computer.

Mike turned and walked over to the computer. "You took what was mine. You're never going to take anything of mine again. Say goodbye, Jack."

"No! What do you—"

Jack's voice abruptly stopped as Mike hit a button and disconnected them. The bidding screen popped back up.

As I sobbed harder, Mike laughed hysterically.

The bidders were enjoying the show. A $7 million figure popped up at the top of the screen. They were getting off from my fear, but I couldn't stop weeping.

He came and put the computer back on the bed next to me. "This stays here, or next time, you'll get more than a slap, do you understand?"

As more tears fell, I bit my lip.

Mike walked out of the room. I laid there trapped. I sobbed, with my body in excruciating pain, and blood still dripping out of me.

Then I heard it...a woman's voice. It sounded so familiar.

Think, Maddie.

New goosebumps popped up on my skin. I had just figured out who it was when she walked through the door.

"I told you Jack Stevens wasn't a long-term strategy," she sneered at me.

My eyes went wide. *What is Evelyn doing here?*

Mike walked in and started laughing again. "Seems you've made a lot of enemies while you've been whoring around."

"Wh...What do you want, Evelyn?"

She walked closer to the bed. I could smell the stench of her perfume. A dark, sinister smile appeared across her face. "To watch you suffer." She then took her hand and slapped me several times across the face, laughed, and left.

The pain stung long after she left the room. Cold chills flew through my body, and a new round of tears and blood poured over my face.

I prayed that Jack would rescue me before it was too late.

JACK

THE CONNECTION WAS GONE. MY MADDIE WAS NO LONGER ON THE screen. I clenched my fists and ground my teeth, then turned to see the horror on Tom's and Collin's faces.

We were still in the car, on the way to the center, when I had received the FaceTime request.

"Can you trace that?" I handed my phone up to the front of the car, where Piper and Creedie sat. As soon as Maddie had been abducted, they put a tap on my phone in case Duponte tried to contact me.

Creedie was already on the phone. He shook his head. "The IP from wherever he called was blocked."

I punched the side of the car door. "Fuck."

I put my hands over my face, leaned my elbows on my knees, and watched the screen. Michael put the laptop in front of Maddie, to torture her and make her watch the vile bids that continued to increase.

My Maddie was sobbing, and my heart broke again.

Suddenly, I heard a woman's voice. My head about snapped off my neck. "That's Evelyn, the real estate agent I fired," I told Piper and Creedie.

"Evelyn?" Tom questioned me.

I nodded. "I know that's her."

"How does she know Duponte?" Collin asked.

My gut dropped. "I referred her to him when he was looking at apartments to move to New York."

"Why—"

Tom stopped talking as Evelyn appeared on screen and started slapping Maddie hard.

"That bitch," I seethed.

Tom and Collin continued to watch the screen, saying nothing.

Think, Jack. I tried to clear my mind. All I could see was Maddie, lying in a bed, in the outfit she picked out for me and roped to her headboard.

"Oh my, God," I sat up. "Turn the car around now!"

"Jack, what is it?" Tom jerked his head toward me.

"I know where she's at! She's in her apartment."

Piper glanced at me, over his shoulder. "Why do you think that?"

"That was her headboard. She's wearing an outfit she picked out for me. I'm telling you, he has her at her place." I knew I wasn't wrong about this.

Creedie picked up the phone, "We need a SWAT team in a second location."

Hang on, Maddie, I thought. *I'm coming, baby.*

It didn't take us long to get there. We pulled up as the SWAT team pulled up to the curb.

Inside the lobby, Piper put his hand on me. "Jack, you need to stay back and let us handle this."

"I'm going to kill that bastard and Evelyn too."

Creedie stepped in front of me. "Listen, Jack, once he's in handcuffs, I'll give you free rein on Michael, but right now, you need to worry about Maddie's safety. Let us do our job."

Liv and Meg ran in. One of the guys must have messaged them.

"Jack, listen to them. They know what they're doing," Liv instructed.

"I want to kill them, too, Jack, but Liv is right." Tom insisted.

I pounded my fist on the front counter. "What would you do if it was Liv? I'm going in."

"Jack, you're wasting time right now. Let them do their jobs for Maddie's sake." Collin put his hand on my shoulder.

Agent Piper came up to me. "Stay back, Jack, or we will have to arrest you. Maddie is going to need you, and you can't help her if you're in jail."

"Come on, man, time is ticking," Tom urged me.

I wasn't happy but realized I wasn't going to win this battle. The SWAT team already cleared the coffee shop that was attached to Maddie's lobby.

"What are you waiting on then? Go get her." I pointed to the agents.

Piper pointed. "We cleared the route. We're going up now."

As hard as it was, I stepped back. It was torture. Maddie was up there, and they were doing God knows what to her. I started to pace and rubbed my hands through my hair.

The SWAT team filled the elevator. FBI agents took over the lobby, and their computers hooked into the security system of the building. One computer showed the SWAT team in the elevator, and they quickly switched the footage to her hallway. The other computer showed Maddie. She laid by herself on the bed, bare-breasted and crying. I wanted to turn away but couldn't.

Meg came up to me and put her hand on my arm. "She's going to be all right."

I know it was meant to comfort and assure me, but all I could think was, *would she?*

25

Maddie

THE BIDDING QUICKLY INCREASED. IT SEEMED LIKE THE HIGHER THE bidding, the faster the new bids came in.

Jack, please save me, I kept repeating over and over in my mind, the memory of his horrified face replaying in my mind as an additional way to torture me.

The timer blinked forty-five minutes on the computer screen. I closed my eyes and shuddered—some from the cold, mostly from fear.

I tried to escape my restraints again. I wriggled my body and moved my arms and legs, but the ropes were too tight. My efforts only resulted in more blood on my body.

Thirty-eight minutes now, $11 million and things so vile I don't know if I would survive to be sold off to my next bidder. My heart raced so fast I thought I would have a heart attack—pain shot through my chest.

There was a loud noise, and I heard Mike scream, "What the

fuck?" and Evelyn's high-pitched scream, then, "Get on the ground now," over and over.

Am I hallucinating?

It was loud. Then it started to get quieter. It couldn't have been long before my door opened, and men rushed in. I closed my eyes and turned my head to the side as I trembled, not sure who they were or what they would do to me.

"Maddie, are you okay?" I heard.

My eyes closed tighter as I didn't trust whoever it was.

"Maddie, we aren't going to hurt you." The voice sounded familiar.

Slowly, I turned to see Piper and Creedie. Not able to speak, I wept like a baby in relief.

One of the SWAT team guys took their baton and smashed the camera that was in the ceiling.

Creedie had grabbed the blanket that normally sat on my couch and covered me up. The other agents started to assess the ropes around my wrists and ankles.

An agent with bright blue eyes gazed down at me. "Ma'am, we are going to take these off as soon as possible, but I have to take my time, so I don't create more damage to your skin. It's a very tight knot, and you are bleeding. There isn't enough room to put a knife through and slice it, so it's going to take a few minutes. Please try not to move."

I looked at Creedie, "Where's Jack?" My voice was hoarse.

"Downstairs, we wouldn't let him come up. He should be up here shortly. I'm assuming after he lands a few good ones on Duponte." Creedie beamed a sly grin at me.

I wish he would beat the shit out of Evelyn too, went through my mind, but I knew Jack would never hit a woman. Regardless, I let out a small smile. It was something I thought I would never do again. The thought of Jack beating Mike to a bloody pulp made me feel a tad better.

My wrist was freed. "Thank you," I told the agent.

"No problem, ma'am. You're doing a great job. Keep this hand still now, please."

My freed hand ached, and my wrist was bloody and bruised.

"The ambulance is already downstairs, and the paramedics should be up here soon to help," Piper informed me.

Exhausted and in pain, I closed my eyes for a moment but was grateful I had been found before anything else happened. Suddenly, I shuddered again at the thought of what the bidders wanted to do to me.

"Find some more blankets." Creedie pointed to another agent.

Jack. I just need Jack.

My second arm was placed on the bed. The agent working on the ropes moved to the other side of the bed and glanced down at me. "Ma'am, you're doing great. I'm going to work on your ankles now."

"Thank you."

"Maddie!" I heard Jack scream.

"Jack," I cried out, rather gruff, as he rushed through the door, with blood all over his hand.

Piper stepped in front of him and pointed to my ankle. "Don't touch her. She'll get hurt."

"Please, stop for a minute," I said to the agent and cried once again. I wanted Jack. I didn't care about my legs being free at that moment and only wanted to feel his strong arms around me.

The agent stepped back. I heard Creedie say, "Let's give them a minute."

Jack rushed over to me as everyone left the room.

"Maddie!" He bawled, his chest heaved with emotion.

"Just hold me, Jack." I felt the safety of his arms.

He kissed me and pushed my hair behind my ear.

"I'm kind of disgusting right now." My breath was shaky from all my crying.

"Shhh." He kissed me some more. "You're the most beautiful girl. Nothing will ever change that."

A new river of tears flew off my face.

I don't know how long we held each other, but there was a knock on the door. Piper and Creedie came back in, along with the agent who cut the ropes off me.

"We really need to get the remaining ropes off you. The paramedics are here too," Creedie said.

"Don't leave me, Jack." I grabbed him, and my heart started to beat out of my chest once more.

Jack shook his head, "Don't worry baby. I'm not leaving you." He arranged his body so he sat behind me and held me. I leaned back into him, and melted into the familiar feeling of his body, as I tried to push the evil I experienced out of my mind.

The paramedics came in and started to clean and bandage my wrists. They quickly cleaned the blood off Jack's hand and gave him some wipes. He gently wiped the blood from my face, chin, neck, and breasts. I tried not to wince, but the bite mark on my breast was deep and already started to swell.

"I'm sorry, baby." Jack blinked back tears.

"Shhh," was all I could say.

My right leg was set free, and the agent worked on my left leg. "Almost done, ma'am. You're doing great."

He had kind eyes and I smiled at him.

Liv and Meg ran through the door. "Maddie!"

Piper put his hand up. "Don't touch her. She can get hurt." He pointed once again to my ankles.

"Hey."

Tom and Collin voices were in the apartment, but they didn't enter the bedroom.

Jack pointed. "Liv, can you grab a sweatshirt and some pajama bottoms out of that drawer?"

Liv went over and grabbed my clothes.

My last leg was freed. "This ankle is worse than the other," my attending agent told the paramedics.

I looked at the agent and smiled. "Thank you for freeing me."

"Ma'am, I hope you have a quick recovery."

I thanked him again, and he left.

The next few hours were a blur. I was taken to the ER, questioned by the FBI, and was exhausted.

The FBI quickly discovered that Evelyn had been Mike's real estate agent and that she had connections with the night security. She was the reason Mike was able to get me into my apartment.

After Jack fired Evelyn, she researched me and discovered that Mike was my ex and the two started working together in revenge. And it didn't take her long to flip on Mike in order to try and save her own ass.

Jack sat by me the entire time, refusing to leave my side.

"I want to go home."

"I know, babe."

The doctor came back in. "You have a concussion, but we're concerned about internal bleeding. Your left ankle is growing redder and continuing to swell. You're at risk for cellulitis and phlebitis."

"What does that mean?" Jack inquired.

"It seems that the rope used on Ms. Burns has sea life on it. We are concerned about the bacteria that were on it, causing a cellulitis infection. The inflammation gives me concern for phlebitis. I'm going to order IVs of antibiotics and blood thinners."

"When can I go home?"

The doctor reviewed his notes. "Ms. Burns, we need to have you under observation. If your symptoms get worse, we will need to take another course of action."

"Can we do the observation at home?" Jack wanted to know.

The doctor sighed. "You would have to have round-the-clock nursing and pay for it out of pocket. It would cost thousands."

"Done," Jack stated confidently.

The doctor jerked his head, "Mr. Stevens, we aren't talking about two thousand here."

Jack held up his hand. "Done."

The doctor nodded. "All right. You will have to set it up on your own. We can give you a list of places at the nurse's station." He left the room.

"Jack, you don't..." Jack's lips were quickly on mine. "Shh. It's decided, don't argue with me. We are going home."

He picked up his phone. "Tom, you guys bored out there?"

Silence and then a brief laugh. "Can you go to the nurse's station and arrange for private care at my place? Maddie is going to need observation, and we need to get her out of here and back home."

Silence. "Thanks, man."

Jack came and sat next to the bed and stroked my cheek. "I'm so sorry. I should have gotten to you sooner, Maddie."

My eyes widened. "Jack, you didn't know! It's not your fault."

"I should've realized where you were when I saw your outfit."

"No, Jack. You couldn't have. The only thing that matters is you rescued me in time." A wave of chills ran back through me, as a flashback of the computer screen flashed through my mind.

"What he did to you—"

"Jack, he bit my breast. I'm sorry you saw that. It could have been worse." I tried to downplay what happened.

Jack closed his eyes. When he opened them, he admitted, "I saw the auction, Maddie."

At first, I was confused. Then, a bad feeling began to climb through me. "But how?"

"The FBI found it. Collin guessed the password. I saw..." Jack stopped and closed his eyes.

"You saw him stick his fingers in me and slap me." I winced.

Jack's face heated with new rage. "I wanted to kill him, Maddie. I still do. And I want to kill Evelyn, too."

I grabbed Jack's face in my hands. "Shh. It's okay."

"No, it's *not* okay."

We didn't say anything for a few minutes. "I don't want you to lie to me, to hide from this, Maddie. What else did they do to you?"

I pulled Jack's face to my forehead. "Besides slap me around? Nothing."

Jack was relieved, but also seemed as if he didn't know whether he should believe me.

"Honestly, Jack. I swear. I'm lucky because if you didn't find me when you did, it was going to get really bad for me."

Jack closed his eyes again and took a deep breath. "I'm so sorry I didn't protect you." Fresh tears streamed down his face.

"Shh. Jack, you couldn't have."

"We should have had the bodyguards following you around inside work, not only standing outside the secured area."

I pulled him closer to me. "Jack, stop. This isn't anyone's fault. You aren't responsible for what others do."

"It's my job to protect you."

"It's your job to love me. That's all. You have saved me so many times from so much, and I love that about you. I love that you want to protect me at all costs, but it isn't your job. You're only job is to love me. You still love me, right?" I whispered, suddenly wondering if what Mike had done to me would be too much for him to get past.

Jack pulled back and squinted at me. "Maddie, why would you ask me that?"

I looked away. "Maybe you're not going to be able to get past seeing Mike put his hands on me?"

Jack picked up my head. "Maddie, don't ever question my love for you. You have my heart, and it's yours until you don't want it anymore."

"You promise?"

"I promise. Just please, don't ever give it back."

The IVs kept me infection-free, and four days later, I was given the all-clear to no longer be under observation. It probably could have happened two days sooner, but Jack wouldn't take any chances.

We hadn't left the house, but we also hadn't been alone. When the nurse finally left, I walked out of the bedroom in heels and turned to Jack. "Go grab the sunscreen."

He raised a brow at me in question.

"It's a beautiful summer day, let's go for a swim."

He laughed. "Let's go get our suits on."

I laughed harder. Grabbing my phone, I hit the music button and Nelly's "Hot in Here" came on.

Jack stared at me in surprise, as his dimple peeked out.

I slowly removed my shirt and threw it on the couch, sauntered over to the staircase that led to his rooftop pool, and swayed my hips. "Since when do we need our suits?"

With a sly grin on his face, he licked his lips.

I sauntered up the stairs, and one by one, threw different pieces of my clothes off. Jack stared at me, enjoying the show.

At the top, I stepped out of my panties and threw them over the rail to him. He laughed, then quickly ran up the stairs.

I tossed my heels to the side, ran to the pool, and dove in. Jack quickly undressed, then jumped in. He pulled me into his body and embraced me for a long kiss.

"Mmm, I missed this," I stroked his hair.

"Swimming naked or my naked body?" he teased.

I pretended to think about it, and he tickled me.

The sun felt good. The noise of the city was far below. The cool, crisp water made me feel weightless. I floated on my back for a few minutes and felt the warm sunshine on my face. Then I dipped underwater and started doing handstands and somersaults.

Jack laughed. "Maybe we should put you in synchronized swimming?"

"Ha, ha!" I plunged into the water and did another handstand.

We swam for maybe an hour. We made out now and again.

I pulled back from a kiss and grinned.

"What?"

"I like making out with you."

He gave me his dimpled grin. "Feeling is mutual. But I'm becoming a prune. You want to get out for a bit?"

"Sure."

We went to the cabana, laid in the bed, and I snuggled into Jack's arms while he stroked my back. I turned to face him and grazed his hard-on.

He kept caressing my back and smiled at me.

"Jack, what's up?"

He raised his eyebrows at me in question.

"Since when do you let me only lie in your arms naked, unless we've just had a mind-blowing orgasm?"

"You're recovering. I don't want to hurt you more. Trust me. This is kind of torturous for me."

"I'm fine, Jack. Let's play."

Jack wasn't sure. I rolled on top of him. "I'm serious."

"Maddie, I don't want to hurt you. I don't think it's a good idea while you are still bruised up."

I put my forehead to his, and gazed at him in the eyes, as I had so many times before. We hadn't discussed anything since the hospital. We kept things light...easy. Numerous times, I woke up with night terrors, but I refused to talk about it when Jack would pull me in his arms.

I choose my words carefully. "I need to feel you, Jack. I need to know you are mine and nothing has changed."

"Nothing has changed. I love you. I just don't want to hurt you."

I fidgeted with my hands. "I know you love me, but I need you to fix my internal bruises."

There. I admitted out loud that the pain I felt outside couldn't even compare to the pain I felt inside.

He pulled my chin up. A slow realization overtook his face that I wasn't okay.

"I need you to bring me back to life, Jack."

He scanned my eyes, nodded slowly, and pulled me into his lips as I slipped into a crouched position and almost brought him into me.

He stopped me and whispered, "Not yet, baby. I want to see your eyes roll first, and feel your body shake in my mouth. I need it as much as you do."

"Okay," I whispered and moved my body away from his bulge. My body pulsed, wet with desire for what I knew only he could give me.

He flipped me on my back and started to nibble on my ear gently. His lips fluttered on my neck, and he gave me butterfly kisses on my collarbone. Like always, Jack knew all my sweet spots and made my insides tingle with every kiss, every touch, every caress.

I moaned loudly. It had felt like forever.

"That's my girl," Jack praised me. His lips fluttered over my breasts, as he carefully avoided the area where Mike bit me. I pushed it out of my mind and pushed him into my bruise. Jack jerked his head to look at me.

"I need it, Jack." I pushed his head back to my bruise. He hesitated, then gently licked it with his tongue, and sucked it gently with his mouth.

I arched my back, and wanted him to take in more, as his lips on my bruise sent a sweet pain through my breast—pain that I wanted—what I needed. I pushed his head on it harder and tried to erase the memory that anyone, besides Jack, had ever touched me.

As I inhaled sharply from the pain, a single tear shed on my cheek. I released my hand from his head and quickly wiped it away, so Jack wouldn't see it and stop. "I've missed you," I whispered.

"I've missed you." He moved to my other breast, lightly caressed my areola with his tongue, and sent a thrill of signals through my body, as my bruise slowly stopped throbbing.

Jack brought his face to mine to check on me. He took my lips in his and reminded me that I was the only person in his world.

I ground my body on his dick. "You feel so good, Jack."

He nibbled my ear again, "You're so delicious, Maddie."

His fingers moved gently in me—one, then two, then three—and caused me to lose my breath.

"That's my baby. You need more?"

"Please, Jack." I drilled my eyes into his, as I wanted to see the familiarity of his face when I begged him.

Jack's thumb swiped my clit.

"Ahh." My breath hitched.

Jack slid his fingers into his mouth.

"Taste your deliciousness." He put his fingers in my mouth where I desperately sucked and tried to push the flashback, of Mike jabbing his fingers in my body and then my mouth, out of my mind.

He removed his fingers and kissed my mouth. The taste of my wetness on his tongue made my cunt clench with desire.

Jack moved gracefully down my body as he kissed my stomach and mound. Skillfully, he began to lick and suck my sex, while I moaned and called out his name.

He brought me to the edge, then stopped me from falling. My body ached and ached, as it waited for my high, and I begged him, "Jack, please, I need it so much." I greedily snatched his head in my hands and forcefully pushed it into my body.

Groaning, he swiped his finger over my G-spot, slowly sucking while he flicked his tongue, creating a lazy ripple that sped up, and became a hurricane within me.

Over and over, my nerves spun in sweet ecstasy, as my body

soared higher and higher, flying as only Jack knew how to make me.

He kissed his way back up and let me relax from my orgasm. But I wanted to feel whole and needed all of him. As I slipped my body onto him, I whispered. "I need more, Jack," then pulled him into me to claim his mouth and taste my orgasm.

My body throbbed against his fullness, and he immediately started to hit my sweet spot.

Slightly dizzy, I closed my eyes and held on to him, digging my nails into his back, trying to forget that anything had ever happened to me and that any evil existed.

"Open your eyes, Maddie."

I opened my eyes.

He pushed my feet to my buttocks, just like the first night we met. "I want to feel you tremble under me."

Like always, Jack knew exactly what I needed. And what I needed was to feel Jack's body on top of mine as I lost all control and forgot about what Mike's body felt like on me.

"Closer," I whispered as I grabbed his ass and pressed him further into me.

"So delicious," he whispered in my ear and sucked a bit harder this time on my neck.

"Jack, I'm close." My voice was hoarse.

He lifted his face to mine. "Stay a bit longer."

My breath was labored, and I refocused.

His forehead pressed to mine. "You feel so good, Maddie."

"I missed you, Jack." A single tear ran down my cheek.

"I missed you," he whispered, as every cell in my body raged with heat, ready to explode, but couldn't fully forget that anyone but him had ever touched me.

"Jack...I..." My eyes started to roll, my body convulsed, as Jack pumped hard into my body. Our bodies trembled together as one, as we cried out each other's names, and at that brief moment, only Jack and I existed.

When it was over, he slowly pulled out of me and rolled onto his back while he held me in his arms.

We didn't say much at first. Jack stroked my back, and his heartbeat slowed. His strong arms kept me close, and I felt like there was no one else in the world besides Jack and me.

Jack spoke first. Slowly, carefully, he found his words. "I've been thinking."

I gazed up at him. "Hmm?"

"I think I need to see someone, and I think you should too."

He wants to see someone else?

"I don't want to see anyone else," I blurted out, as my heart raced in panic, and tears formed in my eyes.

Jack sat up. "No, that isn't what I mean. I don't want anyone but you."

I blinked back my tears. "I don't understand."

Jack, very carefully, admitted, "I have a lot of flashbacks...baggage I need to get past. I never went to therapy after the break-in...when we lost the baby and..." he swallowed hard. "I can't get images out of my head of the night I discovered the trafficking..."

He stopped. I knew there was more.

"Go on."

"And you..."

A tear slipped down my face. Jack kept picturing whatever he saw Mike do to me on the camera. "So you don't see me the same?"

"That's not it, Maddie. If anything, I know, without a doubt, that if I lost you, I would die. But I don't want to keep living in fear and pain. I think I need some professional help and I'm worried about you. It won't hurt to talk to someone just to see if it helps." Jack stroked my hair.

"I'm fine, Jack. Just keep loving me, and I'll be fine."

The last thing I want to do is have to talk to a stranger and relive that nightmare.

Jack shook his head. "You aren't okay, and I can't fix it. As much as I want to...I would give anything to...but I can't. I've been through this before, Maddie. I'm scared to death that if we don't both deal with our pasts, then I will lose you. I can't handle that."

I continued to fidget with my hands in my lap. Jack softly tilted my chin up. "Will you go to a few sessions for me? You don't even have to talk when you get there if you don't want to."

Jack's eyes begged me to say yes.

I closed my eyes; the different parts of my abduction flashed through my head, like a slow-motion movie reel that kept playing over and over.

"Please, Maddie."

Do I really want to talk about all this with a stranger? I opened my eyes. "Why can't I just talk to you about it?"

Jack sighed. "You can talk to me about anything, Maddie. But you aren't able to. Every time you have a nightmare, or I see you have a flashback, I ask you about it. But you won't talk to me about it."

"That's because I don't want to hurt you," I blurted out.

Jack stroked my cheek. "I know, and that's why we both need to go see a professional, sweetheart."

Fresh tears bottled up in my eyes, and I sobbed uncontrollably. "Hey... shhh…" He wrapped me into the cocoon of his body.

"It hurts so bad, Jack." I couldn't hold it in anymore.

He kissed my head. "I know, baby, I know."

I cried in Jack's arms for a long time. He patiently held me and repeatedly told me how much he loved me.

I finally picked my head off his chest. "Jack, I'll go if you want me to."

"Thank you. I do."

26

Jack

WITH CLAMMY HANDS AND A FLIPPING STOMACH, I OPENED THE door and motioned for Maddie to enter.

Maddie promised me she would go to counseling, and I went as well. We both had a few appointments on our own, and the counselor wanted us to start having joint sessions in addition to our individual ones.

Halfway through the door, Maddie stopped and put her hand over mine. "Jack, your hand is shaking."

I hadn't even realized.

Maddie stepped back outside and grabbed my other hand. "We're early. Let's go sit down for a minute."

Blowing out a big breath of air, I let her lead me into the quiet courtyard and over to a bench. She sat down and patted the seat next to her.

Once I sat down, she stood up and repositioned herself on my lap. Taking my face in her hands, she stared into my eyes. "What's going on, Jack?"

"I'm nervous."

She smiled at me and ran her hand on my head above my ear. "I can see that."

"You aren't nervous?" I asked her.

She kissed me quickly. "A little. What are you nervous about?"

I looked away from her, blew out more air, and tried to stop my leg from bouncing.

She pulled my face back toward hers. "Jack?"

I blurted out, "I'm afraid you might see how dark my thoughts are."

Maddie adjusted her body, so it was on both my legs, and I couldn't bounce anymore. She was quiet for a moment but continued to stare into my nervous eyes. Finally, she said, "Jack, there isn't anything you can say that's going to scare me away."

"You say that, but you don't know what goes through my head, and every session I go to, more and more darkness comes out."

"It's the same for me."

I squinted my eyes at her. "There's nothing dark about you, Maddie."

She laughed softly. "You need to take me off your pedestal. I stayed with a human trafficker for six years who verbally, emotionally, physically, and sexually abused me. Oh yeah, don't forget I was kidnapped." She winked at me.

"That's not funny."

Smiling at me again, she stroked my cheek. "I know it isn't, but my point is that we all have some darkness in us. We all are living life, and stuff happens that molds us into who we are. Just because you have dark thoughts based on experiences you've had, that doesn't make you a dark person."

"Maybe it does."

She shook her head. "No, it doesn't. And don't for one minute think I don't know who you are, Jack. I know the real you, the one who no one really knows. Besides, you've already shown me your safe room, so I know dark thoughts are running through your mind. Plus, after what happened to me, there is no doubt I've added more."

I pulled her forehead to mine. "*You* haven't added anything but light into my life."

"And you've added nothing but light to mine. Nothing you can say in any session or outside of any session will ever change that." Her blue eyes drove into mine, and I saw her light, her honesty, and her love for me.

A calm started to sweep over me. I leaned in and kissed her as she grabbed the back of my head and pushed me into her.

We sat on the bench, softly kissing each other. Between kisses, I whispered to her, "So you know, I'll never take you off my pedestal."

She laughed. "Well, you're on mine."

"I'll never stop putting you first, Maddie."

She pulled back. "I was wrong to tell you to put me first."

"No, you weren't."

She put her fingers over my lips. "I was. You shouldn't be number two."

"I've never felt like number two."

"You haven't?"

I shook my head. "Never. You always make me feel like the most special person on earth."

She looked at me like she didn't believe me. "Really?"

"Yes. I think we are each other's number ones."

She kissed me again. "I like that thought."

My alarm started to go off, indicating that our joint session was about to begin. I took another big breath. "We need to go or we're going to be late."

Maddie got off my lap, and I put my arm around her waist. We walked back to the front door. I went to grab the door handle, and she put her body in front of mine to stop me.

Looking down at her, I waited for her to speak.

She reached up, pulled my neck down to hers, and put her forehead against mine. I wrapped my arms around her waist and pulled her in close.

"Remember the first night I met you, when I told you I would take whatever you'd give me?" she asked.

"Yeah."

"That won't do anymore. I need all of you, Jack. The good, the bad, all of it. Every single ounce."

As I stared into the eyes of the most beautiful woman on earth, I wondered for the millionth time how I had gotten so lucky. And at that moment, something impossible happened. I fell more in love with her.

"I love you, Maddie. More than anything on earth, I love you more."

She smiled at me. "I already know that. And that's how much I love you."

The door opened, and our counselor stood in front of us. "Everything okay? Are you ready for your session?"

I kissed Maddie, then looked at our counselor. "Everything is perfect."

EPILOGUE

Over the next few months, I started to feel better. Jack and I both kept going to separate and joint sessions, with Sarah Shepard, the Domestic Violence Counselor, that Tom recommended to Jack.

Apparently, Tom had encouraged Jack, for quite a while, to see Sarah, once he found out about the human trafficking party Jack witnessed.

It was fall now, and New York was full of beautiful colors, and the air had turned crisp. As I walked around Chelsea absent-mindedly, I suddenly stopped dead in my tracks, as I realized I was in front of my apartment and hadn't been back since my abduction. I had subconsciously moved into Jack's.

My heart sped up. My mouth went dry. I started to turn to walk away but stopped. Slowly, I turned and walked in.

The same security officer that ran the day shift was there. "Well, hello, Ms. Burns. It's so nice to see you back."

I smiled. "Thank you." I walked past him to the elevator.

It didn't take long before I stood outside my door. I took a deep breath, dug into my purse, and found the key. I opened the door and slowly stepped inside.

I'm not sure what I expected to see, but my apartment was the same. A tree outside the window started to change it's green leaves to orange and red. The sun shone brightly through the glass. Any sign that anything sinister ever occurred was erased.

Cautiously, I made my way to the bedroom and stood in the doorway. I stared at my bed, and a flashback of bed shopping with Jack and all the good times we had in it, popped into my mind. A small smile broke out on my face.

I stepped into the room farther, then laid on the bed. I glanced at the wall I stared at for so many hours, while being tortured.

Was it Liv and Tom? Was it Jack? The plaster had been redone where Mike drilled the camera into the ceiling, and the evidence of that day was forever removed.

Lost in thought, I wasn't sure how long I laid there when I heard a knock and gazed over to the door. "Jack, what are you doing here?"

"I kept calling you, and you weren't answering. I was worried and tracked your phone," he admitted. Some things, no matter how much therapy we received, would never change. I was okay with it.

I slapped my hand to my forehead. "My phone is on silent. I'm sorry to worry you."

"It's okay. I'm just glad you're safe."

We quickly laid together in our usual position. My head was on his chest, and his hand caressed my back.

"What made you come here?" Jack quietly asked.

I shrugged. "I don't know. It just happened."

"What are you thinking about?"

I smiled. "I was remembering when we went shopping for this bed. That was a fun day."

He gave me his dimpled grin and laughed. "That was fun."

I sat up on my elbow. "I just realized that I sort of moved in with you."

"Maddie, please tell me you aren't moving out now?" Jack peered at me with worried eyes.

I laughed. "Nope. You'll have to kick me out."

"Good!" He leaned in to kiss me.

"But I did love this apartment."

"Me too. Lots of great memories."

"Lots of great orgasms." I giggled.

Jack tickled me. "We can have some more of those right now if you want."

I paused for a minute. "Let's leave this apartment in the past, Jack. I'm happy working on only our future." I sat up. "In fact, I think it's time I moved the rest of my stuff into your place."

He looked at me with his schoolboy grin. "Yeah?"

"Yep. Come on, let's go. I'm assuming your movers can handle this for us?"

"I'll get right on that, Ms. Burns." Jack pulled me off the bed and kissed the top of my head.

We walked out of the building, hand in hand, as the early night air started to turn a bit chilly. Jack pulled me closer to his warm, muscular body.

All is right in the world.

It wasn't long before we were back at the Penthouse.

"Hey, Maddie, let's go up on the roof for a bit, while the weather is still decent."

"That sounds nice."

We walked up the stairs and out into the night air. The night skyline sparkled, and the buzz of the city hummed below. Out of the corner of my eye, near the pool, millions of rose petals grabbed my attention.

I spun to see Jack, on one knee, a massive diamond ring in his hand, and lots of emotions in his eyes. I bit my lip and smiled.

"Maddie, I fell in love with you the minute you fell into my arms. There are so many things I could tell you, but the biggest one is that you're my life and I want you as mine, forever. Will you marry me?"

Tears of happiness fell, and I grabbed Jack's face in my hands, as I pushed my forehead into his. "Yes, Jack, I would love to be your wife."

He picked me up, twirled me around, as both of us laughed. He kissed me again, then snatched my hand and slid the ring on my finger.

"It's beautiful, Jack."

He led me over to a table that had been set up with a bottle of champagne and popped the cork. He poured me a drink and one for himself, too.

I grabbed both the drinks and put them on the table.

"What's up, Maddie?" He looked at me, confused.

"I have a gift for you too."

"Last time you told me that, you gave me a cock ring." His dimpled grin popped out.

Throwing my head back, I laughed. "Sorry to disappoint you, but there's no cock ring." I stopped smiling and gave him a serious look.

"Okay…what is it?"

I sat on the bed under the cabana and patted the seat next to me.

He sat down and looked at me, curiously. I propped my body onto him and put my face right next to his.

"What's up, Maddie?"

I whispered to him, "What do you think about being a daddy?"

Jack froze for a moment, then jerked his head back. He scanned my eyes. "Maddie, are you...?"

I nodded and smiled.

"We're having a baby?" he whispered.

I laughed a little. "Yes."

He jumped up, once again, and twirled me around. "I'm going to be a daddy!" he shouted.

I laughed. "Yes, Jack, and you're going to be the best daddy." Then I kissed him with all my love.

ALSO BY MAGGIE COLE

THE LIE - ALL IN SERIES BOOK FOUR

A Midwestern girl who came to New York with a broken heart. A Texan tycoon who created his own billions.

A lie so devious it still haunts them a decade later.

Laura Aimee's got her life together—until she crosses paths with the man who bootstomped her heart a decade ago. Back then, Blake Montgomery told her a lie so devastating she still hasn't forgiven him.

But she also can't forget the feel of his rough hands on her. The taste of his mouth. How he undressed her with his eyes.

She can't forgive him, and she can't trust him. But Blake will do anything to make her his. One night, she tells herself. Just one night together and then she'll let him go forever.

Why are the men who wreck us the hardest to resist?

THE LIE is the fourth installment of the All In series. At approximately 70,000 words, this sizzling novel features a love-at-first sight romance and a guaranteed HEA. It can be read as a stand alone or after books 1 - 3 of the All In Series.

THE LIE - PROLOGUE

Ten Years Earlier

The knock on the door sent a cold shiver down my spine. It's like I knew my life was about to change.

I thought about not opening the door.

There was another knock.

I went over and opened it. "Sherry, you shouldn't be here."

Sherry had tears in her blue eyes and was holding something in her hand. "I'm pregnant. It's yours."

My mouth went dry. *No, this can not be happening.*

Sherry and I were engaged to be married. Not because either of us wanted to marry the other, but because she was a Rockman, and I was a Montgomery. Upon birth, our parents planned our wedding, so the largest merger of wealth in Texas could occur.

And times were getting harder in Texas. Competition of wealth was increasing. No matter how much Sherry or I told our parents we did not want to marry each other, it wouldn't change our fate.

"Blake, are you going to at least let me in?" Sherry asked quietly.

I opened the door wider. "Sorry. Come in."

Sherry cautiously stepped in.

"It was a mistake, Sherry. I was so drunk I don't even remember it." I rattled off.

And I didn't remember it. A few months ago, I had called Sherry to inform her that I was telling my parents that there was no way I was going through with this wedding. They would cut me off, I knew it, but I was in love with Laura.

It was the wedding announcement in the paper that started it all.

Laura had stormed into my house, with tears in her beautiful brown eyes, and threw the paper at me. "You're engaged?"

My gut dropped. "Let me explain."

"Explain? Explain that you've been fucking me for almost a year and telling me you love me and you're engaged?" she hurled at me through tears.

I grabbed her shoulders. "Sweetheartâ€”"

"Don't call me your Sweetheart!"

"Please, listen to me. Let me explain. I don't love Sherry. She doesn't love me. We don't want to get married," I cried out.

Laura picked up the paper and shook it in my face. "Then why is there a wedding announcement?"

"Our parents planned it. They want to merge our wealth."

Laura's head snapped back. "What are you talking about?"

I swallowed hard. "I come from one of the richest families in Texas."

Laura didn't say anything. She stared at me through tear-filled eyes. "So you've just been lying to me this entire time about who you are?"

I quietly admitted, "I guess you could say that. I'm sorry."

Laura's eyes filled with more tears. "Why would you lie to me, Blake?"

I shook my head. "You don't understand how they are. I've

been trying to tell my parents that there will be no wedding before I even met you."

Laura looked at me with disgust in her eyes. "Then why haven't you?"

I sighed. "It's not that easy. But I will. Tonight. I will go to my parents and tell them. I'll be cut off, but I'm not marrying her, I promise you that."

Laura stood frozen.

I stepped forward and pulled her in my arms. "I'm so sorry. I shouldn't have let this get this far. You're the only woman I've ever loved and ever will. I'll make this right. I promise you."

And I had meant to keep my promise. But I decided I need a little bit of liquid courage to face my parents and after a few drinks, I decided that I need to tell Sherry that I would not be marrying her.

Sherry came over, and we both drowned our sorrows in liquor about our family situations. Well, I thought we were both drinking.

After blacking out, I woke up next to Sherry. Both of us were naked under the covers. I panicked. I had never cheated on anyone and never thought I would have cheated on Laura.

Sherry promised me she wouldn't say anything. I told Laura that I told my parents, needed to get out of Texas for a bit, and we spent two glorious weeks fucking each other's brains out in Cabo.

Except for my guilty conscious hanging over my head, I thought I had gotten away with it.

The plan hadn't changed, and I would tell my parents the wedding was off. I just needed some more time. There was no way I would marry Sherry. I only wanted Laura.

Sherry looked at me with pissed eyes. "Yes, I know it was a mistake. But now I have the consequences of that mistake."

I closed my eyes and took a deep breath. *Stop being a dick.* "I'm sorry I'm in shock."

"What are we going to do, Blake?" Sherry stared up at me, frightened, with more tears in her eyes.

What are we going to do? My heart was about to beat out of my throat, and my stomach was flipping.

Sherry stepped closer to me. "Our child needs both of us, a mother and a father."

Our child.

I snapped my head up at her. "You know I would want to be in my child's life.â€

She looked at me with her lip shaking. "And you know how they are."

They meant our parents.

And she didn't have to say anything else. Unspoken words said it all.

Our parents would never allow me to be in my child's life if I wasn't married to Sherry. If I didn't marry her, I would be cut off. Whenever Sherry or I had tried to tell our parents we didn't want to marry each other, we both were warned. We knew they didn't only make threats.

No, they took action.

If I were cut off, I would never know my child. I would have no money to fight them in court, and I would have a child in the world who was fatherless.

So I made the hardest decision I ever made. It was a decision that would haunt me. I knew when I made that decision that I would never forgive myself or be happy again. Happiness didn't exist without her.

My heart broke before I broke Laura's.

THE LIE - CHAPTER ONE SNEAK PEAK

Laura

The snow fell so hard the wipers could hardly clear the windshield before more snow covered it again.

Phil glanced out the window. “It’s really coming down. I wonder if we’ll take off tonight.”

I let out a big sigh. We were already late for our flight plan, and it had been several long days in Michigan. Nothing sounded better than a warm bubble bath and my bed. “I hope so. New York is calling my name!”

Tom held his finger up. “Hey Cindy, are we going to be able to take off in this storm?” He sat next to Phil, with his phone to his ear.

Please, Cindy, say yes. I prayed quietly in my head.

“Ok, see you soon.” Tom hung up. “Cindy said we are good to go.”

I threw my arm in the air in a victory pose. “Yes!”

Tom laughed.

Phil laughed then absentmindedly looked out the window again. "Hopefully, it stays that way.”

"Let's not put anything bad out into the universe, Dad," I teased Phil.

Tom gave me a fist bump.

"Ha, ha," Phil rolled his eyes at us.

Tom and I loved to tease Phil and call him Dad even though he was only a few years older than us.

Tom's phone rang, and he picked it up. "Hey, Jack."

Must be Jack Stevens, one of Tom's investors.

"Yeah, it's snowing like a blizzard right now. I bet you're jealous you didn't join us on this trip," Tom sarcastically teased.

I looked at Phil. He looked as tired as I did. While Tom should have been tired, he didn't seem as worn out as Phil and I. Maybe it was all his athleticism that kept him full of energy. Who knew.

Tom Marko was the captain of the New York Knicks and a self-made billionaire. He was also my boss, although he never treated me as anything but an equal.

"No, everything is handled. The investors understood you couldn't be here." Tom told Jack.

Yep. It was definitely, Jack Stevens.

Tom continued, "Cindy said we are still good to take off. Tell him he's more than welcome to hop on the jet back to New York. Have him go on in and introduce himself to Cindy. I'll text her now."

I looked at Phil and wondered who Tom could be referring to. Phil shrugged his shoulders and gave me his 'I don't know' look.

"No problem, Jack. I'll see you this weekend." Tom hung up and sent a quick text.

"Looks like we'll have some company on the way home. Jack's friend from college is supposed to be coming out to New York, and his jet broke down. He's already on the runway, so I guess he beat us," Tom informed us.

"I don't care who's in the jet as long as we get home and I get to sleep in my bed tonight." I grinned at them.

"I hear you on that," Phil agreed.

Tom laughed. "I won't argue. I'm ready to see Liv."

Phil grinned and rolled his eyes.

"I bet you are," I teased and smirked at him.

Tom softly laughed, and his face got a tad red.

We sat the rest of the ride in silence, which wasn't long. The car pulled up to the jet, and we quickly but carefully trudged through the slippery snow. By the time I got up to the jet doors, I was covered in white and looked like a snowman.

The three of us got into the jet and removed off our snowy jackets. I laughed, "I guess it's not Michigan if you don't get to experience the snow." I walked through the door to the middle of the cabin.

I shook the snow out of my hair. I turned to go into the last cabin when I caught a glimpse of the back of his body. He was tall and built. His thighs filled out his pants in just the right way. His dress shirt clung to his back and arm muscles. I could see his muscles flex as he ran one hand through his chestnut hair in frustration. His other hand held the phone up to his ear.

My vagina pulsed, but at the same time, I stopped dead in my tracks. The hair on the back of my neck stood up, and my skin quickly was covered in goosebumps.

No, it couldn't be, I thought, as little volts of energy shot through my veins.

"Laura, is something wrong?" Tom stood next to me, but I hardly heard him.

There was only one man who had ever made me feel that way, and that was over ten years ago.

I stood in the aisle, oblivious as Tom and Phil stared at me. Part of me prayed it wasn't him. Part of me prayed it was. I stood paralyzed, except for the beat of my heart which had quickly increased in speed.

"Laura?" Phil now questioned me, too.

I slowly gazed over at Phil. My mouth went dry.

He squinted at me through his glasses. "You all right?"

I slowly nodded and took a deep breath. *Get a grip, Laura. I must be super tired because it can't be him. There's no way it can be him.*

"Just tired," I managed to say quietly.

"Let's go sit down and have a drink. We've all had a long week." Tom motioned for me to go first.

I took a deep breath and willed my body to move. I shuffled my feet into the cabin. That's when I heard the Texan drawl.

"They said it's mechanical. I'm grateful they found it before I took off in this storm."

I froze once more. *This must be a bad dream. This can not be happening.*

But I knew that voice anywhere. That voice haunted me in my dreams. It would pop up when least expected, crush my soul and break my heart over and over again.

I scanned the back of his body once more. He was more filled out then I remembered. But then again, we were only what... twenty-two and twenty-four? Back then, he was just a boy. Standing in front of me was a man. And he looked better than he did at twenty-four.

While I tried to convince myself it wasn't him, my eye caught it on the couch. A cowboy hat: brown, real leather, faded from use. I knew that hat well. *I bought him that hat.*

"Laura?" Tom peered down at me in the doorway and waited for me to move.

Upon hearing my name, he slowly put the phone down and turned around.

"Laura?" A grin started to form on his face.

My eyes widened, and I spun to walk away, but Tom's 6'10 frame was right behind me. I gazed up and saw a frown on Tom's face. "Laura?"

"Move," I hissed.

He jerked his head back and stepped aside. I had never hissed at Tom before.

I walked as fast as I could to the front of the plane. The warmer blanket was over the door. I quickly pulled it back, attempted to trot down the steps, and grabbed the cold, slippery rail. As my blood boiled, tears welled in my eyes, and I heard voices but couldn't comprehend what anyone shouted to me.

I scurried down the stairs. The blizzard gusted all around, and a white blanket loomed in front of me. As the snow pounded down, the cold wind repeatedly slapped me across the face.

There was so much snow. I tried to walk faster, but the thick, wetness slammed into me. My feet moved one in front of the other and slowly crunched through the snow. I didn't know where I was going. I just knew I needed to get as far away from him as possible.

I'm not sure how far I got. Suddenly, I felt someone grab my arm and spin me. I almost slipped and fell, but he caught me in his arms.

He pulled me tight into his chest. "Laura, I'm so sorry."

I sank into him for a brief minute, felt his familiarity and warmth, and inhaled his spicy and intoxicating scent. His strong biceps flexed around me. Our bodies flushed perfectly together, and his hands stroked my hair. The quick beat of his heart banged against my ear.

Then I realized what I was doing. I would not melt in this man's arms. No, I would never again put myself in that position. I pulled back and pushed my palms against him. "Let me go," I screamed, as rage ran through me.

He embraced me tighter. "No! Sweetheart, I'm so sorry," he drawled.

I reached up and slapped him. Hard. "I'm not your Sweetheart!"

Grab your copy of THE LIE NOW!

Or: www.authormaggiecole.com/thelie/

COMING SOON BY MAGGIE COLE

THE ALL IN SERIES *- CLICK ON THE LINK TO ORDER NOW or go to www.authormaggiecole.com*

THE LIE - January 4, 2020

THE TRAP - January 31, 2020

THE GAMBLE - February 27, 2020

If you've not read The Rule, book one in the All In Series, grab it here and read all about Tom and Liv's story!

If you've not read The Secret, book two in the All In Series, grab it here and read all about Collin and Meg's story!

ABOUT THE AUTHOR

Maggie Cole is the pen name of a multi-faceted woman. She's an entrepreneur at heart and loves writing contemporary steamy romance novels that help her readers feel lots of different emotions. Sometimes you'll laugh, sometimes you'll cry, sometimes you'll have little flutters racing through your veins...and that's Maggie's biggest wish for you when you read her novels.

She's a wife, mother, and lives in the sunshine, where she can often be found staring off into space while creating new scenes in her mind.

ACKNOWLEDGMENTS

To my friends who read several drafts and kept pushing me to make this novel better, I thank you!

To my editors, cover artists, launch team and author friends who shared so much wisdom with me, I thank you!

To my readers; from the bottom of my heart, I thank you! I sincerely hope you loved this novel. I can't wait to share the rest of the series with you!

Made in the USA
Middletown, DE
24 April 2020